Britpop summer

angela atkins

First published in the UK in 2024
by What's the Story
Holborn Viaduct, London

First Edition

ISBN: 978-1-4467-4206-8

A catalogue record of this book is available
from the British Library

Gen X author photo © J Trevelyan
Cover Design Athos Boncompagni
dreamstime.com

For Fraser

Britpop summer

To Miranda,
A fellow britpopper!
Love Angel
Nov '22

Before we knew what we were...

We didn't know we were Gen X.
We were just there.
In the '90s.

But it was a where that our parents never understood.
It was a where the next gen couldn't even conceive of.

We didn't have the internet.
No wi-fi.
No google.
We had to wait to find things out.
Or try to remember them.
There were no smartphones.
Mobile phones were the size of bricks,
and only ex-yuppies used them.

We had to turn up when we said we would.
We couldn't tell someone if we were late.
They just had to wait.

We moved out of home as soon as we possibly could.
As soon as we had some semblance of
a low-paid shitty job
that would just about cover the rent.

We lived in crappy flats with crappy flatmates.
We weren't interested in living at home into our thirties
and saving for a house.
We just wanted out.
We wanted our independence.
as soon as we could get our hands on it.

Our parents weren't our friends.
We detested their hypocrisy.
We hung out with our *actual* friends.
People we had chosen to be our new family.

And then there was the music.

After Kurt died, for us, there was a silence in the world.
We weren't sure what would come next.
What would follow?

And then Britpop arrived.

In that blissful summer,
Britpop played everywhere.
At every party.
In every store.
In cafes and restaurants.
On the streets, in houses, on trains and buses.
It played from car stereos and CD players.
It was in the air, it was everywhere.

And that's where you'll find us.
Caught beneath a landslide.
And if you don't know the next line,
then you weren't one of us.

Ethan & Elise
get high

Recommended listening: Champagne Supernova
From the album '(What's the story) Morning Glory' by Oasis
Single released only in Australia, New Zealand and France.
Album released in October 1995, by Creation Records.
While there are many theories about what this song is about,
Noel has said he really hasn't got a clue.

Imagine you are high above a city, looking down through the clouds. You can see a harbour, blue choppy waves catching the sun in bright glittering diamonds that make you squint. You can see a gray city centre, squashed between soaring hills dense with trees. And dotting those hills, multi coloured wooden houses.

Zoom down through the clouds, down towards the grey city centre, down, down, down until you are hovering above the city streets. Then swerve, and fly towards the biggest hill. This is Mount Victoria, rising high above the city.

It's lower slopes are webbed with winding streets and old villas, and on the far prow, a red brick monastery gleams in the sun.

As we swoop up the slopes, past the houses, painted blue and green and yellow, we see gaps between the trees and walking tracks winding their way across and up the slopes. Then, suddenly the trees break open, and an open meadow of green grass appears.

And that's where we find them.
Both lying in the grass.
The sun beating down on them.

Ethan has his arm bent over the top half of his face, shielding his eyes from the glare. He is clean-shaven, with dark brown slightly curling, unruly hair. He is wearing one of the three white and slightly torn t-shirts that he owns and his usual ripped 501s. His Doc Martin boots have rolled away from him and rest in the grass on their side.

Elise has a magazine over her face, but her short dark hair peeps out above the top of it. She is wearing a grey singlet with a red cross on it and a short cream skirt. Her kicked-off Converse One-stars have rolled away and have come to rest near Ethan's boots. Her bare arms and legs are still white from the winter, and she is hoping a few hours of sun might start off her summer tan.

Not that summer should be here yet.
It is only early November.
Summer doesn't usually start down in little old New Zealand until after Christmas. Until January is well set in.
Obviously not this year.
And that's where we are.
Wellington, New Zealand.
Down at the bottom of the world.
And it's November 1995.
The start of Britpop Summer.

*

Elise loved her city. She loved the winding streets going up the hills which puffed you out every time, even when you thought you were fit. She loved the shine from the waves, getting in your eyes, and the constant sound of the harbour. She even loved the uninspired city centre with its 1970s office blocks surrounding the odd historic building.

And most of the time, she even loved the wind.

In this part of the world, Wellington was famous for being windy. She was sure it would give Chicago a run for its money if there was a competition. Because these weren't gentle sea breezes but full-blown hurricane-force gusts that ripped up the city streets and almost lifted you off your feet. Sometimes it was all you could do to hold on to a traffic sign post with both arms, your eyes streaming with tears, your teeth clenched.

Elise truly thought that windy, cold, wet cities were better. She had decided they made people more creative. Wellington was like what she imagined New York was. Frenetic. Everyone rushing everywhere. Of course, half the time it was to get out of the wind or rain, but they were still rushing. It created a buzz.

Yet something strange had happened that morning. No wind. No rain. A clear blue sky. And golden, warm, summer sunshine.

Elise had thrown her curtains open to a beautiful day.

Not really believing it, it was only just November after all, she'd made a sandwich and gone out and sat on the back porch to eat it. Their flat was the top half of an old wooden Victorian villa. You had to come around the back of the house, and climb a set of rickety wooden stairs to their 'front' door, which was actually the kitchen door. A couple lived downstairs and were forever banging on the ceiling yelling they were making too much noise up there. Elise and Harriet just ignored them.

Elise finished eating her sandwich and stretched out in the sun. She had until 4 pm before she had to go to work.

She heard the phone ring from inside. Just once and then it stopped. Then rang again. It was their secret ring. They all had people they wanted to avoid and there was nothing worse than getting caught answering the phone.

When it started ringing a third time, she climbed up and went into the hallway to answer.

It was Ethan.

"Harriet's not here," Elise had seen Harriet's unmade bed and knew she hadn't been home last night.

"I wasn't calling for Harriet," Ethan said. "I wondered if you wanted to go up to Mt Vic? I need to pick some parsley."

"Does it grow up there?" Stupid question. Why would he be asking to go up there if it didn't? The thought of hanging out with Ethan by himself had thrown her. Normally he was always with Harriet.

"It's there if you know where to look."

Elise hesitated. But what else did she have to do this afternoon? It was too nice to sit home and read.

"Sure, why not?" she grinned. "I'll head over now."

"See you soon" Ethan hung up.

Elise went and brushed her teeth. She looked at herself critically in the bathroom mirror. She had short dark hair, she guessed it was a bit boyish, but it kept it out of the way and she liked it. She was having a fad for tank tops after seeing the Tank Girl movie, which she would just like to throw out there, was nowhere near as good as the comic version.

And she liked that tank tops made her boobs look a bit bigger. Not that they weren't a nice handful, which someone had once told her was, in fact, the perfect amount. But when she stood next to Harriet who had enormous ones, she felt a little insufficient.

Today though, they would do. Happy enough with what she saw, she slipped on her favourite sneakers, grabbed a bag with her wallet and keys, and headed out.

*

It was only a 10-minute walk over to Ethan's. He lived on the lower slopes of Mt Vic, near the bus tunnel.

Any Wellingtonian worth their salt had at one time or another run through the bus tunnel. It was extremely narrow, barely more than a few centimetres on each side of the buses that hurtled through it. And it was about 50 metres long so there was a pretty good chance that once you were in there, a bus would come. There were alcoves along the tunnel so if you were caught, you had to throw yourself into an alcove and scream and scream as 5 tonnes of bus barrelled past you. To the people on the bus, you were just a white blur for an instant against the black of the tunnel walls.

It was probably quite dangerous, but it gave you a boom! adrenalin hit. A quick thrill that made your heart race. Like so many things in life that you shouldn't do.

Heading to Ethan's, Elise cut across the top end of the city centre, choosing streets with some shade from the sun. Normally she was looking for cover from the rain because as often as the heavens opened, she never seemed to remember to bring an umbrella with her. Not that there was even a cloud in the sky today.

Heading up Ethan's street the air was hot and breathless, and she realised today there wasn't even a breeze. It would be nice to get up into the shade of the trees on the hill above.

She knocked at the door.

Ethan also lived in an old villa as many Wellingtonians did. In Mount Vic, the suburb that clustered on the lower slopes and edged the city, they were nicely done up and painted in different colours. That is, unless you were renting. Then they were run down, with peeling paint, weeds sprouting out from under the foundations, and mouldering and sagging walls. Ethan's was somewhere in between. In need of repair but it had good bones.

Ethan opened the door. "Hey come in."

It was a typical villa with a central hallway and rooms leading off on both sides. It was cool inside when Elise stepped in, and she followed him past a barely furnished sitting room on the left, someone's bedroom on the right, and then into his bedroom.

Ethan went straight over to his desk under the window and started rummaging there for something in the mess of books and papers covering it. Elise stood hesitantly by the door looking around. Next to the desk, he had a big sagging double bed shoved in the far corner. The corner by her had an old dresser, also piled with books and general clutter.

There were also magazines stacked around all the bottoms of the walls. Elise stepped forward and almost tripped up on one of the stacks.

"Careful, they keep the rats from coming in" Ethan said, and Elise jumped back, pulling a face. She wasn't sure if he was joking.

"I'm not joking," he said with his back to her "and I fucking hate rats".

Ethan pulled the drawer of the desk open, grabbed his wallet, and slipped it into his back jeans pocket. He shoved the drawer shut and picked up a bottle of water.

"Ready?"

She nodded. She'd also brought a bottle of water with her. A few months ago, bottled water hadn't existed, now she couldn't remember what they'd all done without it. She guessed she must have been thirsty a lot. It was funny how quickly small things changed your way of life.

Leaving Ethan's, they headed up the road towards the bus tunnel. Next to the entrance was a kid's playground and that's where most of the walking tracks started that led up the slopes of Mount Vic. She thought it was kind of funny that they had called it a mountain. She thought of it as a really big hill.

"Which way?" she asked realising that she had taken the lead without knowing where she was going.

"Up here" Ethan took a steep track that led up into the trees and then turned out of sight. "Watch out for mountain bikers coming down there." he pointed to a track that cut across theirs.

"Thanks" Elise started up after him.

They didn't talk as they walked. Elise was surprised that she felt quite comfortable with that. Normally with people she didn't know that well, she felt awkward if they ran out of things to say. It felt wrong. But with Ethan, it was actually nice just enjoying walking through the cool of the shade, with the smell of the earth and the sound of the birds. She could hear the hum of the city below them, and a ship tooted in somewhere out in the harbour, now hidden by the trees.

After a while, they came out into a flat grassy patch and Elise drew level with Ethan. The bank dropped off sharply to the city side and they could now see out across the harbour to the hills beyond, and on the prow of the hill below, the monastery gleaming red.

They had stopped walking and were both standing looking out. Ethan took a drink from his water bottle.

"That's a great view," Elise said.

"Yeah, I guess so."

"Come on! It's gorgeous!" she threw her arm out and realised that she was acting like a tour guide. Which she guessed she was in a way. Harriet had told her that Ethan had moved to Wellington without ever having visited it before, so he probably hadn't discovered all there was to discover yet.

"It's a little claustrophobic for me," he shrugged.

Elise looked again at the view. The harbour was completely closed in on all sides by hills that plunged down steeply into it. And even with the sun out, all the hills were covered in dark green bush.

"Huh. I never thought of it like that." She really hadn't.

"I thought it was a dank dripping hole when I first got here. But I'm getting used to it."

"I don't think I could live anywhere but," Elise said.

"Really? How many other places have you lived?"

"Well, I lived in the UK, when I was a kid."

"So you don't have much to compare it to" Ethan took another swig of water.

"I suppose." But Elise was really thinking that you just knew when a city was yours. You clicked with it. It felt like home and even if it had some things that you complained about once in a while. It was the place you wanted to be.

Harriet had said she'd missed living in Wellington the whole time she was away so Elise knew that other cities weren't that great. Harriet had also told her that Ethan could be negative about things.

Now Elise saw what she meant.

Together they started up the hill again, Elise falling in behind when they reached another path that wound its way up through the pines. She was gasping and stopped and drank some water. She was starting to get annoyed with how far this parsley was. Surely it wasn't worth saving the couple of dollars it would have cost to buy a bunch from the shop.

"Here it is" Ethan called out from around a bend in the path. Elise stopped again and got her breath for a moment. She didn't want him to see her puffed.

When she came around the corner, she found they were at the side of another meadow that sloped down to more trees below them. And on the slopes above them, gently heading up towards the top of the hill, were pine trees. There, in the pine-needle-strewn ground between the trees, were indeed clumps of parsley.

Ethan had already climbed up the slope and was picking a bunch of it. Now he slid back down towards her, holding the parsley bunch out like it was a bouquet of flowers. For a moment she almost reached out and took it from him.

But he wasn't offering it to her, he was just making sure he didn't bruise it. He laid it at the base of the nearest tree in the shade and then walked into the meadow. He sat down and kicked off his boots. Elise followed and sat down next to him, throwing her bag down and kicking her shoes off too. She wiggled her toes in the grass and leaned her face back against the sun.

"You can't say this is claustrophobic" she said, regarding him out of one eye.

"I guess not" Ethan lay back in the grass and put his arm over his face. Elise turned and looked in her bag. She had forgotten her sunglasses but found she still had an old copy of 'The Face' in there which she spread out over her own face as she lay back and closed her eyes.

*

Later Elise woke, her mouth gummy. She sat up, the magazine falling to the ground. She rubbed her eyes and took a long drink of water and then splashed some on her face. Ethan was no-where in sight. Elise climbed up and walked up the tree line looking for him. She heard a noise above and peered up through the trunks and saw Ethan coming down one of the tracks towards her.

"I walked to the top!" he said when he reached her. "There's a whole load of people up there, talking about how amazing the view is."

There was a parking look out at the top of Mt Vic that people drove to, walked around for 5 minutes and then felt like they had been and done something. Elise always felt that driving up there was cheating. She was also kind of

ANGELA ATKINS

jealous as she didn't have a car and so couldn't drive up there. Or actually drive at all. She'd never bothered to learn.

"I thought you'd abandoned me" Elise didn't think anything of the sort but she liked being dramatic. She knew Ethan wasn't the kind of person to do that. She'd seen how he'd looked after Harriet, bringing her things when she was ill, getting stuff for her, even though he wasn't even her boyfriend anymore.

"Do you have to head back?" Ethan looked at his watch. Elise came up next to him and looked too. Her arm brushed against his and she felt her heartbeat quicken.

"Whoops it's 3.30!" she said suddenly realising what Ethan's watch was saying. "How did it get that late?" she rushed back down to her sneakers and pulled them on. Ethan stood watching her.

"Where do you have to be?" he asked.

"At work. By 4" She slung her bag on her shoulder and hurried back up to him.

"It's okay, you'll make it," he said.

"You don't even know where I work!" she laughed. Laughter tinged with a little bit of panic. It was a crap job anyway selling a satellite TV package over the phone. She wasn't a born telemarketer and she wasn't doing particularly well at it even after days of practice. But she needed the money so she couldn't really push it too much by being late.

"Somehow I'm sure you'll make it" Ethan went and got his parsley. They hurried all the way back down. It was when they got to the bottom that Ethan started laughing.

"What?" she stopped and looked at him.

"I can't keep it in anymore. It's actually only 2.30" he said. "You read it wrong" he held his arm up and she grabbed his wrist. She looked and looked again. It was now showing quarter to 3. How could she have got that so wrong?

"That's not funny!" she said.

"It was. Watching you panic and do that little half walk, half run all the way" Ethan had seemed to have had no trouble keeping up with her half walk, half run.

"That's mean!" Elise punched him on the arm. "Stop laughing at me!"

"Sorry. It was really cute though." Ethan stopped laughing and grinned at her. She decided to forgive him.

"Don't do it again" she pretended to tell him off.

They were on the street now in front of the bus tunnel. The city felt hotter than it had before. The concrete and tarmac had absorbed and was reflecting the heat.

"I better go home anyway and change before I try and flog people something they don't really seem to want to buy," she said.

"I can walk you" Ethan offered.

"As long as you're not going to pull anything else on me."

"In all fairness, it was actually your fault."

"It was not! You could have told me straight away what the time really was."

He shrugged. "Okay, I'm sorry."

"Thank you." Suddenly Elise stopped and grabbed his arm. "Listen!" she said. Ethan looked around, not sure what he was supposed to be listening to.

"It's Oasis!" From a car stereo somewhere nearby, a song was blaring out. A very British-sounding guy was singing about how many special people change and asking where you were when they were getting high.

"Have you heard this?" Elise asked.

Ethan shook his head.

"It's Oasis! They're huge in England. When I was in the UK for a few weeks at the start of the year there was a huge battle raging between them and another band called Blur. I've been waiting for it to reach here." Magazines and music still took several months to reach New Zealand from overseas.

11

They stood and listened to the song until just when Liam was declaring that someday you would find him, when the stereo switched off and they heard a car door slam.

"Come on, I can play you the whole thing when we get back to mine" Elise said, and they set off across the city.

Later Elise couldn't remember what they talked about as they walked, but that they'd had no trouble finding things to discuss. They had teased each other and had fake punched each other on the arm several times. She remembered having to bend over laughing quite a lot.

They went up the back stairs to the flat and Elise opened the door.

"Hello?" she called out checking if Harriet or Rosalie were home, but all was quiet. She led Ethan down the hall to her room. Closing the door behind them, she went over the stereo to find the Oasis CD that she'd brought in England. She was glad it had finally been released here. It was her favourite album, but no-one knew what she was talking about when she mentioned it.

"This is a great room." Ethan was looking about.

"I know" Elise was distracted, but actually when she'd first looked at the flat she hadn't been able to believe it either. Her room was the front bedroom, with two big sets of bay windows, looking out over the city.

The room was painted white and was about three times the size of the others. There was a bricked-up fireplace and mantelpiece, which she'd stacked her book collection on top of in three towering piles, and a wardrobe hidden behind a white curtain. Her bed was a mattress on the floor in the corner, and her only other furniture was a dresser and a bookshelf. It was even more sparse than Ethan's. Now she put the CD on and clicked it forward until it was on Champagne Supernova.

Ethan sat down in one of the bay windows and stretched his legs out.

Elise sat in the other window, crossing her legs at the ankles.

They listened to the song.

"What do you think?" she asked, desperate for him to like it. There was something friend-defining when you liked the same music.

"It's excellent. I like it." Ethan nodded.

Elise got up and put the CD back to the first song to play the whole album. She felt Ethan come up next to her. He picked up the CD case and looked at it. Then he looked at her. She knew instantly this was one of those moments. She pressed play on the CD player without looking at it.

Ethan moved into her, and Elise closed her eyes as they started kissing. Ethan was a good kisser. They stood there kissing for a little while and then both pulled away at the same moment. Ethan looked over to her bed, and Elise took his hand and pulled him towards it.

That was when Ethan stopped.

"What the fuck is in your bed?" he asked looking at the body-shaped lump that took up half of her double mattress. With the duvet over it, it did look like a human body was under there.

"Just some essentials" Elise stepped over, pulled the duvet down and showed him. There were clothes, books, some muesli bars, pens and paper. A magazine. A large stuffed globe soft toy. The usual.

Ethan ran his eyes over the full extent of it, shook his head and grinned. He pulled her into him, and they went back to what they had been doing, and then somehow were laying on the bed, still doing what they had been doing, and Oasis was still playing.

*

Later Champagne Supernova started to play again.

13

"Shit, this is the last song!" Elise said. They had been lying together, just listening to the music. "I have to get going." She pulled the duvet around her and reached out to grab her clothes, which were somehow strewn on the floor. She could just about reach them.

She knew that if she got up and walked around naked, then anyone walking or driving past on the street below and looking up into her window, would see her. Instead, you just had to keep below the height of the bay windows.

She pulled her singlet and skirt underneath the duvet, and then clumsily managed to put them on, trying not to be totally inelegant. Ethan was lying next to her, propping himself up on one elbow, his back pressed up against the pile of 'essentials', watching her.

Dressed, she climbed out of the bed.

"I'm going to have a quick shower and then I have to go work" she chewed on her lip, not sure how to say what she wanted to say next.

What she really wanted to say was that she wanted him to go now. And never mention what had happened because she didn't know what Harriet would think of it. She didn't want to lose her friendship with Harriet over this.

In the end, after a long pause, she blurted out "Harriet might be back soon."

"I'll head off then," he said.

"I didn't mean that" she said although that was exactly what she had meant. She stood still chewing on her lip.

"Is there something else?" Ethan raised his eyebrows. He was going to make her work for it.

"Listen, this has been great…." Elise swallowed and forced herself to go on, "but I don't think we should do it again. Or mention it."

"I totally agree."

"Oh. Okay then" she hadn't been expecting that. "Okay well I'll go and shower and I'll talk to you later then?"

"Sure" Ethan grinned.

14

Elise hurried down the hall to the bathroom.

While she was plucking her eyebrows in the mirror, she heard him come down the hallway, go through the kitchen and let himself out. She was pretty sure even through the bathroom door, that he was singing Champagne Supernova quietly to himself.

As she turned on the shower she smiled.

Gwen
in the dark

Recommended listening: Girls & Boys
From Blur's third studio album 'Park Life'
Single released in 1994 and reached number 5 on the UK singles chart. Album released in April 1994, by Food Records.
Damon has said it's not about sex, but how people move across borders. The line, "Du bist sehr schon" is German for "You are very pretty".

Gwen was in her darkroom, and it was totally, completely, pitch black. Like the kind of black you can't tell if your eyes are open or closed. Because when you process colour photographs, you don't even get a red bulb. Absolutely no light can enter.

Gwen knew how to feel her way around. It was a small narrow room, only a few steps long. Along the wall was her processing bench, with her developing machine in the centre and boxes of photo paper to the side. That was it. That was all you needed.

Now she slid one of the negatives into the magnifier and put a sheet of paper underneath. This was the part she liked. Playing around with the photographs.

Once you clicked the light on, you had moments to adjust the colour settings, smudge out areas that were too dark, and make the whole thing come alive in a way it just didn't in real life. She loved the tactile-ness of it. The smell of developer on her fingers, the curl of the roll of negatives, the silkiness of the photo paper.

She heard a noise in the corridor outside. It was a small noise. The kind of noise someone makes when they are trying not to be heard.

This went right against policy. As you walked through the maze of corridors that joined up all of the dark rooms you had to yell out that you were coming through. Because the corridors were also pitch black, no-one could see anyone coming and you were likely to smash into someone and break your nose. It had happened before. So Gwen always made sure she started calling out coming through before she even left her dark room.

But this person wasn't saying anything.

She felt, rather than heard, the curtain to her room swing open and someone enter.

"It's me!" Brian whispered in a mock scary voice, trying to be dramatic.

"I know it's you."

"How?" he sounded so hurt and she could picture him sticking out his bottom lip in a pout. He might be in his late forties, but he acted like a child.

"I felt your horny vibes coming down the hall," she said.

At that, he pressed himself up against her back.

"Give me a sec," she said. She was in the middle of developing and would ruin paper if she stopped now. Brian was always talking to them about minimising waste and as the Company Accountant, he knew more than anyone about the cost.

He moved away while she worked, and when she'd finished, she snapped off the machine and was suddenly

17

wedged against the bench, Brian kissing her in a frenzy and pulling her skirt up.

It was semi-uncomfortable having sex up against a developing bench, but she knew that was part of the appeal. It made him more excited, and it made her feel more exciting. No boring hotel beds for them, no back seats of a car. They did it in strange and exotic places that other women wouldn't have dreamed of screwing in.

They were finished moments later and Brian zipped up his jeans, kissed her once on the mouth, and then slipped out. Gwen was used to this.

She turned on her light, and made herself presentable, peering into the small mirror by the door. She had brown shoulder-length hair, which she had started to put a darker hair dye through, to highlight her eyebrows and her long neck, which she always thought was quite elegant. She had a squarish face, and so wore dark plum lipstick and made her brows darker to give a slightly gothic feel. She would never have admitted it and perhaps didn't even realise it consciously, but perhaps she was being influenced by Brian's wife, Samira.

Samira had beautiful dark skin and long gleaming hair and was always dripping in gold jewellery. If Gwen was going to compare to her, then she needed a more compelling look than mousy brown.

Gwen now retouched her lipstick and her brows, thinking about Samira rather than Brian. More than once Samira had decided to come into the dark rooms on some fictitious errand, just to see what everyone was up to. Gwen was a little worried about Samira catching them, but not worried enough to stop. Brian didn't want to get caught either. He was going to leave Samira, but he had told Gwen it had to be the right time. They had two children, and he didn't want them to be hurt.

Gwen understood that. Most of her friends' parents were divorced and it wasn't a great process to go through.

She looked at her watch. It was almost the end of the day. Checking everything was ready for tomorrow, she turned off the light, took the finished photos with her, and walked out into the maze.

"Photographer walking! It's me! I'm here" she called out as she wove her way around several corners. She swept aside the curtain that covered the main entrance and stepped into the light. She stood blinking for a few seconds like an emerging mole.

The main part of the company was a big warehouse space, with light flooding in from skylights. There was an enormous dented and slightly sagging table in the middle of the room, where they did large-scale work. Old couches lined the walls and in the corner was the kitchen. A corridor to the left led to the offices where Brian and Samira were based, along with Deepak and the rest of the senior photographers.

Deepak had started the company after he had graduated with a business degree. His parents had emigrated from India when Deepak was a kid, and Deepak wanted to live their dream for him, of running his own business.

It had started with just him in a tiny studio, doing family portraits. Then his younger sister Samira came to work with him and started doing wedding photographer. As the work kept on coming, they'd had to move to a bigger premise, hire more photographers, and finally an Accountant to run the operations. Samira and Deepak had interviewed a younger and much more studious-looking Brian, who had only graduated a few years before. They'd liked him and hired him. And Samira and Brian had hit it off in another way and been married within 6 months.

Gwen only knew all of this from piecing together things that Samira had told them.

Not that she wanted to be thinking of Samira again.

To the right of the offices was the studio where they did formal portraits. And out in front was the reception area, behind a wall of glass.

Everyone seemed to have left for the night, so she went to her locker to get her bag.

"See you tomorrow" Samira had come through the working space and now stood at the door. Gwen almost jumped out of her skin but felt she hid it well by coughing.

"Yep, see you tomorrow" she gave Samira a half-hearted smile and escaped down the stairs. She came out onto the street and stopped short.

It was a gorgeous day. The sun was out and it was actually warm. She'd put on her jean jacket expecting either the usual chill coming in off the harbour or some sort of drizzly rain that always seemed to switch off and on at the absolutely worse times during November and December. But not today. Today there was not a cloud in the sky.

She looked up, feeling the warmth on her face, and decided she would walk home around the waterfront. In November there weren't many tourists around yet and all the suburbanites who worked in the city and commuted there and back each day, hadn't yet decided to hang about in town and pretend they were urbanites.

She always felt vaguely awed and inspired walking along the waterfront and looking out at the ocean crashing up against the sea wall below her. The road wove around the water, and over towards the bottom of Mt Victoria, the green hills dived down towards her. There was a wooden walkway next to the tarmac there, and she loved clomping along it, although not when it was packed with people dawdling along sight-seeing.

Even though it was just after 5 pm, the sun wouldn't set yet for several hours. Gwen shrugged off her jacket and rummaged in her bag for her spare pair of plastic sunglasses she kept for the odd occasion when it did get sunny unexpectedly.

She put them on, tied her jacket around her waist, and headed down to the water.

*

With the sun out, the whole city felt cleaner and happier. It hadn't been a bad winter or spring. But summer didn't usually just arrive like this. Usually, it showed itself for an hour or two, then disappeared again for weeks, then came back for a whole afternoon, then perhaps one day followed by rain and grey again the next.

But this felt different.

The grass and the trees were somehow greener. The water bluer. The sun was reflecting off the tiny waves into her eyes, winking at her. And people seemed lighter. Less substantial. She felt slightly drunk from it all.

She reached the walkway that looped along the seawall around the waterfront and led to Oriental Bay and the sliver of sand there. Even the sea wall looked brighter today. Not its usual dull grey. Bright grey. Was there such a thing? She'd been in the dark most of the day so perhaps it was making her see things differently.

There were a few local city dwellers out on the wall, like her. Enjoying the sun. Enjoying the walk. Enjoying their city.

She realised without the normal stiff breeze, and without the normal cloudy and grey skies, she was actually breaking out in a sweat. Unheard of for November.

She sat for a little while on the seawall to cool down before she headed up the steep hill to her flat. She flatted on the top floor of an old boarding house, sharing with two couples. She had told them that she was single, even though she wasn't really. She just couldn't tell them the whole Brian situation. She knew somehow, they would disapprove.

She'd always wondered why was it that a room in a flat would cost you a certain amount if you were single but not that much more if you were a couple. It was the same room. Why should each person pay less if they were together? They were together anyway. It made her angry. Not that she and Brian were living together or even got to spend a night together. It was the principle of the thing that annoyed her.

She was breathing hard when she got to the top of the hill and paused before running upstairs, and let herself in. Their flat took up the whole top floor. There was a small lounge and kitchen, three bedrooms, and a family bathroom. Gareth was their newest flatmate and had a bedroom that looked out over the back garden. Ben and Carly, who acted like the parents of the flat even though Gareth was older than them, had one of the front bedrooms – the bigger one, and the other front bedroom was hers.

Gwen liked the view across the trees and down to the harbour and the afternoon sun that slanted in for a couple of hours late in the day. Otherwise, the room was fairly unremarkable. She had a couple of art posters up, a bookshelf jammed with books, CDs, and her CD player, and a chest of drawers, crammed with clothes.

She threw her jacket and bag onto the floor and pulled off her shoes. She put her sunglasses on the chest of drawers and headed to the lounge.

Ben was sprawled out on their one couch watching music videos, eating a bowl of popcorn. Ben and Carly were complete opposites and Gwen wondered sometimes how they didn't argue more often. Ben was lazy and lay around watching TV all the time when he wasn't at the gaming company he worked at. Whereas Carly was super organised and involved in so many charities and events that Gwen could never remember what they all were. She worked for one of them but seemed to get involved in about a hundred other causes too.

Gwen kicked Ben's leg and he moved over so she could collapse next to him. It was MTV and Blur came on.

Damon was wearing jeans and a tracksuit top and singing in front of a row of very fake-looking houses.

"Wow, he went all out for this video," Ben commented.

"It's street." Gwen knew because Blur and Oasis were all Elise had been going on about for weeks. She'd even made Gwen listen to the songs. Gwen had thought it was okay, but the Rolling Stones were so much better. She liked meaningful music.

"Is this song about being gay?" Ben asked listening to the lyrics of the chorus about girls who do boys like they're girls.

"I don't think it's limited to being gay. I think it's about holiday shagging. Shagging anyone." That was what Elise had told her anyway and Gwen didn't really care one way or another.

"Yeah, I'm not sure I like it." Ben had finished his popcorn, pushed his bowl away, rolled himself onto the floor and climbed up. Gwen didn't know how Carly put up with him being so overweight. It was painful to watch sometimes.

He went into the kitchen to see when dinner would be ready. Carly was cooking tonight, and Gwen was pleased. When she'd first moved in, she hadn't liked the idea of having to cook dinner once a week, but actually, it was nice to have a home-cooked meal.

They would usually have sat and watched TV while eating Carly's curry, but as it was such a nice evening, they went outside. There was a shared garden out the back of the house with an old set of almost in-one-piece metal chairs, that held together as long as you didn't sit on them the wrong way, and a rusty table. There was no-one else out there, and they all sat down carefully, putting their curry and drinks on the pitted surface. Gwen felt a little bit sophisticated and European having dinner al fresco.

"Maybe we're going to get a great summer?" Carly said, twisting her long straight hair to one side of her neck.

"I bloody hope so" Ben was a cricket nutter and if it was a good summer, there would be many boozy afternoons for him watching cricket.

"I'm quietly optimistic," Carly took a sip of her water.

"I agree," Gwen said. If it was a great summer, Gwen would at least get to see it in the evenings. The one downside of being a photography assistant was not just being inside but being inside a dark room all day.

Still, it was worth it in so many other ways. Gwen knew that this was a calling. It was art. And that was something neither her older brother nor sister displayed any aptitude for. Being a doctor and an engineer were both highly respected and highly paid – but it was art that was valued in their family. Her parents had owned an art gallery and her father had also sold his own art and Gwen had seen how that had occupied them both. It was more than just having a job. They were making the world more beautiful. She respected her parents for that and knew that this was different from how most people seemed to consider their parents.

It wasn't like she was worried about impressing them or anything like that. But they had lived a life less ordinary and that's what Gwen felt cut out to do too.

That's why she'd moved out at eighteen. To get her life-less-ordinary finally started. She'd flatted with Elise to begin with. Elise had felt her family were as normal as could be and couldn't wait to get away and live life her own way too but in a different way than Gwen. Elise didn't have a calling like Gwen did. Elise seemed to have no idea what she wanted to do, unlike Gwen who had it worked out.

After they'd finished eating, Gwen sat outside with Ben and Carly, talking for a while, until it started to get dark.

"I'm going in to watch TV," Ben said, picking up their plates and putting them into a pile to take inside.

"I have to make some phone calls," Carly said. She always had to make some phone calls. Gwen sometimes felt like that was the other unfair part. They split the phone bill four ways, but Carly was the one who used it the most.

"I'm going into town," Gwen said, following Carly inside with their empty glasses. She grabbed her bag from her room and headed out.

She was a little annoyed with Elise working evenings, so they could never meet up after work like normal people. Not that Elise would probably last long with the telemarketing. Hopefully, once she quit that, she might finally get a proper job where she worked during the day.

Gwen walked along the waterfront and reached the cafe where they liked to meet and managed to get a table by the window looking out at the harbour. It was just after nine and the lights were coming on in the houses dotted around the hills and in the port.

A few minutes later Elise arrived and rushed over to the table. Her face was glowing.

"What's happened?" Gwen couldn't really help but ask.

"Guess what I did this afternoon?" Elise asked, squealing her chair out from under the table and sitting down. She'd obviously been waiting all evening to tell Gwen about it.

"Had sex?" Gwen asked, thinking about what she and Brian had done that afternoon.

"Yes," Elise looked disappointed. "You weren't supposed to guess it that easily."

"Hang on, *who* did you have sex with?" Gwen knew that Elise wasn't exactly surrounded by men interested in her. In fact, she never had been. When they had been at school together Elise had been the gawky, unattractive one. Gwen had been the one who always had a boyfriend. She had tried to set Elise up, but Elise had always seemed to become friends with them. Boys thought she wasn't interested and so they weren't keen on making a move.

"Promise you won't tell?" Elise leaned forward.

"Of course not" Gwen promised. This year she had got used to having things that she couldn't tell anyone. If her family ever found out that she was seeing a married man, they would disown her. And so Gwen had only ever talked about it properly with Elise. She hadn't even told Greer the full story. She'd known Greer would judge her. Greer and Gwen had been friends since primary school and had a different friendship to Gwen and Elise. Greer had had her first boyfriend at the same time as Gwen. Greer had always known she wanted to work in law. Greer was way more mature than Elise and would have had strong opinions about Gwen seeing a married man. Unlike Elise, who was just in awe.

The waitress came over at that moment and Elise sat back in her seat. Gwen knew she wouldn't want to discuss it with anyone listening.

They both ordered hot chocolates and the waitress left.

"Okay spill the beans" Gwen ordered. Elise had literally only had sex twice, so to suddenly be having sex with someone that she hadn't even mentioned before was almost unthinkable. And then Gwen realised she had mentioned some guy that she had met at her telemarketing job. "Oh - hang on, is it Scott?"

"Scott? No, I haven't managed to talk to him yet. Although I smiled at him this evening" Elise raised her eyebrow. "Any other guesses?"

Gwen racked her brains for anyone else Elise had mentioned. There was of course the obvious.

"Not Ethan?" she said.

"Yes," Elise looked puzzled for a minute like she hadn't expected Gwen to guess.

Gwen almost wanted to laugh. It wasn't like there were any other guys that Elise hung around with. It was Scott or Ethan. That was it. But she let Elise go on. This was about the most exciting thing that had happened to her friend for a long while.

"I'm really worried Harriet will find out. I don't know if she'll be okay with it or whether he's off bounds" Elise picked at her nails.

"Whoa, slow down. First of all, what happened?"

And Elise proceeded to tell Gwen about her afternoon and playing Oasis and then falling into bed together. "Then I said something like Harriet would be home soon and he said he'd let himself out. So then I said that maybe we shouldn't mention what had happened and he agreed. And then he left" Elise was wide-eyed.

"Do you want it to happen again?" Gwen asked. She liked this. She was the experienced and wise one when it came to men, and she wanted to help Elise with her love life. Up to now, that had been pretty non-existent. This at least might be the start of something and Gwen would be able to share her wisdom and help Elise through.

Elise really had no idea about men. She really thought that she would fall for her one true love and that would be it for her. Gwen didn't want to burst her bubble completely, but she wanted to show Elise that wasn't how life worked.

Gwen herself had fallen in love four times. The first time was with her first serious boyfriend, and she'd been pleased that she'd lost her virginity to someone who mattered. She'd also fallen for her third boyfriend and then of course there was also Hugh. But she couldn't think of Hugh. And now she was in love with Brian.

But Elise had only ever seemed to have had crushes on celebrities or guys who were with other people. She hadn't really fallen in love. Even this thing with Scott was what Gwen would call lust. It was just a physical attraction. But as usual, Elise had attached far more to it than she should have and decided that Scott was who she was supposed to be with.

"I wouldn't mind if it happened again," Elise mused, "Ethan was really lovely this afternoon and the sex was nice.

But a - I'm in love with Scott and b - I don't want to piss Harriet off."

"Listen, Harriet doesn't have a claim on Ethan anymore. She broke it off with him, didn't she?" Gwen said.

"I think so. But they're still good friends. I just feel like it's wrong. And I know what happened with the whole Jason thing."

Gwen didn't care what the whole Jason thing was. Elise had probably told her at some point, but she couldn't remember.

"You should sleep on it and see how you feel tomorrow" Gwen advised. "Also…" she paused. She'd just remembered something. "Didn't Harriet tell you that Ethan has…." she trailed off.

"Yes, he does!" Elise seemed to know immediately what Gwen was talking about and raised her eyebrows and widened her eyes. "It was huge!"

Their hot chocolates arrived and both of them were trying not to laugh as the waitress put them down. They plopped their marshmallows in. Elise pushed her under the foam with her spoon to melt while Gwen dipped hers in the sprinkled chocolate and then ate them quickly.

Sometimes after a night out drinking when they'd decided to end with a hot chocolate, they'd debated which method was best. Neither would concede to the other.

"You haven't got much to compare it to though" Gwen had to remind her.

"Yes, but Harriet has." Elise wiggled her eyebrows again.

Gwen shrugged. She couldn't argue with that.

"Anyhow you'll never guess what I did this afternoon," Gwen said.

Elise spooned a pile of foam into her mouth and said, "You had sex with Brian again?"

Gwen wiggled her eyebrows up and down. "It was quick, but it was magnificent" she grinned. Even if Elise started having sex more often, Gwen still had the upper hand.

"Just be careful," Elise said.

"We are. Samira's hopeless anyway. Sometimes I'm sure she thinks something is going on because she comes into the darkrooms asking us some stupid thing that isn't urgent at all but then other times she really has no idea, or she'd do something to stop Brian being out all the time. I mean apart from work, we meet up even now for breakfast some mornings."

"What about the guy that owns it?"

"Yeah, he hasn't noticed anything either. We're too discreet. Except last Saturday afternoon Brian took me for a ride on his motorbike. I don't where he tells Samira he's going."

"Will you see him this weekend? Or do you want to go for a drive?"

"Yeah, let's go around the bays. I've got my sister's car for the weekend" Gwen sometimes went and had dinner at her sister Nikki's on a Thursday night and then begged to borrow Nikki's car for the weekend. She didn't want to go for dinner, her sister wasn't a good cook, but on Thursday nights no-one was rostered on to cook and there was often no food in the flat. Putting up with Nikki for an hour saved her the cost of a takeaway. She didn't like having to borrow their car, but no-one else she knew had one, and she loved driving.

In their last year of school, she and Elise would drive around the outer reaches of the harbour, where there were lots of little bays and beaches, the road winding around them like a ribbon. They would listen to the Rolling Stones loudly and talk about men, love, life, and anything else that came to mind. It was a habit they'd carried on over the last few years.

They were just finishing their hot chocolates, sucking out the last few dregs when Blur started playing. It was the boys and girls song again and Elise started singing along.

"I know you love them, but this is not a good song," Gwen said.

"You have no taste," Elise said.

"I don't think it's me who has no taste. Ben said he doesn't like it either." That was a bit of a white lie, but it served Gwen's purpose here.

"Well, I like them." Elise wouldn't be deterred.

"You have to admit it does not compare to the Stones."

"It's just different." Elise could be stubborn.

The music stopped and they realised the café was closing.

"I'm not tired yet. Shall we walk around the harbour?" Elise asked. Gwen nodded. Both of them liked to walk away from the city centre, right to where the promenade turned around the corner towards the airport, where the harbour got more rugged. Around that corner, were some of the most expensive houses in the city. Some of them were old villas, renovated and modernised, and some were new builds. This was actually where Gwen would like to live but they weren't the kind of properties that ever came up for rent, and if they ever did, the rent was too much.

So the two of them left the café and walked together around Oriental Bay and around the far corner. The moon was half full, either waxing or waning, Gwen could never remember, but it shed a ghostly grey light.

They reached the first of the houses they liked to gawk at and slowed down to check each one out. Alongside them, the water was now black with the moon reflecting in it.

When they reached the last house, they turned and wandered back. Soon they were back in front of the steep street that led up to Gwen's.

"Okay I'll call you tomorrow," Elise said.

"Sure, and don't worry. Things will sort themselves out with Ethan. If neither of you says anything, then Harriet will never know." Elise nodded, and then Gwen watched her head back towards the city centre. Gwen turned, took a deep breath, and headed up the hill back to her flat.

Blair comes home

Recommended listening: Common People
From the album 'Different Class' by Pulp
Single released in May 1995 and reached No.2
in the UK Singles Chart.
The song is based on a girl that Jarvis Cocker, lead singer of Pulp,
met at St. Martin's College. She was studying sculpture.

There were a number of things that Blair wasn't thinking as she came off the almost-empty flight, into an almost-empty airport. She wasn't thinking about her best friend Zöe picking her up because Zöe was away. She wasn't thinking about how alive and vibrant Wellington was late on a Sunday night because there was clearly no-one around. And she wasn't thinking that this had been a fantastic idea to come home.

What she was thinking as she lugged her suitcase off the baggage conveyor, and then started dragging it towards the exit, was the same refrain over and over.

What had she been thinking?

What the *hell* had she been thinking?

She trundled her bag across vomit patterned carpet and finally came outside into the warm night air to find there were no taxis.

"Shit" she shouted throwing her arms up dramatically. How was she supposed to get home with luggage? There were no buses at this time of night.

She was looking around to see if there was a pay phone she could use to call a taxi, when she saw a single set of headlights driving into the pick-up bay.

She ran. Fitfully, but she ran. She knew there were a couple of other people who were coming off her flight. She wasn't taking the chance they needed a taxi too. She pulled the door open, hefted her suitcase onto the back seat, and climbed in.

She gave the taxi driver her mother's address and sat back. She rested her forehead against the window. Outside she could see they were driving along the road next to the harbour. The water glistened black like oil. There was a sliver of moon and it reflected on the gently lapping waves.

She leant back slightly and she could see herself reflected in the glass. She had long strawberry blonde curly hair, that she often wound into a messy knot on top of her head. A heart-shaped face and a sprinkling of freckles across her nose. It was her freckles that had made her and Zöe become best friends when they were five. Zöe also had them, despite having dark hair, and they'd had a competition to see who had the most. They'd both hated having them back then although Blair had finally grown fond of hers now.

They stopped at traffic lights. There were no other cars and for a moment Blair wondered if the cabbie would run the light. But no, the meter was ticking.

Compared to where she had just come from, Wellington was silent and asleep. Blair leaned her forehead on the cool windowpane again. They were turning into the city centre now, and it was still deserted. It wasn't even midnight for god's sake. Sydney would still be crowded with people, out drinking and enjoying themselves. Here, as they were stopped at another set of lights, the only movement she saw was a lone cat that shot out of the bushes by the side of the road and disappeared into one of the nearby buildings.

She felt desolate. She wasn't ready for this. She thought it had been the right time to return but she was regretting it and she'd only been home for less than an hour.

They took the right turn, cutting across the north of the city centre. The taxi driver seemed to know where he was going. She was glad. She didn't feel up to an argument tonight about the quickest way to get there. How many times had a taxi driver tried to take her on some long winding route just to be able to charge her more?

They stopped at yet another red light. It was so quiet she could imagine a movie scene with tumbleweed blowing down the street with that eerie wind noise that always accompanied it.

She wound her window down and poked her face out to catch some breeze.

Her hair blew everywhere, and she pulled it into a messy ponytail. She couldn't believe how warm it was. Accelerating away, they were now only a couple of minutes away from her mothers' house. Suddenly, thinking about the house, she realised it seemed so cramped, so packed with remnants of her childhood, so un-cosmopolitan. She didn't want to go back there after the independence of living in Australia.

As they sped on, she slumped in her seat dejectedly. There was no escape. She'd made the wrong choice.

Then suddenly she sat bolt upright and poked her head out of the open window again. They were driving past Elise's house and the lights were all on.

The lights were all on!

"Stop!" she grabbed the headrests of the two front seats and leaned forward to the driver and said it again, with a please, even though he couldn't have failed to hear her the first time. "Can you pull over here?" Her voice was urgent and wasn't really a question. Blair was a girl who was used to people doing as she told them.

The taxi driver frowned and pulled over. Blair saw that it was a dotted yellow line, but it wasn't as if anyone else was going to need to pass.

"Just give me a minute, I'll be right back." She almost fell out of the cab in her haste, slamming the door shut, leaving her suitcase with most of her favourite possessions in the back, and unlatched the gate to Elise's house. She ran up the zigzag path through the garden and then around to the back of the house. She took the back steps two at a time and knocked frantically on the door.

For a moment she thought no-one was going to answer and started tapping her foot impatiently, but then she heard footsteps down the hall. Cautiously the door opened, and a face peered around the gap. It was Elise. When she saw who it was, she threw the door open and hugged Blair.

"What are you doing here?" she asked.

"I just got back from Sydney."

"Like just now?"

"Yep, my taxi's out the front. On the street!"

"Are you going home?" Elise asked.

"I'm kind of bummed out and don't really want to." Blair pulled a face.

"Do you want to stay here for a few days? I've got a spare mattress in my room."

Blair hadn't thought how Elise was going to solve anything, but as Elise finished speaking, Blair didn't even hesitate.

"That would be brilliant. Are you sure?"

"Sure" Elise shrugged.

"Fantastic! I'll just go get my suitcase."

She hurried back down to sort the taxi out. Suddenly things were looking up. She didn't consider the fact that she didn't know Elise that well, or whether it would be an imposition to stay. Those things were not even on her radar. As she dragged her suitcase back up the path, Elise came down to help and they lugged the suitcase together up the back steps.

Blair had met Elise a few months ago. They were both doing a telemarketing job selling car servicing. Neither of them had a car or knew anything about brake realignments, suspension, or oil changes. But the product was good, saved people money, and got the local garage more service so people had been quite keen on it and the pay had ended up okay.

It had been a Tuesday night when Blair knew she had to study for an exam the following day. She'd complained to Elise that all her flatmates would be out and she always found it hard to study alone. Zöe would usually have come and kept her company, but she and Bowie were trying out living together for the first time and had disappeared in a loved-up haze.

Elise had offered to come up and hang out reading magazines to help motivate Blair. After that, she did the same for a couple of other exams. And after that they were friends.

As they reached the top step Blair realised that she probably would have hung out with Elise more but then she'd decided to go to Sydney for a couple of months. It was nothing planned. She'd finished exams, was bored of telemarketing and wanted to avoid a guy she'd had a brief affair with, oh and her flat was kind of breaking up and she couldn't be bothered trying to find new flatmates. Zöe hadn't been pleased but knew better than to argue with one of Blair's schemes.

They got the suitcase to the top of the stairs and wheeled it across to the door.

"What were you doing up anyway?" Blair asked.

"We were watching a bad Sharon Stone movie" Elise shunted the suitcase through into the kitchen.

"Is there a *good* Sharon Stone movie?" Blair laughed.

"Well, if there is, it's definitely not Scissors, the film we were watching" Elise shook her head sadly.

"I've never heard of it."

"Neither had me or Harriet – we were waiting for it to get better." Blair hadn't met Elise's flatmate Harriet yet and once they had dumped the suitcase in the hallway, Elise led her through to the lounge.

"Blair's here," she said, "Blair this is Harriet".

"Hi," Blair threw herself into one of the green armchairs.

"Hi," Harriet sipped her cup of tea and eyed Blair then looked over to Elise. Elise looked back at her. Blair watched the two of them and picked up some sort of tension. Probably some weird flatmate issue they were having.

Harriet took another sip of tea and said "I think I'll go to bed. This movie is really awful". She flicked off the TV, picked up her mug, and brushed past Elise into her bedroom.

Blair picked up a magazine off the floor.

"Hang on!" Elise said and hurried after Harriet.

Blair could hear urgent whispers before becoming engrossed in an article about luxury Russian hotels. Elise emerged and shut Harriet's door behind her.

"She's fine," she said but didn't explain, and Blair didn't care enough to ask.

"This is a great magazine" Blair held it up. She'd never seen it before. Wallpaper* it was called.

"Yeah, I like it," Elise agreed, "although it's really expensive. You can borrow it if you want."

"Thanks." Blair continued to flick through it.

Elise went back to the kitchen, got Blair's suitcase and pulled it down the hall. Blair put the magazine down and followed Elise into her room.

"Hey, this is great!" Blair had thought the room would be a pokey hole, but it was a huge room, with two big sets of bay windows, long curtains, cream carpet and white walls. It was light and felt sunny even though it was night. And had a great view out across the rooves of the houses in the block opposite. "You could have six people live in here!"

"I guess so" Elise shrugged.

"*Why* have you got an extra mattress?" Blair now saw that Elise had her bed in the corner yet there was another mattress leaning against the opposite wall.

"It's Harriet's but her room already has a bed, so I'm storing it." Elise flipped it to the floor. She went over to the wardrobe and rummaged under a pile of clothes and pulled out a sheet. She snapped the sheet into the air, and it billowed out halfway across the bed. Blair caught the other end, and they pulled it tight and tucked it in.

"I've got a couple of spare pillows and a blanket. Will that do?" Elise asked.

"That will be perfect" Blair threw herself down and laid her arms out like Jesus. She'd slept for a couple of hours on the plane so didn't feel tired at all. She propped herself up on her elbows and regarded Elise standing there, looking unsure.

"I'm hungry. Do you want to get something to eat?"

"Sure" Elise shrugged and then did something that Blair could only describe as cocking her head.

"What?" she asked.

Elise seemed to hesitate before replying.

"I'm just really envious of you. It's like nothing's a problem for you. You don't seem worried about anything. I worry about everything". Elise went over to the wardrobe and found a blue zippy top to put on over her singlet and jeans. Blair climbed up frowning. She'd never considered that she didn't worry about things. Why would you worry?

"Actually, my mother will be worried." This just occurred to her. "Can I borrow your phone and just let her know I won't be coming home?"

Blair made a quick phone call. Her mother had been asleep and said she was fine with Blair staying with a friend instead. Blair felt a weight off her shoulders. Yes, she would have go to and say hi tomorrow and get some of her things, but she wouldn't have to revert to being a kid again which she always felt when she went home.

Together Elise and Blair walked through the deserted streets to try and find a shop that might still be open. Blair told Elise about Sydney, the markets, the shopping, and the restaurants. And how miserable she was getting back and realising how quiet and small Wellington was in comparison. Elise didn't say much.

As they walked further and further through the streets, they found absolutely nothing was open. Nothing. Finally, in desperation, Elise suggested a petrol station a couple of blocks over.

"Wow it's actually open" Blair scorned. "In Sydney, everything would still be open right now. They even have 24-hour supermarkets that never close."

"Bullshit!" Elise laughed.

"They do!"

"Did you ever go shopping at 4 am?"

"A couple of times" Blair nodded.

"Well don't think you'll be doing that shit here. 24-hour supermarkets!" Elise laughed in wonder and shook her head. They went into the gas station and loaded up on potato chips and chocolate, then wandered back towards Elise's, eating as they walked.

"I thought you were going to Sydney to be an actress," Elise said after a long silence.

"Yeah, I was thinking about it." Blair realised that had been the explanation she'd told a few people when they asked why she was going to Sydney. It was only something she was half thinking about.

"You could apply to drama school here" Elise suggested.

"Yeah, I'm not sure about that," Blair said. "I can just tell if I got in that it will be all about criticising the hell out of us until we're broken down and crying, then they can reshape us and build us up again."

"What's wrong with that?" Elise steered them back around the corner.

"It's tired. I want somewhere that's going to grow me, not break me down."

"Can you not do acting without drama school?" Elise asked.

"I don't know. I don't know what I'll do. Anyway, let's talk about something important. What have you been doing? Have you fallen in love yet?"

"Well, actually I kind of have." Elise blushed.

Blair took her arm in hers.

"Tell me all about it."

"Do you want the long or short story?"

"I want the long one," Blair said "But wait, let's get organised first" they headed back to Elise's room to sit cross-legged on each of their beds, a pile of chips and chocolate in front of them.

"We need some music" Elise climbed up and went over to her CD player and put on the new Pulp album. She skipped ahead to the song she liked the most. The first few lines talked about how she came from Greece with a thirst for knowledge and studied sculpture at St Martin's College.

"Have you heard this?" Elise asked.

"No" Blair shook her head.

"Listen to this bit," Elise said.

The guy singing was explaining the girl was asking for a rum and coke and then singing that she'd never live like common people.

"That is hilarious," Blair said. "Who are they?"

"Pulp they're called. I think it's great."

"There was a distinct lack of British music in Sydney" Blair snapped off a piece of chocolate, while Elise settled herself back on her bed. They listened to the song for a while.

When it finished, Blair got up and turned the CD player off.

"Okay. You need to spill about this guy you're in love with." She settled back down again.

"Well after you left, I got a job in a cafe."

"Okay, go on" Blair indicated with a piece of chocolate.

"So one day I came out of the kitchen and saw this guy sitting at the table by the window looking out. I went over to take his order and when he looked up at me he looked *exactly* like Johnny Depp. Well, obviously he wasn't, not exactly but pretty much the same. I found it hard to breathe."

"He's beautiful" Blair confirmed "Beautiful men can take your breath away."

"That's exactly what it was like! Anyway, he ordered a coffee, and I rushed off to give the order to the guy who makes all the coffee. Then I went back into the kitchen to talk to the other waitress who was on break and she told me to talk to him when I took his coffee over. So I really tried but I ended up just plopping the coffee in front of him and not being able to say a word."

Blair pulled a sympathetic face.

"Even when he came and paid I couldn't say anything and I never thought I'd see him again" Elise paused and ate a chip.

"But you did?" Blair had almost finished a whole bar of chocolate and was starting to feel ill. She closed the wrapping and threw it at Elise who caught it.

"Well, I got a new job a couple of weeks ago selling satellite TV. The first night of the job I walked in and found that the Johnny Depp guy was sitting at the desk right in front of me."

"Oh my god, that is totally fate!" Blair sat up.

"Yeah, but I can barely speak to him even though I'm in love with him," Elise said.

"What's his name?"

"Scott" Elise said.

"Well, we're going to have to do something about this Scott."

And so Blair gave advice and listened some more and shared her wisdom about men until they were too tired to talk anymore and climbed into their separate beds and fell into a deep sleep as dawn brushed the sky yellow, another day of perfect summer on the way.

Fran
feels chic

Recommended listening: She's Electric

From the album (What's the story) Morning Glory by Oasis

Album released in October 1995, by Creation Records.

Noel said this was the first song he wrote for Morning Glory. Someone asked him if it was about Blur. He said it's not.

It's also not a true story.

Fran was standing looking down at the harbour far below. She was up on the crest of Mt Victoria, leaning against the red brick monastery that stood proud on the prow of the hill, it's crumbling stone shining in the sun. Whenever she drove into Wellington, she always looked out for it from the motorway. It was like a ruby gleaming out amongst the green of the bush and the yellow and white villas dotted around it and that clustered up the slope towards it.

Then her eye would move upwards and to the left of the monastery, to see if she could see her flat. She lived on a hidden street behind the monastery in a light blue coloured villa.

Living up there, was a killer on the legs to walk home at night, but it was great when she was setting out from home to meet someone in the city. Then it was all downhill.

She normally had the choice of either walking down the steep snaking path in front of her that led directly down to Oriental Bay, or she could go the long way, down through the suburbs and then around the waterfront.

Today she was meeting Harriet on the waterfront, so she'd decided on the direct route. Actually, she thought, looking up at the blue sky, it was an exceptionally lovely day. And it had been sunny and warm for days now, which was unusual for November. Maybe it was going to be a great summer.

She needed to watch herself though. Whenever she thought something like that she tended to jinx it.

She was thirsty and so looking out at the harbour one last time, she headed down the path. Going downhill was supposed to be easier than going up, but Fran always found her calves got sore really quickly.

Near the bottom she broke into a jog, tired of resisting the pull of the slope. Finally, on the level, she headed to the little grocery shop on the corner and bought an ice cream.

She wasn't expecting Harriet to be on time. Harriet never had been in all the time Fran had known her. As it was so beautiful out, Oriental Parade was packed. It was a wide promenade that wrapped around the edge of the harbour and went right up the sea wall so people could walk, bike, or skateboard. Nestled below the sea wall were rocks and a little slither of beach that stretched like a smile. There were families down on the sand enjoying the sun and old people sitting on the benches watching the fountain. There were even people sunbathing which Fran thought was ridiculous at this time of year.

Fran found a space on the sea wall, climbed over, and sat down, swinging her legs out over the water, eating her ice-cream contently. She looked across at the opposite

44

shore of the harbour. The waterfront over there continued around in front of the business district and then became the port. At the moment the whole area wasn't that pretty, but she knew it would change soon when they started building the new museum.

She looked the other way over to the Hutt Valley. There were a few boats out on the harbour today even without much wind, and a giant container ship coming in.

Where she was sitting the beach had tapered off and below her was the sea, although it was only a couple of inches deep. She looked down and saw a soggy ice cream cone floating just below the surface, being sucked gently in and out by the waves.

She threw the end of her cone into the waves and watched it join the other disintegrating one.

Behind her, a constant stream of cars made their way around the parade. Windscreens glinted in the sun, and she realised she wasn't wearing her sunglasses. She rummaged in her handbag, found them, and slipped them on. Looking up she saw Harriet's old faded pink VW beetle come around the corner at the end of the parade.

It was a fairly unmissable car and suited Harriet to a t. Fran watched as by some fluke, a black hatch batch pulled out of a parking space just in front of Harriet, and Harriet swerved straight into the gap. Fran wondered if Harriet would straighten the VW up, or leave it angled as it was. Fran would make sure it was completely straight with the kerb, but Harriet on the other hand didn't seem to care.

She had climbed out of the car and was looking wildly around the bay. Fran waited patiently until Harriet looked her way, then waved across the water, and Harriet waved back, seeing her.

Harriet had long deep red hair that was pulled into a ponytail. She was hefting a large purple bag on her shoulder and wearing a yellow sun dress. Fran wouldn't have described her as having any fashion sense at all.

Fran liked to dress non-descript. A lot of black. She felt it was chic. She had shoulder-length hair, and a short fringe a la Janeane Garofalo in Reality Bites. And red lipstick. Lots of red lipstick.

At least Harriet never wore any makeup. Fran hated to think what colours she'd try and pair with her complexion.

Harriet wove her way through the throngs of people and finally sat down on the wall next to Fran.

"Sorry I'm late" she rummaged around in her handbag and pulled out some tortoiseshell sunglasses that didn't go with her hair. Or her dress. Or anything else really.

"I was people watching" Fran had on black John Lennon type sunglasses today, her red lipstick, and a dark grey sleeveless dress. She felt very stylish, especially next to Harriet's kaleidoscope of colour.

"I'm thirsty; do you want to get a drink?" Harriet asked.

"I just had an ice cream."

"Do you want to go to the café over there? We can sit out in the courtyard."

Fran shrugged. She was happy here, but she could sense Harriet needed to go somewhere. They climbed up and walked around the promenade. Parade café was packed as usual, but they pounced on an outside table that had just been left and Harriet went inside to order an iced coffee. She came back grabbing a couple of glasses of water on the way.

"Thanks" Fran took one from her "So how are you?" she said twirling her straw.

"Exhausted!" Harriet flumped down in the chair opposite Fran. "Elise has invited some friend of hers to stay and they were giggling away for hours. I couldn't sleep."

"Who?" Fran didn't know Elise had any friends who hadn't got anywhere to live at the moment.

"Blair. She met her telemarketing. I'll be better when I've had coffee." Fran was pleased her current flat didn't have ridiculous issues like people inviting other people to stay. Most of them were now twenty-five. They were getting too old for that.

"What about you?" Harriet asked.

"Work's a bitch at the moment" Fran was still working in the bookstore where she, Harriet, and Elise had first met each other when they'd all worked there. "They've frozen buying so I've really got nothing to do. No reps to see. No stocktakes. I just have to serve customers" Fran screwed up her nose. Dealing with customers was always the worst part of the job.

Fran paused then said, "Ethan came in the other day."

"Did he?" Harriet leant back in her chair.

"I don't think he really likes me. He kind of tried to avoid me" Fran searched Harriet's face for confirmation and saw she was uncomfortable. Well, Fran didn't like Ethan either, so it was mutual. "I don't know what you see in him." Fran sipped her water.

"Not everyone gets him" Harriet shrugged.

"Have you seen Jason lately?" Fran threw it out there like a challenge.

Her thunder was stolen when the waitress came over with Harriet's coffee and almost knocked Fran's water all over her. By the time she'd left apologising, Fran had missed seeing what Harriet's reaction had been.

Stirring the cream around on top of her coffee Harriet shrugged and said "I saw him the other day. I bumped into him when I was walking down from the university. He seemed lonely."

Fran had gone out with Jason last year when they were flatmates. It had been pretty serious. On the day that she'd moved in, Jason had come down to see if she needed any help and they'd ended up in bed together. They'd decided to keep their own rooms although straight away Fran started spending most nights upstairs, rather than in her room downstairs.

And it had been a truly horrible flat. There was a couple who had lived there forever and had the other downstairs bedroom. They had years of their crap piled everywhere. They also left food all over the house. There had been a pot of beans sitting on the stove, uncovered for days. Fran decided to throw them out and was yelled at. One day she'd seen the cat's food bowl had maggots in it.

After months of putting up with the mess, she'd tried to instigate a cleaning roster and all hell had broken loose. Jason had had to be the mediator between her and the others and after weeks of a stand-off, Jason had told her perhaps this wasn't the best flat for her.

Fran felt attacked and had attacked back.

She'd accused him of taking the other's side.

He'd shrugged and said that they'd been here longer than she had. Fran had then suggested that maybe he wasn't the best boyfriend for her. They'd had a flaming row and she'd said it was over and she'd moved out. He'd come down to help her pack a few days later when she'd found another place and they'd ended up in bed again.

This time the breakup was melancholy.

Fran knew that Jason still felt she'd been in the wrong and they both knew that she wouldn't stand being with someone who wasn't going to side with her. So they left it unsaid so that they might still be able to be friends. And who knew, from time to time maybe even hook up again. Although of course as mature as Fran wanted to be about that she actually found afterwards that she couldn't face seeing him again.

At the same time, Harriet had needed a new place to live. Fran had introduced her to Jason when Harriet had come round for dinner at the house. Now Fran suggested Harriet give Jason a call and see if the room was still free. It was, and Harriet had moved into Fran's old room.

Fran had to then endure the two of them going out together.

She knew that she and Jason were over, but that hadn't meant that she wanted Harriet to get her claws into him. Harriet had of course checked with her first and Fran had said that it was fine, but she hadn't *meant* it.

Even now, now that Harriet and Jason had also broken up, she still hadn't really forgiven Harriet for not actually understanding that it wasn't right. It wasn't done. Exes were off-limits unless you were really okay with it. Which no-one really was.

Although Fran liked to think that she was a good enough friend to try and put it to one side and only occasionally show Harriet that she still wasn't completely forgiven.

"I'm sure he'll find someone else soon" Fran felt a little nasty saying it but she didn't want Harriet to think she was anything special. Jason went through women quickly. Harriet had just been another in a long line. He and Fran had had something special and had been together far longer than most. But Jason was never going to be able to settle down.

"Are you going out with anyone new?" Fran asked.

"No," Harriet said. "I did go on a date with this guy who told me about how he loved to kill and stuff birds. He kept saying it over and over again. I thought it was hilarious."

"He sounds great…." He sounded crazy, like a lot of t the men that Harriet seemed to date. Fran drank some of her water. "So that makes us all single at the moment?" she realised.

"It's funny how we all go through stages when we're all single, or we're all with someone" Harriet took a sip of her coffee.

"What about Ethan? Is he seeing anyone?"

"I'm not sure. He talks a lot about his ex-flatmate Aria. But he doesn't need to be with someone. He's pretty self-sufficient."

"Yes, that was something Jason was not."

Fran now felt like having an iced coffee so went inside to order.

"So how is the flat other than the Elise thing?" she asked once she'd sat back down.

"Rosalie's funny. She was very proud to show me the stain in her bed from when she slept with some German guy. I thought it must have been the night before, but then Elise told me that she showed her the same stain weeks ago."

"That's disgusting" Fran couldn't understand how Harriet found these things amusing. She just seemed comfortable living in grunge.

After Fran got her iced coffee, they moved on to reminiscing about their bookshop days and then talking about books. As she finished her drink, Fran noticed something.

"People are glaring at us."

"They just want our table" Harriet shrugged.

"I suppose I do have to head off. I'm going to a party tonight."

"Do you want a lift up the hill?" Harriet offered.

"Yeah, that would be great."

As soon as they stood up a couple who had been loitering in the doorway rushed in and grabbed their table.

Jack
meets a wanker

Recommended listening: Charmless Man

Released in 1995 as the fourth and final single from the album 'The Great Escape' by Blur.

The single reached No 5 on the UK singles chart.

The video stars French-American actor Jean-Marc Barr (best known from film The Big Blue), in his underwear. It also features some awesome 90's dance-leaping from Damon.

Christof was pacing the front of the room like a bull terrier in a pen, glaring from time to time at his tacky gold watch. Jack looked around the room. Most of them had arrived already, why did Christof have to be such a wanker about it? Jack wished he'd stayed downstairs and had another cigarette if there was going to be trouble.

Christof was short, fat, and kind of greasy with a gold chain lying in amongst the chest hair sprouting out of his open-neck shirt. Jack knew he was kind of portly himself but he was lovable fat, or so his girlfriend Sarah told him regularly. She called him a pudgy Ethan Hawke but in a good way. He liked to believe her.

As Elise, the new girl hurried in and threw her bag under an empty desk, Christof clapped his hands and they

51

all meandered to the front of the room and milled about there, like passengers waiting for a late train. Jack winked at Scott. They both knew how much their fucking around pissed Christof off.

"Form a circle" Christof ordered and infuriatingly slowly the fifteen of them drifted together to make a ring, Christof stood impatiently at the front by his desk. "Now" Christof started, "tonight I was going to congratulate Scott on making 10 sales last night ..."

Scott took a bow, and everyone clapped.

"But instead" Christof continued loudly over the top of the applause, "I'm going to share a customer complaint about Scott. Yesterday you called a Mrs Abbott who told you she was eating dinner and not interested in the deal. She said you then got pushy with her, and she ended up hanging up."

Scott was gazing thoughtfully out of the window while the rest of them watched him for some reaction.

Christof continued, "Now I'm not going to come down on any of you for having a crack, but what Scott did next was not on. Can you tell everyone what you did?"

Scott continued to stare out of the window. Jack looked around the circle. Elise was gazing at Scott and appeared to be holding her breath waiting to hear what he had to say. Jack had seen that look before.

"Scott?" Christof prompted.

Scott picked something out of his teeth, turned, and grinned at each person in the circle, and said, "I called her back and told her she was a fuck-wit." The group broke into laughter and cheers and Scott took another bow. Christof raised his arm until they lapsed into silence.

"It is *not* funny," he said sternly. "I don't want anything like that to happen tonight."

"No sir!" Scott bowed.

Christof's face turned red, but he didn't respond and faced the rest of them. "Alright, let's get to it."

Scott snuck in a low five to Jack before both of them took to their cubicles.

For the next two hours, the room was a noisy babble of the same pitch over and over again, about how great this offer was, what a great time it was to try, and what a great range of movies and shows you could watch. It was punctuated only when someone made a sale with a shout of hurray! as they put down their phone.

Jack found himself reading out the entire sports programme to try and get someone signed up. When they asked if there was any American Football on, he lied and said there was.

Once it turned seven, people finished the call they were on and filed downstairs. Most of them congregated in the car park to smoke and complain. Jack had a hunch that there was more to Elise than met the eye so he made sure to fall into step beside her as they left the room.

"Are you coming for a smoke? I've got a few extra."

She looked at him for a moment and he flicked a strand of hair out of his eyes.

"Okay, thanks," she said and grinned.

Clustered in a circle very different from the one they were forced into upstairs, they all lit up and ended up talking about lying to customers. As they blew smoke into the air, they all cheerfully admitted they'd done it. Whether it was telling people that a movie they wanted to see was on, or that there were more sports that they liked than there really was.

They all figured that because the schedule changed each month, they could just say they got confused about the programming if they were ever pulled up on it.

Elise shook her head and tutted. "So that's how you guys make so many sales? Lying?"

"You're not doing too badly. You've got a couple tonight haven't you?" Jack asked tapping his cigarette ash onto the floor.

"Yeah but with this technique I'm going to double that" Elise grinned.

"Goddamn we've corrupted her" Jack exclaimed.

And sure enough towards the end of the night between calls, he heard Elise telling a customer about the wide range of porn on offer. Jack knew there was hardly anything dirty available but he hoped they would buy it.

When 9 pm hit, they all finished their calls and took their final results up to Christof, before saying goodbye to everyone and wandering out of the room. As they left Jack caught up with Elise at the lift.

"Did the guy buy the porn you were peddling?"

"Oh, you heard that?" Elise blushed as Scott stepped into the lift with them and cupped his hand to his ear.

"Did I hear the mention of sweet pornography? Were you selling them on the non-existent porn? I'm impressed."

Elise blushed some more and shrugged. "Well, it worked. He brought the add-on package too."

"Brilliant, that means you can shout us a beer. You are going to come and have a drink with us?" Jack indicated towards himself and Scott. They had gone for a couple of cold ones after work a few times.

Elise opened her eyes wider and nodded.

The three of them came out of the building to find the sun had just set and the colour was slowly leeching out of the sky. It was still warm and there was a pub only a short walk away. Jack and Scott led the way with Elise trailing next to them.

Once inside, they made their way in single file through the dark and smoky part of the bar, and out the back into the garden area. Soon they were tucked into a table in the corner under a tree.

"I guess it's my shout to start." Elise went inside.

Once she'd gone Jack turned to Scott.

"I think you should invite her to golf." Jack took out his cigarettes and lit up. Scott had decided that they should go and play a round tomorrow and Jack had agreed. He liked the guy. He knew Scott could be a bit of a wanker where work was concerned, but he firmly believed he was good at heart.

"Maybe, she seems a bit quiet." Scott scratched his jaw. He was always scratching and picking at his face, and Jack didn't understand why that seemed to have created some kind of attraction for Elise. Because he had seen her gazing dreamily at him several times.

"I think she could be fun."

"I'll think about it." Scott shrugged.

Elise came back out carrying a jug and three glasses.

"You drink beer?" Scott asked. When she nodded Jack saw her stock had risen.

"I wasn't getting you guys anything stronger. You've already turned me into a pathological liar and that was when you were sober."

"I think you give us waaay too much credit" Jack laughed, took a drag, blew it upwards and looked up at the sky. Now it was getting darker, and the sky was turning black, you could start to see the stars. Even with the strings of lights hanging off the fence and the trees around them, he could still make out the constellations.

Elise followed his gaze.

"Can you see Orion?" she asked.

"Which ones that?"

"See the three stars close together then one at each point. That's his belt." She leaned close to him and pointed up. On the other side of the table, Scott twisted and tried to match where they were gazing.

"Whoever thought that looked like a belt was stoned" he shrugged. "I thought Orion was supposed to be a pot."

"Well yeah they do say that too" Elise nodded. "The line of stars is the handle."

"Oh yeah, I see it!" Jack thought he did.

"I think you two have been at the pot." Scott gave up cricking his neck and drank his beer. "I'm getting another," he said and scraped his chair back on the pavers. Elise picked up Jack's pack of cigarettes. They were in a wooden holder with pictures of the Beatles laminated all over it.

"My girlfriend Sarah made it for me" he shrugged.

"You like The Beatles?"

"Don't you?"

"No, I'm a Rolling Stones girl."

"Wash your mouth out! The Beatles are superior in every way to the Stones!"

"Oh really?" Elise was obviously up for a fight. Jack sat back happily. He hadn't had anyone to argue his case to for a while. All his other friends had given up on his Beatles obsession a long time ago.

"Do tell!" Jack said happily.

"The Beatles didn't know a thing about rock and roll. They are pop through and through." Elise seemed to feel this was unarguable.

"And you're saying rock is better than pop?"

"Definitely!"

"Sergeant Pepper is actually considered to be a milestone album that changed the face of both pop and rock. The Stones didn't do that."

"Phooey" Elise said and took a sip of her beer. "They just took experimenting to new heights. The Stones honed what a great rock song is all about."

"Your argument is phooey?" Jack laughed. "Have you really listened to Sergeant Pepper?"

"Have you really listened to the Stones?" They narrowed their eyes at each other and laughed. Scott had been standing listening for a couple of minutes, now he sat down again.

"Have you two finished? They're both ancient history."

"Actually they're going to release a new Beatles song that was never released" Jack leant forward excitably.

"Enough!" Scott banged his fist on the empty pack of cigarettes. "If you're going to talk about music, it had to be from this decade."

"Sure" Jack shrugged. "Who are you into at the moment?" he asked Elise.

"Oasis and Blur" Elise shrugged.

"But which specifically? Oasis OR Blur?" Jack leaned forward.

"Oasis. They're more rock and roll." Elise said.

"So they're the Stones are they?"

"Yes, and Blur are pop. They're the Beatles."

"It's interesting to me that Oasis steals their lyrics and concepts from the Beatles though, not from the Stones." Jack raised his eyebrows at her.

"That was one song and one line, it proves nothing," Elise said.

"Oh my god, what have I started!" Scott threw his hands in the air. "You two are as bad as each other."

"You'll have to give me your number. We'll have to get together and discuss this when we haven't got a musical Neanderthal with us" Jack winked at her. Elise grinned.

*

While Elise visited the bathroom the boys analysed. It was a quick discussion and that, for Jack, was one of the biggest commendations for drinking with the boys. You did not have to discuss your feelings like he had to with Sarah and her friends when they roped him into coming with them. The entire conversation was:

"Okay she's hot" Scott admitted.

"And witty" Jack added. "And I think she likes you."

"You don't say?" Scott seemed to take this suggestion and mull over it. Otherwise, that was that. She had the thumbs up.

When Elise got back to the table Scott leant back and took a long drag on his cigarette. Exaggeratedly slowly. And then blew the smoke up into the air. Jack shook his head. He was beginning to wish he hadn't said what he'd said if Scott was going to act like he was Hefner.

"We're playing golf tomorrow," Scott said, raising one eyebrow. "Do you want to come?"

"Me?" Elise asked. Jack hoped she wasn't going to stuff it up now. "I've never played golf."

"It's not that hard. I can show you" Scott shrugged.

"Okay, what time are you going?"

"Early. I'd have to pick you up at nine".

"I can do nine". Elise explained where she lived which was right round the corner. She looked at her watch. "I have to head off," she said and picked up her beer for one final sip. "See you tomorrow then."

"Cheers" Jack waved, and they both watched her backside as she weaved between the tables. Jack looked at his watch. "I better get home to the little woman," he said.

"Yeah, I suppose I should get home to mine too" Scott finished his beer and put the empty glass on the table.

Jack looked at Scott. Scott looked back.

"I didn't know you had one," Jack said cautiously. Sure, he didn't know Scott that well but they'd had drinks a few times and you mentioned something like that. He didn't want to think he'd just tried to set Elise up with a wanker.

"Yep, going on two years now." Scott ground out the end of his cigarette in the ash tray.

Jack was bothered. He didn't get bothered by much. He prided himself on being pretty laid back about what life threw at you. If you didn't, you just got wound up and made yourself miserable or sick. He'd seen his father rant about how unfair life was until his heart attack, which stopped him dead.

"Why did you bother inviting Elise tomorrow then?"

"Well, you never know what might happen."

In the silence between songs, Jack hoped he hadn't unleashed a monster. He'd underestimated how nice Elise was and what a wanker Scott could be.

With beers drained, they headed through the bar to the exit. There had been several Brit Pop songs played over the time they had been there and Elise and Jack had caught each other's eye, excluding Scott, but now Blur's Charmless Man started to play.

Damon started to sing about meeting someone in a crowded room and how he ended up being a charmless man.

Jack couldn't help shaking his head. Tonight he'd seen a bit of a charmless man in Scott, and it hadn't been pretty. Thankfully he would be at golf tomorrow to protect Elise if Scott was going to be a wanker. And then she'd hopefully see and lose interest in him.

At least he hoped she would see.

"Catch you tomorrow" Scott nodded and headed off.

Jack nodded and headed the other way for the walk home.

Ethan
in the sun

Recommended listening: Cast No Shadow

From the album (What's the story) Morning Glory by Oasis

Album released in October 1995, by Creation Records.

Written about Richard Ashcroft, lead singer of the Verve, who Oasis supported on tour before releasing Definitely Maybe.

Ethan woke up to sun bright against his curtains. His window was only inches away from the wall of the house next door, and the only time in the day the sun made it down the chasm was for half an hour or so around noon.

Groggily he rubbed his face, ran his hands through his hair, glanced at the glowing red numbers on his clock next to him on the bedside table, confirmed that it was, in fact, midday, and climbed out of the bed.

The mattress sagged, the springs made rusty gasps whenever he moved and every time he got up the whole frame creaked alarmingly. He no longer noticed its protesting.

Aria had left it behind when he had moved in and not having a bed himself, he had taken it under his wing.

Now he pulled on a white t-shirt thrown over the end of the bed and shrugged on his frayed ripped jeans that were splayed on the floor. He opened his door and turned towards the bathroom. At that moment the front door opened. A petite woman with a sleek black bob stepped inside. She looked Ethan up and down and said in a strong French accent:

"Who are you and what are you doing in this house?"

Ethan peered at her. He had no idea who she was so shrugged and went into the bathroom. He emerged a few minutes later feeling more human and up to facing the world. As he opened his door and stepped out into the corridor the French girl sprung out of the spare room with her hands on her hips.

"You will not ignore me! Where is Aria? Why are you in her room?" It took him a moment to gather his thoughts against the tirade.

"She moved out 3 weeks ago."

"Merde, this cannot be right!" The girl looked distraught. He took a moment to check her out. She was in bleached jeans and some sort of hoodie but managed somehow to make it look chic.

"I can take you to her, she's house-sitting near here" he offered.

"Oooh you are fabulous!" She came over, put her hands on both his cheeks, and kissed him. She was wearing Issey Miyake. He knew the scent as he'd brought some for Harriet.

"Issey Miyake," he said, forgetting himself.

"You know my scent? You are like a Frenchman!" she narrowed her eyes and looked impressed. "When can we go? I have important things to discuss with her."

"Just give me a minute." Ethan didn't have to work today and had wondered what he would do with himself. He was pretty sure that he had a few dollars left on his credit card so had been planning to buy himself a book and a Big

Mac. He guessed he should find out who the girl was at some point, but she'd had a key, so he guessed she was an ex-flatmate he hadn't been told about.

In fact, all he'd been told when he moved in was that the fourth bedroom was spare at the moment. He'd met with the guy who owned the house and lived in the room at the back and was a bit of a freak, and Aria who had been on her way out and had told him he was welcome to look in her room, which was the one he'd be renting. Later he'd met the other one Lynn, who's room was on the other side of the hallway, and who was such white trash and with such a strong Nuzulund accent that he'd had trouble even understanding her.

The other room had always been called the 'spare room'.

Aria had actually been the only one he'd liked and of course, she'd moved out as he moved in.

They left the villa. It was bright outside and Ethan stopped on the path to put on his sunglasses. The sun was overhead, and he cast no shadow. As they headed out down the street the black bobbed girl hooked her arm in his.

"I am Cèline by the way. I 'ave been away for a few weeks with my mother and sister in Nouvelle Caledonia. You have been?"

"To New Caledonia?" Ethan asked. He knew it was one of the pacific islands that were a few hours' flight from New Zealand.

"Oui," the girl said.

"No, never." Ethan shook his head.

"But it is so near! Everyone should go!"

"Is the food good?"

"It is expensive" she shrugged. She continued to tell him about growing up there after her mother got divorced. Her mother had wanted to get as far away from France and Cannes where her ex lived. But Céline had always loved going back to France to visit. Finally, her mother realised that New Caledonia was too small and moved to New Zealand, where Céline had then gone to university.

Ethan listened amused, barely needing to add anything. They reached Aria's house and Ethan knocked at the door, Céline still attached to his arm and now chattering about how quaint the little garden and path were that had led them here.

Aria opened the door.

"You are here!" Céline launched herself into Aria's arms, hugging and kissing her and abandoning Ethan. When she had pushed past into the house, Aria turned to Ethan.

"If Céline didn't explain her room is the spare room. She paid for a few weeks but none of us were sure when she was coming back."

"I was kind of hoping for something like that" Ethan grinned.

"She's loony but in a French way. Do you want to come in for a coffee?"

"Sure, thanks" He followed her inside. Céline had thrown herself onto the couch and was playing with the small pup that was running around the floor in circles, yapping happily.

"I'm making Ethan a coffee. Do you want anything?" Aria asked.

"I will help you" Cèline went into the kitchen with Aria where Ethan could hear her talking frantically.

He lay back on the couch and let the little pup jump up on him and run round in circles on his stomach as he stroked its tiny little body. He'd always loved dogs although this one was closer in size to a rat.

Growing up they had had a golden Labrador called Nugget that Ethan had adored. Nugget had been so tremendously stupid that when they had tried to take him to dog obedience, even the dog trainer had told them to give up. Almost every day Nugget had run down the hallway in the middle of their house and smacked into the glass door, never understanding you couldn't run through it. They had even put stickers on the glass to help, but it hadn't. If they tried to give him some chocolate as a treat, Nugget would eat the wrapper. He constantly tried to eat the cat's food and so was constantly being scratched. But Ethan missed him. It was one of the only things he missed about his childhood.

The little pup now sprang up and started licking his neck, and Ethan scooped it up and put it on the floor. As Aria came back through and handed him his coffee, he sat up. He listened to the two of them chat for a few minutes. Céline was telling Aria about some man she had been with who was good friends with her father.

"Call me old fashioned but I don't fancy men who are old enough to be my dad," Aria said.

"You do not know what you are missing" Céline laughed. "Young men are good, but old men have money."

"They also have wrinkles and sagging backsides. Unlike young men" Aria said and nodded over to Ethan, who raised his eyebrows at her.

"On that note," Ethan said, "I'm going to leave you two to catch up" He had finished his coffee and stood to take his empty cup through to the kitchen. Aria came over and took the cup from him.

"Call me," she said, and he nodded. She let him out the front door and he headed down the street.

*

He walked into town. In normal weather, you could walk the entire city and not even work up a hint of sweat, but with these weeks of endless sun and blue sky, he was getting tired of feeling clammy. As he rounded a corner near the harbour, he found there was actually a slight breeze coming from the water.

He kept to the shade and by the time he cut back away from the water into the city, he was feeling good. He went into one of the tiny little bookshops that was hidden on a side street. He liked it more than the chain bookstores as it had a more weird and wonderful selection. He spent some time browsing and half-reading. He had so many books he wanted to buy but so little money to buy them. Although he decided that today he could buy one. One would still leave just enough money for the rest of the week.

As he came out Harriet was waiting at the crossing on the other side of the road facing him. He didn't really feel in the mood for her today but there was no way he could avoid her, so he stood and waited.

She hurried across once the green man appeared.

"What have you brought?" she asked.

He lifted the brown bag in his hand.

"A book."

"What book?"

Ethan sighed. If he'd wanted to tell her he would have said it. Now it was going to sound like a big deal but really, he just couldn't be bothered defending the author today.

"I'll show you later," he said as they turned and started walking the way Harriet was going.

"Is your credit card working today then?" She knew all about his spending habits.

"Just."

"Do you want to get a cup of tea?"

He didn't like tea. Harriet knew this. He drank coffee.

"I would *love* a cup of tea," he said.

"Or a cup of coffee then" Harriet pouted. She knew exactly what he was saying.

The trouble was that so much hanging out involved food or drink and it all cost money. He wasn't going to blow his last few bucks on something he could make at home. He would blow it on Big Mac. No-one knew what was in that special sauce.

His credit card only had a pathetic amount on it, but he perpetually had it over its limit. Several times a month he

ANGELA ATKINS

arrived home to an automated telegram from the bank telling him that he needed to make a repayment. Sometimes the repayment required was less than two dollars, and he was sure the printing and postage cost more than that to send it.

It wasn't that he was irresponsible with money, he just needed a certain level of income to support his lifestyle, and his job just didn't quite get there. The one time he'd been paid a lump sum from his student loan, he'd gone and spent it in one go.

He'd been living with Harriet at the time and she'd been excited when he'd told her he was going to go see if his next loan payment had been processed. They had a number of bills they needed to pay and the rent was a couple of weeks behind. When he'd got home a couple of hours later, Harriet had been sitting at her desk studying.

"Did it go through?" she asked looking up.

"Yes," he'd been hesitant, pushing his hands into his jeans pockets.

"How much?"

"$400". It was a lot of money. Weeks of rent, months of phone bills, many, many takeaway dinners.

"Perfect, we could go out for dinner" she had closed her textbook and with her eyes shining started to suggest a couple of possible restaurants.

"There might be a problem with that" Ethan had said.

Harriet had paused and looked at him, narrowing her eyes. She sat down hard on the desk.

"What have you done with it?" she said.

"I brought something" Ethan was shifting his weight from one foot to the other and looking at the floor. Suddenly Harriet had noticed the belt that he was wearing. It was shiny black patent, with a peace sign, a smiley face and a red heart as the buckle.

"That belt?" she asked. Ethan looked down at the belt and nodded.

"How much did it cost?" she asked.

"It's Moschino" Ethan explained, still looking at the belt. He knew Harriet knew he had a perchance for designer goods, even though he couldn't afford them. He'd once taken her into the menswear store in the centre of the city that sold Armani, and showed her the clothes he liked. She'd seen the prices then. She knew.

"Is there anything left?" she asked quietly.

"Not really" he shrugged.

"That's very naughty" she had come over to him and fingered the three buckles on the belt. "You could take it back?" she suggested and they looked at each other. Ethan shook his head, grinning.

"What am I going to do with you?" she asked but she was smiling.

"We could go somewhere cheap and I can wear my new belt?" Ethan had suggested and she had laughed.

*

Now he followed Harriet into McDonalds where she slid into a seat by the window. He slid in opposite her and put his brown bag with the book inside, on the tabletop.

She went up to the counter and ordered a cup of tea and for him, a cup of water. It would have to do. He was starting to feel hungry, but he wasn't going to get anything with Harriet around. There'd been enough times when they'd gone for lunch and she'd insisted she didn't want anything, then had eaten half of his fries and several bites of his burger. It drove him crazy. He had offered to buy her something so why the hell had she said no? He didn't know if it was Harriet thing or a woman thing but that didn't make it any less infuriating.

It was the same when Harriet got tired. He would ask if she wanted to head home and she would insist she was fine but then get snappy and frankly no fun to be with.

Not that she didn't have some redeeming features he thought as he watched her rummaging in her bag for some lip gloss. She was great fun when she wanted to be. She seemed completely unaware that the stories she told were hilarious.

Now she looked at him.

"I'm worried about Elise," she said as she stirred her tea. Ethan knew this meant she wasn't worried, she just wanted to complain, and he resigned himself to it.

"Why are you worried?" He may as well get it over with.

"Blair is taking advantage of her. Elise is so suggestible. I mean she told me that Blair's father is rich, but I doubt that Elise is charging her rent. And if she is charging her rent, then really me and Rosalie should get a discount."

Harriet continued on her monologue, engrossed with her own complaining, and Ethan stared out of the window. He'd quickly guessed that Harriet was annoyed as she was no longer in control of Elise and so his thoughts had turned to thinking about a Giorgio Armani tie he'd seen in a men's suit store. The problem was if he saved up to buy it, he would need a suit to go with it. And a shirt for that matter. And his credit card wasn't going to stretch to that. He needed another credit card.

"What do you think?" Harriet asked.

In all their time together, Ethan had only once let Harriet know that when she rambled on, he thought about other things. Once she'd been talking about some deep emotional issue and asked what he was thinking, and he'd said he was thinking about going and getting a burger. She had been horrified, not with the idea of a burger but that he'd been thinking of something so insignificant to what she'd been telling him.

So he'd had to tell her he'd been joking and from then on never made that mistake again and made sure he listened enough that he could get the gist of what she was moaning about.

"Elise can look after herself" Ethan shrugged.

"But she can't! It's not just how Blair treats her. Gwen talks down to her too. I heard them talking one day and Gwen was basically saying that Elise didn't understand about sleeping with married men. So I went out and said I'd slept with a couple and you didn't have to get all tortured about it. That stopped her dead in her tracks!"

"Sure" Ethan nodded.

"And Elise is so at her beck and call. We were sitting watching TV and Blair goes that she was hungry, and Elise ended up going out to get pizza. Leaving me having to talk to Blair. And I wanted to watch the movie that was on."

"Yeah, that is pretty rude," Ethan said. Although it made him remember something that Harriet had once done. After he and Harriet had broken up there was an awkward period when they'd both been angry with each other and had both been determined not to contact each other. Ethan had been especially angry as he'd been ripped away from all his friends to come to a new city with Harriet, and then she'd ruined it.

Actually, he supposed that wasn't true. They'd never been particularly good as a couple but her timing had been perfection to decide they should split just after they had organised a flat together. So he'd said some things he shouldn't have and she'd got angry with him and him with her.

It wasn't until she rang him late one night, crying and saying there was a rat or something in the flat, and could he please come and help that he'd gone up to get rid of it, even though he hated rats. He'd ended up staying there that night after kicking the rat out, and then stayed a couple more days as Harriet had come down with the flu and had always been terrible at being sick.

The goodbye sex seemed to clear the air between them and that was when they'd started to have lunch together as friends again. Ethan hadn't quite forgiven her, but he didn't know many other people.

Then, a few days later, Harriet had invited him for dinner and when he'd arrived, he'd found Elise there. It was the first time he met her.

Harriet had sat and chatted for a few minutes then announced that she needed to have a bath and went into the bathroom. Elise had seemed a little perturbed by this and Ethan had had to explain that this was usual Harriet behaviour. Elise had coped fairly well with being dumped with a stranger and the two of them had got themselves a drink and gone and sat on the back steps and chatted.

When Harriet had emerged almost an hour later, she'd told them she didn't really have anything to cook for dinner even though she'd invited them just for that, so they had piled into her VW and driven to McDonald's instead.

But it was typical Harriet that she was now feeling that Elise popping out for 10 minutes and leaving Harriet alone with a stranger in her own home was rude.

Ethan smiled ruefully.

Harriet sipped her tea. "Do you think I should talk to Blair about the rent issue if she's going to rip Elise off?"

"Sure" Ethan didn't care one way or another. But if it was annoying Harriet, he was going to hear about it again, so perhaps she should get it sorted.

Ethan had long ago realised that while most men wanted to fix an issue, women actually just wanted to talk about it for a while first. He guessed that was why he got on with women; because he'd stopped making suggestions about how they could fix the issues they were complaining about and just listened. While thinking about other things.

He listened to another half an hour of Harriet's complaining before deciding he'd had enough. He looked at his watch.

"I have to go. I have to go to work for a couple of hours for a meeting."

"Okay, well I'm going to go home and see if Blair is there." Harriet squared her shoulders.

They parted ways and Ethan headed home.

He didn't need to go to work. He wanted to go home and read his book. He'd finally managed to find a copy of American Psycho which didn't have the warning label stuck across the front cover and wanted to read it again. He'd already read it a couple of times, but he was pretty sure that it was going to be one of his all-time favourite books. He knew Harriet didn't like it and that in showing her, he would have got her tight-lipped disapproval glare.

Luckily her problems with Elise had made her forget all about it and now Ethan could enjoy re-reading it in peace.

Blair
at the beach

Recommended listening: Sorted for E's and Wizz
Released as a double A-side single with Mis-Shapes
From the album Different Class by Pulp
Single released in September 1995, by Island Records.
Inspired by a line that Jarvis Cocker overhead while at a rave.

Blair slammed the door to Elise's room and stood with her back to it, like shutting the door would make whatever she had just seen disappear. Elise's head popped out from under her duvet and she looked at Blair quizzically across the room.

"There is a naked man with a Mohawk in your hallway," Blair said. First thing in the morning before she'd had a cup of coffee was not the time for springing such things on her.

"Oh, so he didn't have his kilt on?" Elise said. "When I first met him, he was sitting with his legs up on the exercycle in a kilt and I could see everything underneath."

"Who the hell is he?" Blair climbed back into her bed.

"Some guy Harriet knows from Dunedin who's visiting for a couple of days."

"Are they sleeping together?"

"I guess so" Elise shrugged.

"Well, when he's gone, do you want to go to the fruit market?"

"Sure, what's the fruit market?"

"Elise! It's the best – much better than the supermarket!" It was the one part of Wellington that felt more cosmopolitan and a little bit Sydney. And it was where Blair found things like sprouts. Yet no-one ever seemed to know about it.

"Okay, sure" Elise agreed.

"Great, and then we'll go out to the beach." For Blair, it was a perfect day.

*

Later that afternoon, the two girls were laying on a sliver of beach, under the dappled shade of a tree, on the peninsula out past the airport, the sun shining off the water.

Blair was enjoying hanging out with Elise. Elise didn't know every little detail about Blair's life like her other friends who had all gone to school with her. It was also nice to do something different than going out drinking and dancing, then sitting around hung over and gossiping about what had happened the night before.

Elise didn't know any of Blair's friends so there was no point in gossiping and while Blair had now met some of Elise's friends, she didn't know much about them except what Elise had told her.

Blair gazed out across the water, over to the hills on the other side, dotted with only occasional houses. Out of sight were the monastery and city centre. Blair liked coming over to this side of the city.

The other side of the peninsular was covered in Wellington's outer suburbs, but on this side, nearer the airport, the hills were too steep. The road twisted and turned around the coastline next to it. In many places on the other side of the road were rocks and the sea, but there were several coves where trees grew and provided excellent shade for parking your car and lying under them on the beach.

Elise was telling Blair that she had driven round here a hundred times with Gwen, but she'd never actually stopped to get out.

"I thought you grew up here?" Blair checked.

"Yeah, but out in the suburbs," Elise hadn't really gotten to know the city centre until she'd moved out of home when she was seventeen. "I had to catch the train home after school every day."

"Oh, you were one of those."

Unlike Elise, Blair had grown up on the fringe of the central city. Her mother's house was in Aro Valley, only a few minutes away from where Elise now lived. There had been some girls from the suburbs at her school, but they never came into town and hung out at McDonald's because they had to go and catch the train. Blair had never envied them. She hadn't realised Elise was one of them. Not that they'd been at the same school. That was one of the things you quickly found out about anyone new you met here. What school they went to.

"Actually, we did stop out here once when we were first learning to smoke. We wanted to practice without being caught so we parked on the headland just around there" Elise pointed. "It was really windy and Gwen didn't want her mother's car to smell of smoke, so we had to smoke with our backs to the wind."

"I didn't know you smoked at all."

Elise told her about them going and picking their cigarette brands. Unfortunately, Elise had picked Camels because she liked the packet. She didn't realise they were quite strong. It had put her off smoking for a long while. But now she told Blair that "I've had kind of had to start again because they all smoke at work."

74

"Smoking is gross" Blair proclaimed propping herself up on her elbows.

"Men used to buy me drinks more often when I smoked" Elise shrugged.

"Elise, you really should look after yourself more" Blair was on a health kick at the moment. This morning when she'd taken Elise to the fruit market she couldn't believe that even though it was right in the middle of the city and only a couple of minutes' walk away from Elise's, Elise hadn't even known it existed.

"I just want to get some bean sprouts and snow peas. Then we can make some salads" Blair said, picking over the stalls.

"I've never eaten either of those" Elise said.

"What?" Blair stopped and looked at her. "How can you NOT have eaten bean sprouts? They're fantastic."

"I grew up eating stodgy root vegetables and over-cooked meat. I think the only salad we ever had was some lettuce and cucumber sliced up."

"Okay well, you have to try this" Blair picked up a packet of snow peas and started to crack it open.

"You can't do that" Elise gasped.

"Can we try this?" Blair asked the man behind the stall. He nodded. Elise had seemed amazed.

"People just do what you want don't they?" Elise had said shaking her head. Blair had shrugged. She was into the packet of snow peas and held one out to Elise. "Eat," she said.

Elise tried one gingerly.

"It's really sweet."

"It's delicious. You will eat snow peas all the time from now on" Blair ordered. They got a few other salad ingredients and had gone home to make the salad for lunch. Elise had to agree that it was the best salad she had ever eaten.

As she was making the salad Blair had shaken her head. "You guys have no food in this house. What do you normally eat?" Blair was genuinely interested. In Sydney, her father's house had been fully stocked, and even at her mother's, there was always enough to make something healthy.

"Harriet and I do a shop every now and again. But most of the time we eat at the charcoal chicken place down the road. They do a roast meal for only a few dollars."

"Elise, that's terrible."

"No, the chicken's cooked on a spit roast so it's not fatty."

"I don't care. This is much better for you. Harriet must want to eat healthily. I see there's some soy milk in the fridge."

"Oh, don't touch that" Elise warned. "It's been in there for months. It's solid."

"I was going to use it….." Blair pulled a face and stayed clear of it.

*

Now back on the beach, Blair sat up.

"Time for a swim?" she asked.

"You're joking?" Elise said. "I haven't swum in the sea since I was a kid."

"What's the point of living by a harbour if you don't go swimming?"

"To get a sea view?"

"See, in Sydney, people get out on the harbour sailing and windsurfing and swimming. But here it's just about the view."

"Because it's too cold to swim!" Elise argued. "Maybe I'll paddle, but I'm definitely not swimming."

"Rubbish" Blair was now stripping off her sundress and had a little red and white spotty bikini on underneath.

She jammed her straw hat under her towel and got up. "Come on lazy."

Elise hesitated. "My bikini is horrible," she said.

"What? What are you saying? Come on in!" Blair was already running across the tiny bit of sand and wading straight in and diving under. She came up, water streaming through her curly hair.

"It's warmish!" she called out.

So Elise peeled off her singlet, slipped off her cream skirt, and stood up. She'd worn her dark blue bikini. She walked into the water up to her thighs and then stood there.

"What are you doing?" Blair called out.

"I'm waiting for my legs to warm up, then I'll come out a bit further. I have a method!" Elise called out.

"Just dive in!" Blair was bobbing about further out.

"There's seaweed!" Elise screeched as a big clot of dark strands floated by.

"Yes, it's the sea. It's where seaweed lives!" Blair swam over and splashed her. Elise slipped and landed up to her neck. After a moment of shock, the water was actually quite nice once you got used to it. The two of them swam about splashing each other.

The odd car that drove past tooted at them, probably as most people knew the water was normally far too cold to swim in. Maybe the weeks of summer weather had warmed it.

Finally, they both ploughed out and collapsed on their towels. Blair twisted her hair into a roll to squeeze the water out and then shook herself like a dog. Elise laughed.

When they had dried off a little, Elise brought a magazine out of her bag and rolled onto her front, flicking the pages.

"Good thinking" Blair smooshed over so she was against Elise so she could see. They read companionably for a few minutes.

"Ethan turned up and said he brought it for me," Elise said after a while.

"That was nice of him."

"What do you think it meant though?" Elise rolled onto her back and put Blair's straw hat over her face. "I slept with him the other week."

"What? You didn't tell me that!" Blair snatched the hat off. "Well, this changes everything. What exactly did he say?"

"He said 'I brought this', I think. And I said thanks and took it from him."

"Do you think he'd brought it himself and he wasn't actually giving it to you at all" Blair shrugged.

"Oh god, do you think so? And I assumed it was for me because of what happened. But we both agreed to just be friends because of Harriet."

"I wouldn't worry about it," Blair said. "Men usually say what they mean. Perhaps it was for you. Do you like him though?"

"As a friend. I'm in love with Scott. I told you about him."

"You did" Blair hadn't really liked the sound of Scott. Elise seemed to half be in love with him because he reminded her of Johnny Depp. Blair liked to think of it as lust by association. She had met a boy once who so reminded her of her first boyfriend that she'd spent the night snogging him to find that he was in no way like her first boyfriend, and she'd felt entirely cheated.

"Are you in love at the moment?" Elise asked.

"No. I had a fling with a boy in Sydney but I'm happy being single at the moment" Blair said. It was less complicated, and she was enjoying not having to worry about someone else, about what they said, how they were feeling about you. She felt very free being single.

"I guess it is simple being single" Elise sat up and hugged her knees. "I can never believe all Harriet's men and all the problems she has."

"Like?" Blair closed the magazine and turned onto her back again.

"Well she and Fran both went out with the same guy Jason, and they have this sort of feud about Harriet stealing him away even though Fran had dumped him. That's why I'm a bit worried about Harriet finding out about Ethan."

"She won't if you don't tell her. And don't get all funny about being honest. If it didn't mean anything, then there's no point in Harriet knowing." Blair had made that mistake when she and Zöe had been younger. Zöe had had a huge crush on this guy that Blair had ended up kissing at a party. To be an honest friend she had told Zöe. The guy had after all made the moves on her, she hadn't approached him. But Zöe had been angry for weeks and if Blair could go back in time, she wouldn't tell her.

Elise looked at her watch.

"I'm going to have to go to work soon" she pouted.

"Is this the TV marketing job?"

"Yeah. Hey, you should come and work with me. They always need more people to telemarket. And you've got experience."

Blair sat up. "Actually, maybe I should."

"I can ask Christof tonight. He's the guy who hired me."

"Sure" Blair yawned and stretched. Her money stash was running low so this might be the perfect solution.

*

When they got home Elise changed and headed off to work. "I'll let you know about the job" she promised before she left.

Blair called Zöe, and Zöe came over with ingredients for nachos, and they watched a bad movie. Then the boys arrived. Zöe had been going out with Bowie since they were fourteen and everyone knew that one day they would get married. Hang out with Zöe and you had to be friends with Bowie and his group of lads. They set up in Elise's room, incase Harriet returned, and the plan was that once Elise came home, they would all head into town to Barneys, and dance the night away.

*

Blair was sitting on Elise's bed laughing at something Zac had told her when she saw the bedroom door open hesitantly and Elise poke her face around. Elise looked at the five of them sprawled across her room. Blair leapt up and ran over and pulled Elise into the room.

"Elise this is Zöe, Zac, Simon, and Bowie. We're going to go dancing. Do you want to come?"

Elise looked hesitant. When several of them urged her to come with them Elise finally nodded and took a seat on the bed next to Blair.

They were talking about drugs. And the lack of them here.

"In the UK you can get an e for less than it costs to go out drinking for the night," Zac said. He'd lived for a year in London. "All we can get here is weed."

"You can get all sorts of things in Sydney. But I couldn't bring anything back" Blair said.

Elise went over to the stereo and found the tape she had found at the record shop the other day – imported straight from the UK.

"I have the perfect song for this discussion," she said to Blair. She fast-forwarded the tape, then had to go back a bit, and finally pressed play and the beginning of 'Sorted for E's and Whiz' came on. None of Blair's friends had heard it before.

"This is fucking hilarious!" Bowie said as Jarvis Cocker sang about it being a long way from home and wanting to ring your mother but you've left some of your brain in a field.

"Who is it?" Simon asked.

"Pulp. They're a British band."

"Yeah, I could tell that from the accent" Zac laughed.

Elise glared at him and retreated to the window seat. Blair came over and sat down with her arm around her.

"Will you come into town with us?" she asked, forgetting that they'd already asked.

"I said I would" Elise relented.

"You girls haven't even finished these yet" Zac lifted some plastic cups down from the windowsill with jelly vodka shots in them. Once they'd eaten them, Zöe shrieked that they needed to do their make-up so she and Blair sat cross-legged on the mattress and with the boys watching, leaned over and did each other's makeup. Blair beckoned for Elise to join them and she sat down making a circle. They dabbed some eye shadow on and some of it went into Elise's eye.

"Shit," she said, "it's gone in my contact" and she reached into her eyeball and squeezed and popped her contact out. Instantly the guys were fascinated.

"You just poked yourself in the eyeball and you didn't mind?" Simon said.

"No, why?" Elise got up and found her contact lens holder. She put the lens in, shook it so the liquid cleaned it, and then took it out. She went over to the mirror, held her bottom eyelid down, and popped the lens back in, turning it around on her eyeball.

"That is so gross!" Zac had been watching carefully "I can't touch my eye. It freaks me out."

"What like this?" Elise moved her other lens around.

"Argh!" Zac mock screamed and threw himself back on the bed. And Blair smiled. Finally, Elise had bonded with her group.

When they were finally ready, they headed down the hallway like a herd of elephants and stampeded down the stairs. Then they all stopped and grouped together in the back garden. Blair made sure she had taken Elise's arm so she didn't drift off.

"Who's got a lighter?" Zac asked bringing out a joint.

"You do smoke don't you?" Blair whispered.

"Sure I do" Elise whispered back.

"What are you whispering about?" Zöe whispered, turning to them. They all started giggling.

"And you haven't even taken a hit yet" Zac handed it to Zöe, and she took a drag. They were all talking quietly, the smoke weaving its way up through the struts of the stairs above them, when Blair took a really strong drag and then started coughing. "I swallowed a bug!" she laughed, her eyes watering. Then they all started laughing.

The light came on in one of the downstairs windows.

"Oh fuck, the guy downstairs hates us," Elise said. "We have to get out of there." Bowie was sucking down the last hit and found suddenly he was left behind as all of them started running towards the zigzag path, then down it and out of the gate. He stubbed it out and followed them.

Blair, Zöe, and Elise were running down to the corner and past the charcoal chicken shop. The boys were close behind.

"Why are we still running" Zöe half panted, half gasped.

"God, that smells good," one of the guys said behind them.

"We're not allowed to eat it. It's not as healthy as snow peas" Elise said stopping and pulling everyone else to a stop.

"Snow peas?" Zac said joining them.

"Blair's been corrupting Elise" Simon figured. "Soon she'll be making you drink spirulina."

"I will not" Blair laughed as they all started walking again. "Although actually, it is very healthy."

"It's disgusting. Don't listen to her" Zöe was on the other side of Elise.

"I don't know who to listen to" Elise murmured.

Noisily they made their way down Cuba Street. It was dark now and for once there were people about. This made Blair very happy. It made her feel like she was civilised again. Zac climbed up on the ledge of the bucket fountain and started tipping them out. The fountain had about 8 different coloured metal buckets of different sizes attached to an 8-foot-high structure. The water fed from the top and as the buckets filled, they tipped and emptied the water out to the bucket below.

"You'll get wet!" Bowie warned.

"No, I'm in complete control," Zac said, not realising there was one bucket at the top that he couldn't reach and was now full of water. It creaked ominously and then suddenly with a rusty squeal, tipped. Water splashed everywhere and Zac jumped away just a little too late.

"I told you" Bowie laughed as Zac ran after the girls, trying to hug them with his now wet t-shirt.

"Where are we going?" Elise asked as she and Blair ran down the mall.

"Just here" Blair ran over to a narrow doorway and disappeared inside. Elise followed. Blair was halfway up a long flight of stairs and she waited and then grabbed Elise's hand and pulled her up the rest. At the top, the stairs opened into a long narrow bar. But what they had come for was the dance floor. In Sydney, Blair had gone to a rave which had been brilliant. There was nothing like that in New Zealand yet but a good night at this little hole in the wall was okay.

The music was loud, and she pulled Elise with her onto the dance floor. Within moments all of them were dancing. She and Zöe threw their arms up in the air and writhed

83

against each other. Blair loved the feel of the music vibrating through every pore of her body as she danced with abandon, not thinking about who you were or where you were.

The strobe lights lit the crowd for a moment, plunged them into darkness, and lit them up. The bass throbbed. Around them bodies heaved. Hair swirled.

Blair danced over to Zac and wrapped her arms around his neck and then curled herself behind him. She could feel a thin layer of sweat covering her. She knew it made her skin shine, and her dress hug her tightly.

*

At some point that night Blair noticed that Elise had drifted off. She had talked to Zac for a while, but then she'd lost track of her. Stoned and a little drunk Blair waltzed over to Zöe. The music had lulled into a quieter patch, and they had moved away from the dance floor to the back of the bar.

They could see down through the glass windows to the street a floor below. There was no one about. Blair pulled her hair off her neck and wound it into a bun on top of her head.

"Has Elise gone?"

"I think so" Zöe hadn't really been paying attention.

"I thought you would get on with her," Blair said.

"Just because you like her, doesn't mean we're all going to get on with her," Zöe said.

"Why not?"

"Because it doesn't work like that."

"Oh god, you've got your wise Gaia thing happening haven't you?" Blair snorted. Zöe became incredibly mellow late in the night and started stating things like they were ancient wisdom. When the rest of them realised it was happening they decided it was time to go back to Zac's and eat pizza and consult Zöe the oracle. Blair just had to assume Elise had got home safely.

Jack & Elise
get ballsy

Recommended listening: High and Dry
Released as a double single with Planet Telex
in February 1995 in the UK only, by Parlophone.
From the album The Bends by Radiohead.

The small battered red car careered around the corner. Jack could see Elise standing waiting as the fiat came back down onto two wheels. He was sitting in the back seat but leaning forward and holding onto the two front seats like they were ski poles, and he was in a slalom.

Scott was a terrible driver. The morning traffic had cleared but for some reason, Scott would accelerate and then brake and skid around nonexistent cars. And he was taking corners like a rally driver.

As they pulled up beside her, tires smoking, Jack could see Elise was disappointed. He decided that like him, she'd probably thought it was just going to be three of them. But it wasn't. She could see who was in the front passenger seat and he saw the little frown on her face. Jack hoped he hadn't been quite so obvious when he'd seen who Scott had also decided to invite.

Scott had seemingly decided to invite Christof to make up for the Mrs Abbott incident. Jack didn't think it had been needed, but it was too late for that.

Christof had spent the drive so far telling them about all the golf courses he'd played and describing the hardest holes that he'd aced. Scott had been adding the odd story of his own. Jack had nothing to add. He'd never played before.

"Hey, we're late!" Scott called out of the rolled-down front window. "Get in!"

Elise looked like she'd tried to dress for golf. She had on a pair of red tartan trousers, a white singlet, and a green cap. She was wearing little round orange sunglasses. Jack had made no such effort, in a happy face t-shirt and baggy jeans. Jack shifted over as Elise opened the back door and climbed in with him.

Scott turned and gave her a grin before speeding away from the curb. Elise was immediately thrown against the door.

"Buckle up" Jack warned her as they fought to put their seat belts on.

"So, what's your handicap?" Christof turned and asked her.

"Um, whatever's highest? I've never played golf before" she said and clearly had no idea how a handicap worked.

"Me neither! This should be fun!" Jack wasn't going to let the two golf nerds make him and Elise feel like idiots. Everyone had to start somewhere. Christof resumed his description of golf holes of the world for the rest of the drive. Jack looked over at Elise from time and time and shrugged his shoulders. She shook her head and smiled ruefully.

Finally, they arrived at the course.

For a moment Jack had been worried that it would be some exclusive club, with luxurious buildings and a dress code of ties and jackets just to get in. But as they parked next to a cluster of trees and got out, he found the car park was muddy gravel and the club house was an old wooden building, with paint flaking off, and he was pretty sure it was leaning slightly to one side. He didn't think the dress code wasn't going to be an issue.

"Do you want to share hiring some clubs?" Jack asked as they walked over to register.

"Sure" Elise nodded.

Once they'd paid, the four of them headed out to the first hole. There was hardly anyone on the course, just one group they could teeing off a few holes further on, and a couple of pairs of golfers who were near to finishing up.

"You guys will need a lesson before we start," Scott said. He put his ball on a tee, stood with his legs apart and positioned his club next to the ball. He explained how to swing, demonstrated a few dummy hits, and then whacked the ball straight down the runway.

"It looks easy" Jack shrugged.

Christof took his turn and also gave them a lecture on how to tee off before also whacking it fair and true. It arched into the air, gleaming in the sun, and then thudded down near Scott's.

"Okay, your turn" Christof stepped away for Jack to make his debut.

Things went downhill from there.

After Jack had hacked at the ball eight times, he finally managed to hit it. It hardly went into the air and only went a pathetic distance. Jack saw Christof and Scott look at each other grimly.

Elise went next. She did a little better and managed to hit it after four attempts. And it even went further than Jack's.

Scott and Christof humoured them for the first 2 holes. After an excruciating fourteen over par from Jack and ten over par from Elise, Scott cleared his throat.

"Look why don't we go on ahead and you guys can practice as you play and then it doesn't matter if you take a while," Christof said.

So he and Scott played the whole hole, and Jack and Elise stood waiting at the third tee area until they'd finished.

Jack sensed that Elise was disappointed. He felt like he had to cheer her up somehow.

"Look we'll have much more fun this way – and at the end, we can catch up with them and you'll have some great stories to tell Scott."

"I don't have much choice, do I?" she said.

And then Jack and Elise proceeded to have one of the best rounds of golf that either of them would ever play. Not in terms of actually getting a good score, but in terms of having fun and laughing than they ever had in living memory.

They ricocheted balls off trees, sunbathed in a sand bunker, and made their own miniature golf course on the putting green with their other clubs. On one hole Elise actually got it in on par and proceeded to do a dance that she would have been far too embarrassed to do if Scott had been around. Jack had teased her about it knowing that luckily there were a lot of trees on the course, and she was hidden was view.

On another hole, there was a water feature at exactly the correct distance for both their balls to land right in the middle.

Which they did.

Elise walked up to the edge of the water and looked at the ripples of where the ball had disappeared.

"What do we do?" she asked.

"We have to add a point to our scores and tee off again," Jack said. So both of them did and again, both of their balls went splash straight into the water.

"Whoever designed this course was sadistic," Jack said.

"We've only got one ball left" Elise looked in the golf bag.

"Fuck this," Jack said "I'm not paying for more balls" and he took off his shoes and socks and waded in, to the sound of Elise laughing so hard she started snorting.

He couldn't find the balls so started doing a little dance feeling around with his feet.

"Use your club!" Elise yelled laughing harder.

Finally, he found the balls and dribbled them with his club to the edge of the water. They sat on the grass for a while so Jack's feet could dry.

They say the definition of stupidity is to do the same thing and expect different results. And stupidly both of them teed off again and both hit the ball right into the middle of the pond again. It had taken Jack about 10 minutes to dry his feet and put his shoes back on and he couldn't face doing it again, so this time he waded in with his shoes on.

Elise stood laughing so much she could now barely stand up. They completed the next hole with Jack's shoes squelching at every step.

As they were halfway down the 10th hole, they both realized that the course was designed so that the 18th hole started near the end of the 10th.

"Are you thinking what I'm thinking?" Jack said.

"Abandon all hope?" Elise said.

"I think so."

They finished the hole, abandoned the 11th to $17^{th,}$ and walked over to Scott and Christof who were just reaching the 18th.

"Right, we've had enough practice. Now we're going to give you a run for your money" Jack said, squelching over.

"Should I ask what happened?" Scott looked down at his waterlogged shoes.

"Best not to" Elise replied.

They all played the last hole together. Jack may have been bragging about having enough practice, but actually, Elise seemed to finally get the hang of it. It was her best hole and suddenly she saw that Scott and Christof were quite impressed when she got it in on one over par.

Jack decided the gentlemanly thing to do was to make her look good, so stuck with putting it in for 10 over, saying he wanted to go out with a high score.

Afterwards, they went to the club house for a drink and just like Jack had suggested after they had split from the golf geeks on hole three, he and Elise did most of the talking telling stories of their round.

Scott and Christof listened and laughed. Their round had been serious and they'd done enough bragging already. Jack had no problem telling them about the finer points of their best tree ricochets, the time Elise's ball had got stuck in the fence and when Jack had sent his ball down a small rabbit hole.

At one point Scott asked them how they did with the water hole. Elise started laughing before Jack had even started telling them.

*

As they finished their drinks, Scott said something that made Elise's face fall, although at the time only Jack noticed. Scott said: "I'm going to tell my girlfriend how much you improved. She thinks she'll be crap at golf but now I have proof that even if you haven't played before, you can get one over par by the end."

"And she didn't even play every hole!" Jack added helpfully seeing Elise's crestfallen expression.

Elise was fairly quiet after that. Jack carried on joking with the lads to distract them. On the drive back to the city, Elise stared out of the window, her chin resting on her elbow and her forehead resting against the glass. Scott wasn't driving like a maniac anymore which Jack thought, somehow made it worse. If they'd been thrown around like before, at least Elise would have had something to focus on.

Jack tried drawing her in a couple of times, but she answered in one syllable and he gave up. Scott continued to talk about his girlfriend and it was obvious that they were living together. Elise seemed barely able to muster a goodbye as she climbed out outside her house.

"See you at 4:30," Jack said.

"Okay," she said fleeing up the path and round the side of the house.

*

Jack got home to find Sarah out. He felt awful about Elise. He felt like he'd set it up and then hadn't even broken it to her while they'd played that Scott had a girlfriend. He'd meant to, they'd just been having so much fun.

He put some music on and sat outside having a cigarette, but it wasn't working. Finally, he left a note for Sarah and headed back to Elise's' on foot.

He went up the same zigzag path he'd seen her disappear up less than an hour before. There was a small porch that shaded the front door and he strode up to it and knocked. There was no answer.

But he was worried. So he walked around the back of the house and saw there were stairs. He went up and knocked at the second door he found there, which looked like the kitchen door.

Again, no answer.

He turned and was halfway down the steps when he heard a window open behind him.

"Jack wait!" Elise called out. "I didn't know who it was!" She disappeared and a moment later came and opened the door.

"You need one of those little peepholes they have in hotel doors," he said.

"No, we have something much more complex. If you angle the mirror in Harriet's room just right, you can see who it is without them seeing you" Elise was putting on a brave face. Her eyes were red. Strangely Jack didn't feel that uncomfortable with women who had been crying. It was just like a guy smashing his fist against a wall and then going on a binge drink. It just meant someone was upset.

"Are you okay? Scott's an arsehole" he said.

"He is an arsehole! But I had a pretty big crush on him."

"I figured."

"God, was it obvious?"

"Well, I noticed you giving him moon eyes. But I'm pretty switched on with the ladies" Jack did his little smooth move hand movement.

"Oh, are you?" Elise laughed.

They were still standing in the doorway.

"Hey, do you want something to eat?" Elise asked. "We've got some sausages and bread. I can make some hotdogs."

"Sure" Jack realised how hungry he was.

He took a seat on the step that led from their kitchen up the hallway. He leant backwards slightly and sniffed. "Why is there a horrible smell in your corridor?" he asked.

"Oh, that's Rosalie's shoes. One of my flatmates. She only has two pairs of shoes and they both stink. They're actually in her room, in the cupboard and her window is open. And you can still smell them."

"Jesus" Jack leaned forward. Elise was grilling the sausages and that was a much better smell.

"I think we've even got a couple of beers left" Elise found one in the fridge.

"This is my kind of flat" Jack took a swig.

"Can I ask you something?" Elise asked.

"Sure, that doesn't mean I'm going to answer though."

"I'll take a chance" she held up some slices of bread to the light and checked each side for mould. With each day still breaking as summer, even with putting their food in the fridge, things were still growing little green spots. "Do you think if Scott was single, I would have had a chance with him? Because he's really good-looking."

"Really? You dig the ear picking and scratching?"

"It's kind of sexy" Elise shrugged.

Jack shook his head. "To be honest, I think he would have been lucky to be with you, not the other way around."

"Awww thank you" Elise grinned. Jack couldn't be sure whether he believed her or not. He'd listened to Sarah and her friends talking enough to realise that women put themselves down all the time. It seemed a little easy that Elise had instantly believed him. Elise finished making the hot dogs.

"Let's go to my room. I want to play you something."

"As long as it's not the Stones."

"No, it's Oasis. I feel you need a proper education on their albums."

"Sure" Jack stood up and took the plate from her.

"You might want to hold your breath until we get to the end of the hall" Elise warned as they hurried past the smell.

*

Elise put on Definitely Maybe and they each sat in one of the bay windows eating their hot dogs.

"This rocks!" Jack said.

"I can do a copy for you if you want" Elise had a blank tape somewhere.

"Excellent."

"Hang on, does that mean I've converted you?"

"Converted me to what?"

"Well Oasis are more rock, they're more Stones. So if you like Oasis you're coming over to my side of the fence."

"Don't even try it" Jack laughed. "Oasis have taken lines from John Lennon. They love the Beatles. You're coming over to my side."

"Alright, we'll call it even."

"For now."

After Oasis, Elise moved them onto the Stones. Jack had heard the stuff that got played on the radio, but Elise insisted that was just a small selection of the Stones. "I'm going to play you some songs from Tattoo You," she said, taking out the Oasis CD and slipping in the Stones.

Listening, Jack had to admit that some of it was okay. Not a spot on the Beatles, but then nothing was.

After a while, Elise looked at her watch.

Jack realised they needed to go to work soon.

"I don't want to go," she said. "I don't want to see him".

"Listen just put your head down and ignore him. Let him stew. Don't let him cost you sales, okay?"

"Yeah, I can't afford to not go." Elise pulled herself up like the weight of the world was on her shoulders.

*

Jack watched over her that evening. Elise put her head down and made her calls and he saw her manage to sign 3 people up. At the break, Scott didn't seem to notice anything was wrong and chatted away normally, although Elise hung back from the main group.

Jack went over and gave her a cigarette and for once Elise smoked one.

"I deserve this damn it," she said to him. "I've had my heart broken."

Jack nodded.

"He sat me down and so began" Jack sang quietly.

"The story of a Charmless Man" Elise finished. "You are so right." And she even managed to smile.

Just a little bit.

Gwen
plants a tree

Recommended listening: Creep
The debut single of Radiohead was released in September 1992.
From the album Pablo Honey by Radiohead.
Reissued in 1993 to become a world-wide hit.

Gwen picked Elise up at 10 am. It was another gorgeous day, and she had the windows of the car down, the wind blowing her hair. This had been a glorious summer so far and it was only early December.

As a photographer, sunny days actually posed some challenges, but Gwen wouldn't swop them for the world. The sun lifted her spirits.

Although today would be bittersweet. They'd be celebrating Hugh's life but only because of his death.

Gwen pulled up outside Elise's and pressed the horn. She peered up and saw Elise at her window wave down. Gwen sat back. Elise better be quick. She'd pulled up on dotted yellow lines. Why wasn't there any parking anywhere on this street?

Today they were going to plant a tree in one of the parks that were dotted around the city. It had been Brian's idea that they had needed to do something to commemorate Hugh's life and have something to remember him by that wasn't a grave. Everyone had been keen on the tree.

Gwen had been desperately in love with Hugh. He was disarming, modest, and funny, not to mention good-looking. As a senior photographer he hadn't needed to work with Gwen at all, but he'd spent time with her on several jobs, asking her to develop some of the photos and do the touch-ups. And she was sure that he'd felt something for her too even thought he had a girlfriend that he'd been living with for several years.

"Hey," Elise interrupted her thought, getting into the car, puffing from running down the path.

Gwen, her hand always on the gear stick like a racing car driver, peeled away from the kerb and accelerated up the street.

Elise looked over at Gwen.

"Are you okay?" she asked.

"No not really" Gwen didn't expect Elise to understand. She was remembering the morning tea they'd had at work when Hugh had put his arm around Gwen, laughing and joking about her being the company protégé. Gwen was sure his arm had lingered just a moment longer than it needed to.

And then he was dead.

He'd been killed by a drunk driver going through a red light and ploughing straight into Hugh's car. The guy had basically murdered Hugh but had only got a few months in prison.

Gwen had been devastated when she'd heard about the accident. She'd rung Elise, sobbing her heart out and Elise had barely been able to understand what had happened. Elise had known how much Gwen had loved Hugh and like many of their conversations about men, didn't know what to say to someone who was facing a death.

ANGELA ATKINS

Gwen had seen how lost Elise was to know what to say, and somehow that had made Gwen feel older and wiser. She was experiencing things that Elise was just too young to know about. She'd really only then got involved with Brian as a rebound. Brian had been flirting with her right from when she'd first got the job, but at Friday night drinks a few weeks after Hugh had died, Brian and Gwen ended up being the only ones who could stay. Samira was out of town taking the children to visit their grandparents, and everyone seemed to have somewhere to be.

So Brian had broken open a bottle of red wine and said that the two of them deserved a drink because she was the hottest employee he'd ever had.

Gwen had to admit she liked being fawned over, liked being flattered, especially by someone she knew had been around the block. The only trouble with unrequited love was that it was rather one-sided. You could only spend so many hours imaging what might be before you longed for something to really happen.

With Brian, the something really did happen. In the lift. Gwen had always laughed at the scene in the movies when the guy presses the emergency stop in the lift to tell the girl something, or propose, or kiss her. But after they'd polished off the wine and Brian had suggested they go for something to eat, they'd taken the lift. It was only 2 floors and the floor below had a small accounting firm. As the lift pinged to show they were stopping on level 1, Brian had punched the emergency stop button. There was no squealing of lift brakes, or whatever they had, the light just came on red.

"Listen I can't go a moment longer without doing this" Brian had come over to her and leaned in and kissed her. He was stubbly and Gwen remembered the stubble grazing her chin. None of her other boyfriends had really had stubble, or if they had it wasn't hard and prickly like this. She had got right into the kiss, feeling very

98

sophisticated pressed up against the corner of the lift, feeling Brian's leather jacket creaking against her.

She may have moaned out loud.

"Is there someone in there?" a male voice said loudly just outside and banged on the lift door. "Is the lift stuck?"

"What do we say?" Gwen whispered.

"Nothing, he'll get bored and go away" Brian grabbed her under the arms and lifted her up onto the handrail that went around the middle of the lift. She found herself wrapping her legs around his waist as they kissed again and soon they were at it.

The man outside banged a few more times and called out then at some point left them to it, and Gwen forgot about him.

Once she'd had sex with Brian she felt strangely dissatisfied. He was married. Surely it should have felt more elicit than it had. And that's why she had continued. For the thrill that she felt sure she would feel at some point and make her forget about Hugh.

And then as these things do, although Gwen wouldn't have admitted that she had fallen into the inevitable, because that was boring, she did start to care for Brian. And started to believe the things he was telling her. That he would leave Samira for her. That was exciting and that was the excitement she had wanted.

But now the two parts of her world were colliding.

Samira, Brian and most of her workmates would be at this tree planting as well as Hugh's girlfriend. Gwen wanted to remember Hugh her own way, not with these people who didn't know how she felt. So, she was taking Elise. Because Elise did kind of know what it meant to Gwen. Elise was experiencing the same thing at the moment for this guy Scott. Obviously, it wasn't actual love like Gwen had felt for Hugh. But it was a lesser level.

Elise was wearing a light blue singlet, a jean skirt, and sneakers. Gwen personally felt that Elise didn't dress femininely enough. Gwen's look this summer was a range of little floral skirts that flipped up in the wind when they finally got some wind, and white short-sleeved tops. She wore them low cut showing off her cleavage. Elise's singlets were kind of butch to Gwen's mind. Not that she would tell her that because when Elise wore them, it made Gwen look better.

Now Gwen sped through the city streets. She loved driving. She always kept one hand on the wheel and one hand on the gear stick to change up and down at an alarming rate. She felt like she was in control of the car, making it work for her.

"Where are we going?" Elise asked.

"Out to that park that's up on the hill" Gwen didn't really feel like talking so turned on the tape deck. She and Elise always listened to the Stones when they went driving and now Brown Sugar filled the car. But it didn't feel right so Gwen hit the eject button.

"Can you find my Simon and Garfunkel tape in the glove box?" she asked.

Elise opened it and rummaged through the tapes until she found it. She put it in and pressed play. Gwen listened for a minute and then pressed the fast-forward button while steering with her knee. When she pressed the stop button there was a hiss and pause and then Bridge over Troubled Water came on.

This was right.

Gwen was pleased that Elise seemed to know you didn't talk over this song. That she just wanted to listen.

They pulled into the car park at the bottom of the park, and Gwen turned off the engine.

"You know that Brian's going to be here," she said, looking at Elise.

"Don't worry, I'll pretend that I haven't met him before." Elise had come with them to breakfast a couple of times when Gwen hadn't wanted Brian to get too carried away.

If they both turned up late for work, Samira was going to put two and two together at some point. She couldn't be so stupid as to not see what was going on.

The only way Gwen had come up with to cut their illicit breakfasts short was for Elise to come along and stay for a while after Brian had left. Elise had complained and moaned about it. Gwen knew that she was working till 9 pm but it was her choice to stay up until 2 am. Some people had normal jobs and had to go to bed before midnight. And Gwen had done enough stuff for Elise, she owed her.

"I don't want to stay long. Can you make an excuse for us to leave after about an hour?" Gwen was worried this was going to be awful.

Elise nodded. "Sure. Are you ready?"

The two of them headed up the path into the park.

Brian had set up a BBQ and had the charcoal just lit. It would take a while to get hot enough. He was busily tending to it, as well as marinating steaks and opening packs of sausages in the chilly bin.

Samira had laid a blanket out on the ground and was setting out bread and salads. Several people's kids were running around screaming, hanging off trees. The rest of Gwen's colleagues were hanging around the BBQ area drinking and laughing.

"Hi," Gwen walked up to her workmates. "I didn't know this was a party." No-one seemed to notice her tone.

"Don't worry we've got enough for you both" Samira called out from the blanket.

Poor oblivious Samira. Gwen shot Elise a look. They both got a drink and hung around on the edge of the group.

"Right let's plant this tree" Brian finally caught Gwen's eye and smiled. He strode over to the trees by the side of the meadow and picked up a two-metre-high spruce, it's roots wrapped in sacking. The group followed him down the slope to where there were a few trees but lots of grass and open space.

"I thought here would do nicely" Brian looked around for agreement.

"Have we got some sort of permit to do this?" someone asked.

"We don't need a permit" Brian took the spade from Samira who had brought it down to them. He handed the tree to Hugh's ex and stuck the spade into the grass. He pushed down with his boot and put the first lump to one side. Then each of them took turns digging a couple of clots until the hole was the right size.

Brian cut the sacking off and held the tree so the roots were centred in the middle of the hole.

"We're planting this tree to remember Hugh. He was a bloody great guy, and this world is a worse place without him."

"Hear, hear!" a few people said.

"Whenever any of us miss Hugh too much we can come up here and remember him" the ex (Gwen refused to give her a name) choked and another woman put her arm around her shoulders. Gwen bit her lip determined not to cry. It was okay for the ex. Everyone recognised that she loved Hugh. No-one realised that Gwen had too. Still, she had Brian now.

A few others spoke about Hugh and then they all took turns to spade the earth back in and stamp it down. They stood back admiring their work.

"Okay, let's go eat," Brian said and slowly, in ones and two's, they all headed back up the bank to the picnic blankets and BBQ.

Later after everyone had eaten, Elise came over to Gwen who was sitting listening to a conversation, but not participating. "I have to go soon," Elise said, quietly but loudly enough for a couple of people to hear.

"Oh sure" Gwen looked up gratefully. Thank God Elise had remembered. This whole thing was getting depressing, and Gwen wanted to be out of there. Elise followed her as she went over to Samira and made her apologies, and then the two of them headed back to the car.

"Are you okay?" Elise asked her.

"Yes," Gwen couldn't really say more. Everyone had been sharing stories about Hugh and she hadn't had any to add. It was almost like her and Hugh's thing hadn't had time to develop into anything. And they had no stories together. It had brought Gwen down.

"Let's go for a drive around the bays" she suggested.

"Sure" Elise agreed.

They didn't talk much on the drive, just listened to music and watched the scenery blur past the car wind screen.

They stopped in a bay that had a little shop selling ice creams and sat under a tree looking out at the ocean to eat them.

"Do you miss him a lot?" Elise asked.

"I do," Gwen said. This thing with Brian was distracting and exciting, but she missed the conversations she'd had with Hugh, sitting smooshed on the old couch next to the kitchen, the late afternoon sun coming into the high window and hitting the back wall of photos. "But I have to get over him and move on."

"Are you in love with Brian?"

"I'm falling in love with him. And he's very much in love with me."

"Doesn't it bother you that he's married?"

"It does bother me a little. But it's good in a way." Gwen didn't expand. Elise wouldn't understand anyway.

They didn't talk much on the drive back home.

*

"Do you want to go to the movies?" Elise asked. They had spent the late afternoon and evening watching TV and eating pizza. Gwen had been feeling sorry for herself, but it got tiring after a while. "It might take your mind off it?"

"Maybe it will" Gwen agreed.

So they walked into town. They hadn't been able to check what was on or at what time as none of Gwen's flatmates had brought a newspaper that day, but in the foyer of the cinema they found a film that Elise had heard of and wanted to see. It was starting in 30 minutes, so they brought tickets.

"Oh, there's Fran!" Elise said as they brought some popcorn.

Gwen trailed after her as she made her way through the crowd. She didn't really like Elise's friends. They all seemed slightly crazy. She watched Elise and Fran hug. She and Elise never hugged. It had never really seemed necessary.

"Gwen you've met Fran before." Elise turned to introduce her.

"Hi," Fran said.

Gwen said hi back and looked Fran up and down. What was wrong with the woman? She looked like she was wearing a crumpled sack. And couldn't she have brushed her hair?

Fran and Elise started talking about the movie which Fran was also going to with a friend. Then Elise told her that tomorrow night Ethan was cooking dinner for a few of them at her and Harriet's, and Fran should come.

Once Fran had headed off to meet up with her no doubt crumpled friends, Gwen pulled Elise to one side.

"Ethan is cooking you all dinner?" she asked.

"Yeah, Harriet arranged it all. She was going to cook but Ethan offered which is good because Harriet's cooking is awful" Elise grinned.

"Do you think this is a good idea?" Gwen raised her eyebrows. "Have you talked to Ethan since it happened?"

"No, but I'm sure it will be fine."

"Are you?" Gwen frowned and Elise hesitated. Gwen saw she now had Elise looking worried. Poor naïve Elise. It wouldn't just be fine. When two people had slept together there was going to be some tension, and if Elise was worried Harriet might suspect what had happened, then not being able to talk to Ethan was going to be the biggest sign in the world.

"Oh, there he is!" Elise gripped her arm.

"Who?" Gwen had been thinking about the signs that she and Brian had given that Samira should have picked up on.

"Ethan" Elise hissed.

Coming through the crowd was a guy in a pair of ripped jeans and a white t-shirt. So, this was Ethan? He had dark hair and Gwen supposed she could see why Elise though he was kind of cute.

He saw them and waved.

"Hey!" Elise sounded tentative and scared.

"Hi, you must be Gwen?" Ethan said looking at her.

"Yes hi, you must be Ethan" Gwen smiled. She could see that Elise had lost it completely. She'd just meant to warn her that the first conversation might be tricky.

"What movie are you seeing?" Ethan asked Elise. She blinked and looked at Gwen, who answered.

"S.F.W. Elise said she'd heard it was good."

"So did I. It was on at the film festival but I missed it."

"Are you meeting someone?" Gwen asked, looking over his shoulder. Perhaps he was here with Harriet which would make this even worse for Elise.

"No, just here by myself. I'll just go and get something to eat." Ethan headed off.

"Oh god, I don't know what to say to him!" Elise said.

"Well try and say something. Or it will be horrible tomorrow" Gwen said.

Ethan came back over.

"I brought you some snifters," he said and handed Elise the packet. Snifters were these weird minty chocolate candies.

Elise's face lit up. "I love snifters!"

"I know, you told me" Ethan grinned. "I'm a Jaffa's man myself" he shook his box of the little round orange-flavoured chocolate balls.

"I prefer Jaffa's too," Gwen said but neither of them seemed to hear her.

"I just invited Fran to dinner tomorrow. I hope that's okay?" Elise suddenly seemed to have found her tongue again.

"Sure" Ethan shrugged. "I'm just going to make a big pot of pasta so I can add a bit more."

"That sounds great. Far more edible than the lentil and vegetable soup Harriet was talking about making."

"Yep it's an experience trying to eat some of her creations," Ethan said and the two of them laughed together. Gwen could see no tension between them at all. She frowned. Elise couldn't have got over it already.

The doors to the movie theatre opened, and the crowd started to make its way in.

"Do you want to sit in the front?" Elise asked.

"I always sit in the front, it's the best row" Ethan grinned.

"The middle's good too," Gwen said but neither of them were listening and heading straight for the front row. The Paramount was also a theatre and put on plays, so there was a very low stage in front of the screen. It meant that the front row had a fantastic view of the movie.

"You're right. This is good" Gwen said once they'd sat down. It was like being right in front of the world's biggest TV screen. But unlike other theatres where the front row was metres below the screen and you had to crick your neck looking up, this one was the same height as the seats.

"Remember when we went to see Braveheart and we were in the front row?" Gwen asked Elise.

"God yes. I wanted to lie on the floor my neck was so sore" Elise laughed. "And it happened to us twice."

"You went to see Braveheart twice?" Ethan asked.

"Actually, three times" Elise admitted. Ethan shook his head.

"Come on, Braveheart was brilliant" Elise chided.

"Listen I think there might be some crazy Mel Gibson fans in the area so I'm going to with it and agree that yes, Braveheart was brilliant."

"Hmmm," Elise narrowed her eyes at him.

The adverts came on and they sat back to watch. Every so often Elise would lean over and whisper something to Ethan and he would laugh.

Gwen ignored them. She was continually surprised that Elise seemed fine to be living without knowing what she was going to do with her life. She felt like Elise was stuck deep in the black hole, whereas she had leapt nimbly over it.

They had talked about the black hole in their last year of school. From their point of view, it seemed that when people finished school or university, they kind of went into this black hole for a few years, and then miraculously at the end of it they came out finished. Knowing their career, having fallen in love with a great guy, and for all intents and purposes being fully grown up.

And Gwen was making progress on most of those. She knew she wanted to get married one day and have children and she had dreams of travelling the world photographing for National Geographic.

She knew Elise had once said she wanted to be a famous actress but that was hardly likely to happen.

She loved Elise like a sister but there was nothing spectacular about Elise. Elise would really be nothing without Gwen. Gwen had helped her with men, with jobs, with flatting.

And Elise was just floundering about in the black hole. Telemarketing wasn't a career. Even Elise had admitted she was going to quit before the end of summer. Then what?

Gwen shook her head. She despaired of her sometimes. She really did. Elise needed to find a bridge to climb onto soon or she would be left behind forever.

Once the film started Gwen stopped worrying about anything.

Halfway through they got to a scene where Stephen Dorff walked in slow motion down a street, his cigarette hanging out of his mouth. Gwen saw from the corner of her eye that Elise nudged Ethan. Gwen realised that the song playing was another of the Brit-pop bands Elise had been rabbiting on about. Evidently, she'd been rabbiting about them to Ethan too.

It was a good song. About how the guy was a weirdo and a creep and didn't deserve the girl.

A few minutes after that Ethan suddenly dropped his box of jaffas on the floor. The floor was wooden and the sound of them rolling about was deafening. Gwen shrunk lower in her seat with embarrassment, but Elise turned and said sorry to the rows behind them, while she and Ethan sat there laughing.

"Look there's one by the screen" Elise whispered. Gwen didn't care. She just wanted them to stop but Ethan and Elise were still laughing about it.

When the movie finished, they stayed in their seats watching the credits, and waiting for the rest of the audience to file out.

"That was great," Elise said. "And did you see that trailer at the start for Love and Other Catastrophes?"

"That was fucking hilarious!" Ethan said.

"Was it? What was?" Gwen had seen the trailer, but it hadn't looked that funny to her.

"When the girl goes backwards and forwards trying to get her form signed. That is *exactly* what university is like" Elise said. Elise had done half a year at uni before deciding that it wasn't for her. Gwen had gone straight from school into working.

"We'll have to see it," Ethan said and somehow Gwen knew she was not included in the invite. They filed out and in the foyer, Fran came up.

"Did you like it?" she asked them.

"It was great," Elise said.

"Did you hear the Radiohead song? When he was walking in slow-mo?" she asked.

"I know! That was fantastic!"

"That's a Britpop band isn't it?" Gwen said to feel included. She may as well contribute now she knew about this stuff.

"Well, they're really British alternative," Elise said. "But close enough."

"Creep was the song I wanted to play you when we were in that record shop the other day," Fran said "but they didn't have it. Anyway, I better catch up with Jill. I'll see you tomorrow?"

Elise nodded.

On the pavement outside, Ethan turned to Gwen and said it was nice to meet her and then said to Elise that he'd see her tomorrow. He turned and headed off.

"I don't know what I was worried about," Elise said, "We're just friends like we were before."

And suddenly Gwen felt like Elise was moving away from her somehow.

She wouldn't show it.

"That's good. That keeps it nice and uncomplicated, not like me and Brian" she said. "Did you see when Samira looked at me at the BBQ? Let's go for a hot chocolate so we can discuss it" Gwen said.

And Elise, who had been glancing down the road after Ethan, pulled her attention back and nodded.

"Sure," she said distractedly.

Ethan
cooks pasta

Recommended listening: Beautiful Ones
The second single from the album Coming up by Suede
Released in October 1996, by Nude Records.
(This was after Britpop Summer but Suede were one of the big four
of Britpop so they're an honorary addition!)

Ethan closed the door to Harriet's room and stood, shaking slightly, white-faced. Harriet looked up from the bed where she was laying on her back, propped up with pillows, reading.

"What's wrong?" she asked.

"I just saw something disturbing" Ethan came back over to the desk and sat down hard.

He'd been playing on Harriet's Apple Mac. She had a game called Factory where little burgers went along a conveyor belt, and you had to put the right ingredients on. The graphics were basic but much better than the game Harriet was currently obsessed with. That was a black screen and you had to move a white asterisk around it. Ethan couldn't see any point in it, but Harriet had played it for hours.

But now, after what he'd just seen he couldn't even focus on the burgers.

"What?" Harriet sat up.

"Your flatmate," Ethan said slowly. "She opened her door at the same time I went into the hall. She was completely naked."

"Wasn't that a good thing?" Harriet asked.

"No! I've never seen anyone so hairy. There was hair...." he paused "...everywhere. I didn't want to look at her.... chest so I looked downwards and there was so much hair and then so much more hair on her legs, so then I looked at her feet. The worst thing was she was wearing a pair of white running shoes. Those are going to be emblazed on my mind forever."

"She exer-cycles in the nude!" Harriet said.

"Don't make it worse" Ethan said rubbing his head in his hands, like that was going to remove what he'd seen. "My god, I haven't seen legs with hair that thick...." He trailed off, lost for words.

"When she shaves them, the sink is covered in stubble," Harriet said and then shrieked with glee when Ethan picked up a pencil from her desk and threw it at her.

"I don't want to hear another word about it," he said as Harriet ducked while reaching up and catching the pencil, still giggling.

"This isn't funny. I've been traumatised." Ethan pouted.

"Oh, you poor thing" Harriet laughed again.

Ethan shook his head, turned and started a new game of the burgers.

"Are you going to be okay to come with me to the supermarket?" Harriet asked a few moments later. "Or are you too disturbed?"

"I'm not leaving until I know she's back in her room" he nodded towards the hallway where they could hear Rosalie on the phone. The phone cord wasn't very long, so you had to sit in the hallway when you were on a call.

"I refuse to see that sight again."

"Okay, we'll wait" Harriet settled back down with her book and tried to wipe the smile off her face.

A little while later they heard Rosalie hang up and go back into her room.

"Right, we're off!" Ethan leapt up, grabbed the book out of Harriet's hands and put a bookmark in it. Harriet climbed up and they crept across to the bedroom door like criminals.

Ethan opened it as quietly as he could, to find Rosalie open hers at the same time.

"What are you two up to in there?" she asked.

"My eyes!" Ethan yelled covering his face and careening down the hall towards the kitchen. Harriet couldn't speak for laughing. Rosalie now at least had a towel wrapped around her. Harriet raced after Ethan who was waiting for her outside the back door.

"It's okay, she's semi-clad" Harriet grinned.

"Have you got your keys? We're out of here" Ethan didn't care at this point if Rosalie was covered neck to ankle. He hurried Harriet down the stairs.

Soon they were safe in her car.

"City or sheep?" Harriet asked.

There were two options of supermarkets. The one on the edge of the city centre was only a 5-minute drive away but was expensive. The other one was in the suburbs. You had to take the motorway and wind your way up the steep gorge that was the only way out of the city. It was much cheaper but was almost 15 minutes away. For some reason that supermarket had giant model animals of cows and sheep hanging above some of the aisles. So they called it sheep.

"Sheep," Ethan said. It was cheaper and he felt like a drive, something pleasant to look at. Harriet put the radio on as they sped through the streets to get to the motorway. Once they were up to top speed, the VW chugged along happily. They slowed considerably up the gorge, and near the top were barely faster than someone walking, but they made it and reached the supermarket.

Ethan got a shopping basket and decided to gather the ingredients he needed quickly. Harriet was not only a dawdler but also an impulse buyer. He wondered if Elise normally kept her in check when they came here together.

And just as he knew would happen, once he had what they needed, he had to stand waiting for Harriet to emerge from one of the aisles.

She had a small pile of jars and packets in her arms.

"What are these?" he asked walking up to her.

"Just some things I'll pay for," she said.

He eyed them. There wasn't a vegetable in there or anything even fresh. It was all packaged. It seemed Harriet hadn't taken on any of the cooking lessons he'd given her.

"What is this?" he said plucking a jar from her hand. He looked at the label. It was processed cheese but in a jar. Like peanut butter. He hadn't even known spreadable processed cheese existed.

"That's for Elise. She loves the stuff" Harriet said. "I'm buying it for her as a present."

"Why?" Ethan suspected there was something more here.

"Blair has her eating snow peas. I'm just reminding her there are other things she likes."

"Yes, this is much healthier than snow peas."

"Well, I'm buying it" Harriet took it back.

*

Getting home they found Rosalie had gone out.

"Hang on…. she's not here for dinner tonight, is she?" Ethan asked.

"Well, yes, but I'll make sure she's dressed" Harriet had put the bags down on the counter and now seemed to have lost interest in the groceries and was putting the kettle on for a cup of tea. It was typical of her not only to ask Ethan to come and cook dinner but also to then invite people that he didn't like.

Luckily he was used to it and shaking his head, he started on the prep. It wasn't easy as he now found they didn't have many kitchen utensils. There was only one knife which didn't look like it was that sharp, and half a wooden chopping board.

"Where's the rest of this board?" he asked Harriet who was making her tea.

"I think that's Rosalie's."

"Yes, but where's the other half?"

Harriet shrugged.

Ethan sighed.

"I think I might go to my room for a while. I should do some study" Harriet said, holding her finished cup of tea.

"Sure" It would be easier for him to prep.

Once she'd gone, Ethan sliced the peppers and fried them off. He checked the time. People would be arriving soon. He chopped the garlic and started to sweat it on a low heat.

"That smells fabulous" Rosalie arrived home first and was now standing in the doorway, Ethan thought in what she possibly thought was a seductive pose. She had pulled her hair up into a bun and was looking at him through her eyelashes and was sort of smiling strangely. She came into the kitchen and stood by him to look at what he was doing. "Harriet said you were very good," she said smiling at him.

Ethan smiled thinly back.

Rosalie went and poured herself a glass of lemonade, leaned against the kitchen cupboard and chatted obliviously to him. She had on a skirt that was slit to her thighs and Ethan could see far too much of the hairy legs again. He averted his eyes. Did she think she was flirting with him? Couldn't she see he wasn't into it?

ANGELA ATKINS

Thankfully after a few minutes, Elise arrived home too.

"Hey that smells great," she said coming into the kitchen.

"Thanks" Ethan rolled his eyes towards Rosalie who was looking down adjusting her skirt to show more leg. Elise seemed to get it immediately.

"Shall we go through to the lounge and leave you to cook?" she asked.

"Thanks" Ethan nodded. Elise linked her arm with Rosalie's who seemed reluctant to leave but Elise pulled her. She looked back and Ethan mouthed thank you to her. She grinned at him and mouthed back 'You owe me.'

Jason arrived next. He poked his head around the door and seemed unsure about coming in. Ethan stirred the sauce. "You must be Jason," he said.

"You must be Ethan."

Jason was a weedy-looking guy with sticking-out ears. He appeared to be completely socially inept. Yet again Ethan found himself wondering what some women saw in some men.

"Harriet is through there" Ethan motioned down the corridor. It was typical Harriet to still be in her room and not here to welcome everyone.

Fran turned up shortly afterwards.

"We meet again," Ethan said as she came into the kitchen with a bottle of wine.

"What are you cooking?" she came over and looked into the pot.

"Red pepper and tomato pasta".

Elise came into the kitchen and came over to Fran, conspiratorial.

"I better warn you that Jason is here," she said.

"What? Why?"

"Harriet invited him."

"I wouldn't have come then" Fran looked sour.

116

"Sorry. If it's any consolation Rosalie's cornered him and is flashing her hairy legs" Elise laughed.

"Jesus, whatever the guy's done, he doesn't deserve that," Ethan said and went back to stirring his sauce.

*

Dinner had been declared delicious and Ethan had been given the best seat. Blair hadn't turned up so there had been plenty and everyone was feeling very happy. They were crowded into the lounge, drinking and telling tales of weird flatmates.

"I had some really strange flatmates when I was at university" Fran told them about a student flatmate she had with such crusty socks they stood up in a row on his floor, one girl who liked to do pagan rituals in the corner of the living room before they ate and the guy who liked to set fire to plastic forks.

"I can top that," Elise said. "The guy that lived here before Harriet and Rosalie was pretty strange. He was called Oxford and…"

"Hang on" Ethan interrupted. "What sort of name is Oxford?"

"I think his parents met there. Kind of tacky" Elise shrugged. "Anyway, he was single but he'd told me when I first looked at the flat that he'd recently broken up with someone."

"Potential flatmates tell you the weirdest stuff" Fran poured herself another vodka and lemonade. They had made a jug of it for the girls. The boys were on beer.

"I went to look at a flat once and they told me to come at 7 pm but then they were all watching Shortland Street on TV and when I said I didn't watch it they thought I was some kind of freak," Ethan said.

"Maybe you are some kind of freak," Rosalie said suggestively.

Ethan took a long gulp of his beer.

"Anyway, Ethan interrupted your story," Fran said.

Elise continued. "So a couple of days after I moved in, Oxford was out and there was this knock on the door. I opened it and this girl was outside and she said that she was Oxford's ex."

"What did she want?" Fran asked.

"She said she'd come to pick up a couple of things she'd left behind. She seemed very nice and reasonable about it."

"You didn't let her in?" Fran tutted.

"Well, she seemed okay. So I let her into his bedroom. Then I went out as me and Oxford were meeting with the lawyers to sign the lease."

"Elise! That was crazy" Rosalie said. Elise pulled a face and Ethan had to laugh. It so clearly said that if the weird hairy flatmate considered something crazy, then it must be absolutely insane. Elise caught his eye and grinned.

"It was crazy! I don't know why I did it. And then I was really worried about mentioning it to Oxford. So it wasn't until we'd finished signing the lease and we were walking down the hill towards here that I said to him that she had turned up at the door earlier. He went *completely* white."

"Poor guy," Jason said and both Harriet and Fran's heads swivelled to look at him. Ethan sometimes wondered if women knew how obvious they were being.

Elise shifted in her seat. Everyone was waiting to hear what happened next. She knew they would never ever guess.

"Oxford asked me in this really shaky voice what I had done when she'd showed up. So I had to say that I'd let her in but I was sure that she'd be gone now. And he just broke into a run towards the house."

"Did you run after him?" Fran asked unwrapping a toffee. The box of toffees was Harriet's contribution to her own dinner party.

"No, it was too hot to run. You know how the weather's been. But I did hurry."

"Oh, you're cruel! So he had to face her on his own?" Rosalie frowned.

"Well I was right that she had gone so he didn't have to see her" Elise paused "but that wasn't the worst thing. I got home a few minutes later and called out to him. There was this muffled sob from his bedroom. So I went and pushed the door open. The room was a mess with his stuff thrown everywhere."

Elise reached down for a toffee.

"You can't stop there" Harriet scolded her.

"Okay, we'll you're not going to believe what the ex had done. On the wall above his bed, she'd written a message in giant letters in some sort of brown liquid that we worked out was furniture polish. The message said: 'This is not blood, blood is red'."

"Poor guy," Jason said again. This time neither Harriet nor Fran looked at him but actually looked at each other for a moment.

"And on his bedhead, she'd scratched something horrible."

"What had she scratched?" Ethan asked.

Elise looked at him.

"It's pretty awful if you think about it."

Ethan did a drum roll in the air.

"She'd scratched the word 'mediocre'."

There was silence.

"That is *awful*," Fran said.

"Yes, that's not nice at all" Jason agreed.

"We spent the afternoon standing on his bed scrubbing his wall down," Elise said. "I felt so absolutely awful about it. He was crying when I got home but I hardly knew the guy and didn't think he wanted me feeling sorry for him. So I called her a bitch and said I couldn't believe what she'd done. And kind of ignored him sniffling away and went and got cloths and water. We actually had quite a good conversation as we cleaned up and he told me about the whole relationship. So that's my weirdo flatmate story".

"Okay, well I think that might win it for the night," Harriet said. "Although Ethan and I have a good one…"

"Who are you thinking about?" Ethan asked.

"Sean. And the toaster."

"Oh yeah," Ethan nodded.

"When Ethan and I first moved up here we stayed with a friend of ours called Sean. He started acting a bit strange after a couple of days, peering out of the window and running out of the house when you were in the middle of talking to him. Then one day Ethan and I got back, and his door was closed. We thought he was just asleep. The next morning Ethan went to make toast."

"And then I realised the toaster wasn't there," Ethan interjected. "And so we opened Sean's door and he'd taken off. With everything in his room but also the toaster."

"And it was our toaster!" Harriet added.

"And then the bailiffs arrived to try and take all our stuff because he owed so much money and we had to try and convince them Sean wasn't there and had nothing to do with us" Ethan finished.

"Yeah good try but that's not as strange as Elise's story" Fran declared.

"What about you Jason?" Harriet asked.

"No, my flatmates haven't been that strange. We did once have the weirdest evening though when one of the women in my flat was having a bath upstairs which was above the lounge. We were watching television and then heard this creaking sound from the ceiling, and then the bath actually fell through and landed on the floor in front of us. And she was still in it."

"She was still in it?" Ethan was sceptical.

"Well, maybe she had got out and was standing above looking down through the hole. But I thought it sounded more dramatic if she had been in" Jason shrugged.

"Do we have any other contenders then?" Elise said.

"Well, I flatted with this crazy redhead in Christchurch" Ethan started, and Harriet threw a toffee at him. "No mine are all pretty normal. I flatted with a girl who used to wear a boob tube that always fell off. Now I think about it she may have been coming onto me" Ethan grinned.

There were a few more stories and more drinking. It was getting late, and Jason was the first to say he had to head off.

After a few minutes more Fran said she should also hit the road as she had work in the morning. Once she'd left, Rosalie tried flirting with Ethan again for a few minutes but when that didn't seem to be getting any reaction she went to her room.

*

Elise stood up and picked up the last few toffees. "Shall we go and listen to some music?" she asked indicating her room. Ethan picked himself up and followed Harriet.

"Is Blair still staying?" Ethan asked.

"No, she moved out," Elise said. "I keep meaning to get rid of her bed."

"Well, I'm glad you haven't" Ethan folded the mattress so half of it was up against the wall and half on the floor, so it was more like a couch. He threw himself down on it and sprawled out.

Harriet sat down in the window seat.

Elise went over to her CD player.

"This is the first Oasis album" she explained as she pressed play. She sat down on the floor under the other window. They listened and talked. When they got to Married with Children which Harriet had heard many times before, she and Elise sang along loudly that your music's shite, it keeps me up all night.

Ethan laughed. After a while, he got up and went and looked at the books Elise had piled in stacks on top of the mantelpiece of the bricked-up fireplace.

"What's your favourite?" he asked.

"The Secret History by Donna Tartt" Elise answered without hesitation. Ethan turned and looked at her.

"That's a great book!" he said. He pulled a couple out of the pile that he hadn't heard of, and then slowly, so slowly, the whole pile toppled in slow motion and fell around him onto the floor.

"Sorry" Ethan hated damaging books. He started to pick them up and Elise came over and helped him.

When they were all back in place, he brought the two over that he'd pulled out to create the cascade. They were both by Japanese writers he hadn't heard of.

"Any good?" he asked holding them up so Elise could see.

"Yes, I liked them both," she said. "The Banana Yoshimoto one is very sparse on language which is quite strange to read, and the Murakami is the opposite, sort of very floral."

"Ethan's favourite book is American Psycho," Harriet said.

"I've heard of that. Is it about two people driving across America killing people?" Elise asked.

Ethan looked up from reading the back of the Yoshimoto novel "No it's not."

He realised his voice sounded cold, but he got tired of defending a book to people. The only person he'd met who had liked it too was a woman he'd worked with when he'd first moved up to Wellington. He'd mentioned her so much that Harriet had used it as ammunition when they broke up saying that he was obviously in love with this woman who liked American Psycho.

Ethan had replied coldly that it was just nice to meet someone who didn't taunt your taste in books or music. Harriet was a fan of some weird alternative bands and Ethan had never once made fun of her taste.

He had in fact made the mistake once of saying he liked the Pixies and then had to endure listening to them over and over.

When you were first trying to impress a girl, you said anything, but it was different when you were then living with them and suddenly had to find an excuse for why you accidentally stepped on the Pixies tape and then stepped on it again until it had cracked. The really annoying thing was the tape hadn't broken enough and Harriet had managed to stick it together and make it still play.

"I must be thinking of another book" Elise seemed contrite.

"And he likes Jay McInerney," Harriet said. Ethan looked at her. He wasn't sure what she was trying to prove tonight.

"Bright Lights, Big City?" Elise asked. "I've read that. It was great. Unlike the terrible film with Michael J Fox."

"The film had its charm, but books are always better" Ethan agreed. They talked about it for a little while. Harriet started making snoring noises.

"I think someone needs to go to bed," Elise said.

"No, I don't" Harriet looked annoyed. Ethan knew what she'd been trying to say. He liked the fact that Elise had either misunderstood or decided to pretend to misunderstand. He also knew that it meant it was time to leave.

"I'm off," he said.

"I'll call you tomorrow about that thing," Harriet said.

"Sure" Ethan was amused. There was no thing that he knew of.

"Thanks for dinner" Elise stood up and walked him down the hall.

"I'll call you tomorrow," Ethan said.

On the walk home, he realised he was whistling an Oasis song.

Blair gets stuck

Recommended listening: Cigarettes and Alcohol

From the album Definitely Maybe by Oasis

The Fourth Single released from the album in October 1994.

Album released in August 1994, by Creation Records.

The song is about the appeal of cigarettes and alcohol as a remedy to the futility of a working-class life.

Blair woke to a pounding headache and dry mouth. She felt around her trying to figure out where she was.

"Hey, how are you feeling?" a voice asked from across the room. Blair recognised it as Elise. She was at Elise's. But she didn't live at Elise's anymore. And why couldn't she remember getting here? The room was bright, and she put her hands over her eyes.

"I'm feeling bad" she croaked. "I need water and drugs."

She heard Elise leave the room.

The bed felt like it was rocking gently under her. She'd almost forgotten about how nauseous that always made her feel. She hadn't been this hung over for a very long time.

Elise came back and made her sit up slowly and take a few sips of water and a low-level pain killer.

"Haven't you got anything stronger?" Blair complained.

"Let's see if you keep that down first."

"Fine." Blair sunk back onto the pillows and noticed the bucket at the side of the bed.

"Oh god I'm sorry" she moaned. She didn't want to know if there was anything in there.

"It's okay. Why don't you try and get some more sleep?" Elise helped her lie back down and pulled the sheet and blanket up over her. Blair drifted off immediately.

*

It had to be a few hours later as the sun had moved across the room. Blair woke up feeling a gnawing hole in her stomach. She had never been this hungry in her entire life. She sat up and rubbed her eyes. Elise was sitting on her bed across the room, reading a book. She must have heard movement and looked over.

"Hey, you're awake. How do you feel now?" she asked, putting the book down and sitting up.

"Hungry" Blair picked up the glass of water from the floor and drained it in four gulps.

Elise laughed. "Careful" She climbed up. "I'm going to make a sandwich. Do you want one?"

Blair nodded.

While Elise was in the kitchen, Blair carefully climbed out of bed and walked slowly to the bathroom. She didn't look too shit hot. She was still wearing yesterday's clothes and her mascara was streaked. Her hair was tangled around her head and she noticed there were some bits of vomit in it, which she bent down and washed out.

She had got back into bed when Elise brought the sandwich through and handed her the plate. She put it in her lap.

"What happened last night?" she asked.

"How much do you remember?" Elise sat down cross-legged on the end of the mattress.

"I remember playing pool, I remember eating pizza. Then I'm not sure" Blair was struggling. She knew this was never good.

"Well after the pool and pizza, you got a bit drunk and disappeared. By the time I went to find you, you were in the bathrooms, and you were yelling blue murder." Elise paused. "Do you really want to hear this?"

"Why what did I do?"

"Well you'd got yourself completely wedged down the side of the toilet, under the toilet roll holder and you were stuck. I tried to get you out but I couldn't and you were yelling so loudly that several other people came in to see what had happened."

"Oh my god" Blair was looking white.

"That's not the worst of it" Elise picked at her fingernails.

"What do you mean? Tell me!" Blair demanded.

"You then sort of went into a coma and were still trapped under the toilet roll holder, so we had to call an ambulance. You were carried out on a stretcher."

Blair composed herself.

"And everyone saw?"

"Everyone saw" Elise wasn't making this any easier. This was embarrassing on a mega scale. Blair had watched others succumb to this type of thing many times but had avoided it. Now she had dallied in it, she seemed to have done it fantastically.

"I'd never actually been in an ambulance before. It was really cool" Elise enthused.

"Yes, I don't actually remember." Blair tested joking about it, but she wasn't ready. "So what happened?" she may as well know the whole story.

"Well once they figured out you were fine, just really, really drunk, they drove us here. I thought it was better than you having to go across town."

"They drove me here in the ambulance?"

"Yes, but they didn't have the lights or siren on."

"That makes me feel so much better." Blair looked down at her sandwich. "I can't go to work tonight," she said.

"Of course you can. Everyone was drunk, no-one will remember what happened" Elise said tucking into her sandwich. "You should stay here until then. And you should eat. Or you'll feel worse."

"I couldn't feel much worse than this" Blair said. But she decided maybe the sandwich would make her feel better, so she took a tiny bite. And then another.

*

"Come on" Elise pulled at her arm.

"You're hurting me" Blair moaned, scuttling next to her, although Elise wasn't holding her arm that hard. She was actually feeling a bit better now. After she had eaten and showered, she had let Elise convince her to come to work. And now she was letting Elise drag her down the road to get there.

As they got to the front door of the building, she tried to talk Elise out of it one last time. Tried to say that she wasn't feeling that good and wouldn't be any use on the phones tonight, but Elise was having none of it.

In the lift, Elise let go of her arm for the first time and they were silent. As they stepped out, they could hear the babble of voices down the hall. Blair tried to turn around, but Elise linked her arm in hers again.

"Come on. Just walk in with your head held high. No-one will say anything."

And so they walked toward the door and stepped inside.

Blair couldn't look up and let Elise guide them round the back of the room. It took a moment before anyone noticed that they had come in and the suddenly there was a hush.

"Hey, the legend has arrived!" Scott stood up and started clapping. All at once everyone else was up out of their seats and the whole room broke into applause. Blair looked up from the grey carpet she'd been studying and saw them all cheering her. She looked at Elise and shrugged. Then she took a bow.

There were wolf whistles.

And the rest of the night had a kind of festive feel. The people they were calling, who were more focused on their upcoming summer holidays but in a good mood because of it, seemed more jovial when saying no. A few of them actually signed up saying they were happy to pay the low sign-up price for 3 months, even though they wouldn't be watching it much, with it being such a great summer. But this way they had it paid for if summer did decide to disappear as it often did.

At their break, Scott and Jack raced over to Blair and gave her a fireman's lift, carrying her out of the room to more whoops and cheers.

"You guys, I'm actually really embarrassed," Blair said.

"Bullshit. You're a legend" Scott said.

Blair rolled her eyes at Elise. How could Elise have thought this guy was cool? He was an idiot. They carried her to the stairs and then put her down.

"Doesn't a legend get carried to the bottom?" she asked.

"Yeah, don't push it" Jack grinned.

Once they'd gathered in the car park and all lit up, and taken their first drag, they started discussing the party. While Blair remembered a little of it, she was happy to hear what she had missed.

She remembered arriving. Christof had told them it was a sort of Christmas/end-of-year party, and it would start sharply at 12 midday. She remembered that none of them had been on time. They had drifted in, arriving alone or with some of the others, half an hour, an hour later.

It was another glorious day and they took over part of the garden bar area of the pub. Blair arrived with Elise and they sat at a table with Jack. Blair hadn't been planning on staying long. She didn't really know any of these people and had told Zöe that she would go out with them later.

Once they were all there, Christof ordered some pizzas. He seemed to be acting like this made a big man.

"Does he think he's being generous? The company will be paying for the food" Jack said. "And what kind of party would it be without pizza?"

"It would be worse if there were no drinks either" Elise laughed.

The garden bar was a little oasis of peace and shadiness. Blair had noticed the last couple of weeks that this end of town was very concrete. There needed to be more parks.

There was a slight breeze now and the tree that was shading Blair rustled its leaves above her. There was a dark little pagoda in the corner that had several people hanging out in it, but then they got up and left. Jack leapt up, almost knocking over the table.

"To the pagoda!" he said, and he and Elise were off and into it.

It was shady and cool inside. Blair followed and curled up on the corner seat. They sat there looking out. It was a little voyeuristic. People didn't seem to notice they were in there so they could do a Rear Window. Scott was holding court at a table nearby, going on about something and picking his ear out.

"This is seriously the guy that you liked?" Blair asked watching him.

"Yeah," Elise shrugged. "I feel weird about it now. I know he's got a girlfriend so there's no point, but I still like him."

"Well you can't just turn off when you like someone," Blair said. "But you can get over them by flirting with someone else. What about Rob?" Rob was another telemarketer who was currently chugging a beer by the pool table.

"No, I can't yet. I need some time" Elise said.

"What about Christof?" Blair said.

"Yuck! What do you mean?" Elise asked.

"What do you think his problem is? Small penis?"

Jack snorted and beer came out of his nose. He was choking and laughing, and Elise handed him some napkins. They were all laughing now.

"It's probably like this" Elise held up her little finger and wiggled it. They all started laughing. Blair glanced out and saw Christof glaring at them. That just set them off again. Blair could see now why Elise liked Jack. He was great fun.

"Do you guys really discuss dick size?" he asked.

"Sometimes" Blair shrugged.

"You'd be surprised what we talk about," Elise said raising her eyebrows at him. "Surely guys talk about girls.... you know, our pieces."

"Pieces?" Jack said. "Sure, we assess tits and arse. But for us, it's about personality and caring."

"Yeah right" Blair drained her beer. "I'm getting something stronger to drink. Are you in?" They both were, so she went and got some tequila shooters. Christof intercepted her coming across the garden.

"Ah, you're onto the good stuff. I'll come and join you" he said.

"No there's no room," Blair said and weaved past him. She told the others what she'd just said, and they burst out laughing again.

And so, the afternoon passed and the party swirled about them. Little groups formed and split up, the party gained energy at some points and then slowed, as parties do.

At one point, Jack and Elise heard the song at the same time. Elise sang along in her best imitation of a Manchurian accent.

Jack was lighting a cigarette. When she sang the next line which ended with the words cigarettes and alcohol, Elise grabbed one from him and put it in her mouth and they all raised their glasses.

"Is this Oasis or Blur?" Blair asked. She was still catching up.

"Who does it sound like?" Elise said.

"Northern. It's Oasis" She was across the whole Blur from the south, being rich boys, and Oasis from the North coming from nothing. She didn't want to start Elise and Jack on that discussion again.

Later again they went inside to play pool. They took over the area and created a pool tournament and soon the others were also signing up and having a round. Elise was surprisingly good. Blair lost interest when she had a round where she ended up potting not one ball.

"Stupid game," she said.

She had meant, she really had, to not drink much and leave before 5 pm but things didn't transpire like that. Christof shouted a few rounds of tequila. He seemed to get very offended when he offered his hand around to lick salt off and most of the girls screamed yuck and ran away. Or wiggled their little finger at him.

And it was after that that Blair had disappeared. She really didn't remember even going to the bathroom and definitely did not remember being wedged under the toilet roll. A fact that everyone seemed to find most amusing as they headed back up the stairs for their second bout on the phones.

"You must have blacked out before," Jack said, "when you were really drunk?"

"I don't think I've ever been that drunk before. I've never been rushed home in an ambulance." Blair said.

"Well now you've got your drinking wings you can come out for one with us after this," Jack said. "We're going to that pub across town for a poetry reading."

"A poetry reading? Are you serious? That's brilliant" Blair laughed.

Blair wondered now as she sat quietly working through her list of people to call, whether Christof knew that he'd lost any modicum of respect or authority that people had for him and now everyone just thought he was a small-dicked wonder. She guessed not. How would you live with yourself if you thought that? He probably thought it had been a great event and he'd been a wonderful boss.

She was going to have to resign soon. Christmas was coming. She'd hardly sold anything and she was less and less likely to. Most people said that if they brought a TV subscription, they were now thinking it would be for next winter.

*

After they finished, (two sales for Elise, one for Blair and three for Jack), they headed back to Elise's and Blair's to find some poetry books.

"I want to do a reading this time, but I don't have anything to read," Jack said.

"Elise will have some poetry. She's got a wall of books" Blair said.

"Actually, I'm not really a fan of poetry," Elise said, "I don't know that I have anything". But they trooped back to hers anyway and soon they were pawing through her books.

"I've got it" Elise said suddenly pulling out a small book and hiding it behind her back. "Jack, if you don't want to read it, I will."

"What is it?" he looked suspicious.

"The greatest poet of all time. And he even rhymed" Elise held up her copy of the Cat in the Hat.

"I love Doctor Zeuss. This is perfect" Jack grabbed it and was flicking through to find a passage to read.

And so later Blair found herself with another drink in her hand. She decided this would be her only one of the night. She was not going to put in a repeat performance under any circumstances. Even if Jack was trying to convince her she would be a total legend.

They had taken a table near the back and were piled in with a couple of Blair's friends that they had bumped into on the way. The table was really only big enough for four, so they were squashed together and having a fine time.

And then it was time for Jack to read. He made his way into the crowd and disappeared for a moment before they saw him climb above the masses onto the stage.

He walked over to the mic and paused dramatically. When he started to read, there was a moment of hush in the room and then people realised it was the Cat in the Hat and started to cheer and wolf whistle. Jack read his section, took a bow, and then made his way through to the bar back to them. The MC announced that was the perfect note to finish on and the DJ came on and the music began to blast.

"Time for dancing," Blair said and even though she'd felt like death that morning, now she felt like grooving.

Fran gets lucky

Recommended listening: She Bangs the Drums
Second single released in May 1989.
From the album The Stone Roses, by the Stone Roses.
Album released in May 1989, by Silverton but was still being played on the radio in the mid 90's.

Fran liked to take a casual approach to parties in general and especially birthday parties. Yes, she would go and buy some drinks and put together a few bowls of potato chips and dip, but that would be it. It was too hot to do anything else.

She and Elise were sitting leaning against the outside wall of Fran's flat, their legs stretched out on the grass, reading magazines. The back garden wasn't big, but there was a squarish slice of lawn and a few trees. The hill then plunged downwards towards the next level of houses below, and you could just see the different coloured metal rooves in between gaps in the leaves.

Up behind Fran's house was a band of much denser trees. When they'd first come out, Elise had looked up the slopes behind them and narrowed her eyes.

"I think just a bit further up on this hill, past these trees is where the meadow is" Elise turned to her.

"And? What's so special about this meadow?" Fran had asked.

"Nothing" Elise shrugged, deciding not to tell her about that afternoon up there with Ethan a few weeks ago.

They sat down against the house. There was dappled shade against the wall, but their legs were in full sunshine. Both were wearing skirts and kicked off their shoes. Fran couldn't help noticing Elise had a better tan but then white was more interesting, wasn't that what they said?

Fran had used her staff discount to buy some NME and Rolling Stone magazines and they both sat engrossed.

"Oh my god – this article about the whole class thing with Oasis and Blur is really good. I didn't even know about it when I first started listening to them. Did you?" Elise asked.

"Of course," Fran said crossly. Elise was so naïve.

Jason had been big on class differences and was sort of a communist. Fran liked to think of herself as very politically astute. She'd voted in the last election, and she didn't think Elise would have bothered or known what party to vote for. She guessed she was more left-wing but didn't really think communism sounded like a good idea although she'd pretended to consider it to impress Jason. She'd even told him that she'd read the Communist Manifesto when actually she'd just flicked through the Cliff Notes.

Funnily at work, they didn't actually stock Cliff Notes, but some inferior version that was much cheaper and shorter. She'd never looked through those, she did have some standards. She hadn't even realised there was a whole rivalry in the book world between publishers of things like Cliff Notes or dictionaries until the Collins Rep incident.

It had happened once when Harriet was in-charge of non-fiction but had asked Fran to sit in. The Collins Rep (she couldn't remember her name), her whole selling point for why they should have the Collins rather than the other brand of dictionary, was that in the Collins the first definition of the word gay wasn't happy, unlike the other brand. The Collins dictionary's definition of gay was being homosexual.

Fran could remember how the Collins Rep had gone red when she'd explained the definition like Fran or Harriet wouldn't know what other definition there could be apart from happy.

The Rep had explained that that meant that Collins was more up-to-date and should be the better dictionary to stock.

She and Harriet had conferred for a moment and then agreed. In this day and age, you couldn't have a dictionary that was behind.

The rep had also sold them a book to stock called '100 books you must read' which basically had two books a week to read. Fran was pleased that she'd actually read a good number of them. She liked to think of herself as well-educated and somewhat literary and she'd felt that having already read over half of the 100 showed that.

The '100 books' also gave you a good rundown of what the novel was about the themes or questions that it raised. She was thinking of buying a copy for Elise for Christmas except that it was quite expensive and even with her staff discount, Elise didn't really deserve that.

While Elise had books piled everywhere, she didn't seem to have read any of the classics. Fran was forever saying 'have you read xxx'' and Elise would shake her head. Fran was thinking a better birthday present would just be compiling a list of a few books Elise should really attempt.

*

Fran put her magazine down and rested her head against the wall.

"Did you know Jason and I spent one afternoon where he drew all over me with a squirty tube of chocolate and then licked it off?" she said, turning her head sideways. Fran loved shocking Elise with tales of her past or present boyfriends.

"Wow," Elise looked impressed and nodded.

"Have you ever had someone do that?"

"No. Ethan and I drew tattoos on our arms with permanent markers the other week" Elise volunteered.

"Yes, but that's not the same thing at all. You and Ethan don't have any sexual tension between you."

Elise seemed to want to say something.

"What? You don't do you?" Fran sat up slightly. Finally, something interesting. She was already thinking of what she would tell Harriet.

"If I tell you, you have to promise not to tell Harriet," Elise said.

"Sure" Fran waved her hand as if swatting away a fly.

"Promise" Elise seemed quite serious.

"Okay, I promise."

"Well, Ethan and I slept together. We've gone back to being just friends again though."

"Hang on!" Fran cut in "When did you sleep with him?"

"A few weeks ago."

"And you didn't tell me?"

"I didn't want to tell anyone. I don't know if Harriet will be okay with it. She gets funny about her exes. And I know the problems you two had over what happened with Jason" Elise looked down at the magazine in her lap and started fiddling with the corner of the page.

Fran was not pleased that she'd brought that up.

"Well, maybe you shouldn't mention it to Harriet. But you and Ethan are just completely friends like it didn't happen?"

"Yes completely. I was kind of hoping that maybe he wouldn't have been able to go back to how it was before.

138

You know.... that he would like me after it." Elise sounded rueful.

"But he doesn't."

"Well, he doesn't seem to. It's okay because I just like him as a friend anyway."

"So that's fine then" Fran went back to reading her magazine. Elise's love life was just so juvenile.

*

Fran looked at her watch.

"Crap!" she said, throwing the magazine down, the pages fluttering and turning in the grass. She was up and hurrying into the house. She stopped in the doorway and looked at Elise who was doing a 'what is it?' face.

"It's only an hour until the party starts! We have to get the stuff ready" Fran said. Elise climbed up and followed her and they hurried down the hill together. They were hot when they got to the supermarket but inside it was cool, and they both stood for a moment enjoying the chill.

Fran loved supermarket shopping. She'd been really pleased when one finally opened in the city the year before. And it was at the bottom of the hill near her, just a short walk away. It saved so much time not having to drive out miles to get groceries.

There was a current fad for people to make signs with their shopping baskets. If you were single and looking for a man, then you had to put some upturned bananas in your trolley and then walk pointedly to the freezer section. Fran had tried it and had actually been approached by one guy who started a conversation over the asparagus. It hadn't led anywhere but it had been fun.

"What do we need to get?" Elise asked now.

Fran had decided for the party that they would just have some chips and dips but that she'd also make something a little fancier. She wheeled over and put some smoked salmon and cream cheese in her basket.

"What are we going to do with this?" Elise asked.

"We need to get some French bread and make little rounds then put some smoked salmon and cream cheese on top."

"Okay. I don't think I've had smoked salmon before" Elise picked it up and had a look at it. "God it's so expensive."

"I know," Fran said. But this party was actually for her birthday after all, and she was feeling slightly generous.

They wheeled over to the alcohol section. Some cheap sparking wine would be fine. Fran grabbed four bottles and put them in the trolley.

Once they were back home, Elise was put on strawberry duty. She washed them and then cored them and cut them in half. "I love the smell of strawberries."

"You wouldn't love it so much if you've ever picked your own" Fran remembered back to last summer when she and Harriet had been driving back from the coast. They'd gone to spend the weekend at Fran's parent's beach house. It was when Fran had been having problems with Jason and the roster and had wanted to get away. She'd probably told Harriet far too much that weekend. Things that she then used against Fran when she got together with Jason.

On the way back they'd passed a sign saying 'pick your own strawberries' and neither wanting to get home quite yet, had turned off and parked.

They had both had some romantic notion of wafting through the strawberry fields, wind in their hair, putting strawberries in baskets. What they didn't realise was that strawberries grew right on the ground, and they had to bend over to pick them. Within minutes both of them had sore backs and were moaning like old women.

They both managed to pick a pathetic half-punnet and then decided to call it quits. Sitting under a tree a few minutes later eating the strawberries was much better although whenever Fran smelt strawberries from that moment on she always felt a twinge in her back.

It always surprised her how much smell could take you back to a memory or a place. When she smelt cut grass she was back at her parents during her first university holidays, sitting under a tree reading a book. Her father seemed to be out cutting the lawn every day and it just triggered that straight away.

Music was the same. There were albums she'd listened to after breaking up with boyfriends that whenever she heard them made her incredibly sad, even if she had been feeling happy moments before. Or albums you listened to when you were getting ready to go out that now when you heard it you thought about one of those nights.

Elise had put on the Oasis album while they prepared for the party and she wondered if she would remember this album when she heard it in the future.

*

It was the tense time. The time you'd said people should arrive but so far no-one had. Fran and Elise were sitting in the lounge with their glass of bubbly with a strawberry in the bottom. Elise had brought her party dress with her so had changed into it. It had daffodils printed all over it.

"Where did you get that?" Fran had asked. She was pretty sure she'd seen the entire contents of Elise's wardrobe, which wasn't much to start with. And it certainly didn't contain any dresses.

"Blair moved out, so we swopped a few things. She gave me this and I gave her my blue zippy top."

"But you love that top." Every time Fran had seen Elise before this summer had descended, she'd been wearing that top.

"I liked the dress more" Elise shrugged.

The Oasis CD had finished so Fran went over to the stereo and put on the Stone Roses. She loved She bangs the drums.

She sang along but Elise didn't sing the next line.

"Don't you think the Stone Roses are a bit morbid?" Elise asked.

"Morbid?" Fran took a sip of bubbly.

"I know it's still Brit Pop but it's just really dour."

"No, you're wrong" Fran heard the front door open and headed into the corridor. Her flatmates had arrived, and they turned the music up and went out into the garden. Fran decided to leave the front door unlocked so she wouldn't have to keep running and opening it. Everyone who was coming would know.

Fran was drinking under a tree when she heard more voices inside.

"We should put some more food out," she said to Elise, and they went into the kitchen. Fran grabbed a bowl of chips and went out into the lounge where she found Harriet had just arrived and walking in straight behind was Jason.

All three of them froze for a moment.

Fran was angry. Hadn't Harriet thought about this? This was Fran's birthday. She didn't want Jason here. How dare Harriet just bring him along without a thought?

"You look great" Jason broke the silence, looking at Fran.

Fran for some reason she couldn't fathom, looked down at herself. Did she doubt what Jason was saying? She did look good. She had on her little black party dress and her new red lipstick. She looked back at him. He seemed sincere.

"Thanks," she said. She wasn't going to tell him he looked good too. He hadn't earned anything like that from her.

"I hope you don't mind," Harriet said without explaining any further or sounding like she really cared.

"No, not at all" Fran sometimes hated being polite. She actually wanted to tell Harriet to fuck off. On second thoughts she looked back at Jason.

"You look great too," she said. "Come through here and I'll get you a drink" and she took his hand and pulled him away from Harriet, into the kitchen. Jason allowed himself to be pulled and Fran smiled to herself. If Harriet wanted to be a bitch about it, Fran would show her that she still had some tricks up her sleeve too. Jason wasn't something that Harriet owned. Fran still had a claim on him and tonight she'd stake that claim again.

She saw Harriet later in what looked like a deep and desperate conversation with Elise. Fran smiled. The party had progressed indoors and currently, Fran was sitting half in Jason's lap at the end of the couch. There were people sprawled everywhere and even a stack of presents. Fran had told people not to bother but they had, and she was secretly pleased. And Jason's mortification at the party being Fran's had meant he was being far nicer than he had ever been before, to Fran's advantage. Didn't he realise that he'd abandoned Harriet?

Still, Jason was the kind of guy who seemed to be swayed by whoever was in stronger need of him. Fran was sure that if some needy woman came onto him, even if he was in a committed relationship, he would cheat and then say that he couldn't help it. The other woman had needed him.

Fran was glad she wasn't with him anymore, but she didn't want him to be friends with Harriet. Harriet had enough men hanging around her after all.

Fran was surprised neither Harriet nor Elise had brought Ethan along. He seemed to be like a second appendage to both of them whenever she bumped into them at the moment. Although she had seen him with some other woman the other day. A woman with a short black bob. She'd have to ask Elise who it was.

Now she knew Elise had slept with Ethan, that changed things a little.

The party was developing nicely. There were people packed into the lounge and kitchen, as well as more out under the trees. Fran had hung a couple of paper lanterns with candles in and someone had lit them. There was talking and laughing, and the music poured out into the night.

*

Fran was drunk. She knew it when she realised she was dancing on the couch and several people were actually holding her up. She stopped abruptly and the helpers lifted her down.

"Come with me" Jason was there and put his arm around her. Fran looked around wildly for Harriet. Earlier she'd seen her and Harriet in the kitchen but now as Jason led her through the room, she couldn't figure out where they were.

Jason was guiding her towards her bedroom.

She looked around for Harriet one last time but couldn't see her anywhere. Tough. Fran was here and Jason was here and that was that.

Ethan
Wakes up

Recommended listening: Something Changed
From the album Different Class by Pulp
Single released in March 1996, by Island Records.

Ethan often fell asleep when he was stoned. Now he woke to find himself sprawled across Aria's couch, the sun burning the leg that was hung over the padded arm. His mouth was dry, and he climbed up in search of a drink. The remains of the Christmas lunch he had cooked them had dried out on the table.

He filled a glass of water and drank it straight down noisily. He put it back in the sink and went to find Aria.

She was asleep in the back garden in the shade of a tree. As he crunched across the gravel path, she groaned and groggily sat up rubbing her eyes.

"Hey what time is it?" she asked as Ethan collapsed on the grass beside her and stretched out for another nap.

He held his watch in front of his face but had to blink several times before he could focus.

"Nearly four" he finally surmised.

"Shit, I have to head over to my aunts' soon." Aria sat up and rested her head on her knees and looked at him sideways. "What are you going to do for the rest of the day?"

Ethan shrugged. "Read. I've got a book I haven't started yet."

"I'd invite you to come with me but my aunt's real uptight." Aria didn't realise that Ethan wasn't bothered about hanging out alone for the rest of the day.

He didn't usually do anything on Christmas Day and didn't really get this whole 'you must hang out with your family' thing.

Last year he'd gone to Harriet's parents with her and while that had been amusing in many ways, he realised he couldn't be bothered with family politics. Her parents had bitched and moaned to Harriet's face, asking her constantly where her career was going and when was she going to get a nice boyfriend and settle down. Then when she left the room, they said how proud they were of her.

The boyfriend remarks had been particularly hard not to comment on. Ethan hadn't found out that Harriet had told them he was her gay flatmate until they were driving down the street towards her parent's house.

"You told them what?" he'd said.

"I had to tell you were gay or they'd give me a hard time about us living together" Harriet accelerated down the street obviously wanting to get out of discussing this. But Ethan wasn't letting her off the hook.

"Don't they want you to be in a relationship?"

"You'd think so" Harriet had turned down the driveway.

"So, I have to pretend to be gay for the rest of the day?"

Harriet slowed the car down.

"Please," she said.

Ethan shook his head and sighed.

The car rounded a bank of trees and there they were. Harriet parked in front of the house and the fun Christmas day antics had kicked off soon after. Ethan had sworn to himself that he wouldn't do that again.

This year he had been happy to sit home but then Aria had said she was going to be by herself for most of the day and did he want to come round for Christmas lunch?

Ethan knew that meant she wanted him to cook. He didn't mind. He had trained as a chef for a year before deciding he didn't like the politics of the kitchen. All this rigmarole of ordering people around and shouting 'Yes chef!' just wasn't him.

Now with his eyes closed and feeling himself drifting off again, he suddenly asked "Doesn't your aunt live like an hour away on the train, up the coast somewhere?" Why that piece of trivia chose to pop up right then he had no idea.

"Yeah, I'll have a sleep on the train" Aria had lain back down again next to him, despite saying she had to leave soon.

"I don't like the suburbs" Ethan declared. He had always lived in the inner city. He liked the buzz of constant noise, buses, cars, and people going places. He always found the 'burbs were eerily quiet, empty streets with houses hidden away behind fences or hedges and the occasional scream of a child. Oh, he was sure all sorts of nasty things were being gotten up to, there must be to break the monotony, but he didn't feel like it was somewhere he belonged.

A few minutes later he woke again with a start, feeling some sort of insect climbing across his face. He swiped it off and sat up. Aria had dozed off again next to him.

He shook his head. He was drifting off again.

"Wake up," he said shaking Aria's shoulder. He climbed up rubbing his face. Aria moaned and then sat up.

"What's the time?" she asked.

"Déjà vu time" he looked at his watch. At least the numbers were a little clearer now. "Four-thirty."

"Crap, I really have to go!" Aria climbed up and rushed into the house, and Ethan meandered after her. He sat on the arm of the couch watching her mad dash to gather up the contents of her handbag which seemed to be scattered around the house. Throwing it over her shoulder, she grabbed his arm.

"I'm leaving now, you have to go!" She pulled him to the door and pushed him through. She gave him a quick kiss and then headed off down the hill towards town.

"I can walk you to the train station!" he called out after her.

"You'll slow me down" Aria called back. "I'll call you later!"

Ethan shrugged and turned and trudged home. He felt grimy like he'd been to the beach all day. No one was home. They had all dispersed to family events. So he took a shower and changed into his other white T-shirt.

He was surprised to find he felt a little lonesome. He tried to start his book but couldn't get into it. He wasn't sure what was wrong with him. He'd been looking forward to having a quiet Christmas unlike the Christmas before at Harriets' parents. All the tedious introductions of her family and her parent's friends, all sitting out on the patio by the back lawn on rackety metal chairs, and children running around screaming.

Ethan realized with a start that he was almost reminiscing, something he couldn't stand in others and didn't think he would ever do. He shook his head and tried to concentrate on his book but just ended up reading the same paragraph three times.

When the phone rang, he didn't answer. Everyone he knew including his flatmates had people they wanted to avoid and so didn't answer. He'd only met one person who just couldn't help herself answering the phone and that was

Céline. She had been amazed and astounded when they had been hanging out in the lounge one day and the phone had started ringing and Ethan had just let it ring.

"Are you not going to answer this?" she had said wide-eyed.

"No, I'll wait and see if they leave a message."

In American TV shows, they had answer phones where you could screen your phone calls but when he had seen one of those for sale it had been expensive. All they could afford was call-minder. You had to wait until the person had finished leaving a message and then dial in to check who it was.

"I must answer it!" Céline had leapt up and taken the call which was for another of their flatmates.

"See they would have left a message" Ethan shrugged.

"But what are you scared about?"

"Afraid of. Nothing. I just don't want to talk to anyone."

"You are a strange man" Céline had laughed.

Now the phone rang again, once, and stopped. It was the secret ring that a select few of them used to mean it was friend not foe on the other end of the line. When it started ringing again, Ethan climbed off the bed and answered it.

"Hi! Happy Christmas!" It was Elise.

"You too. What are you up to?" he sat down on the floor by the phone.

"I've been at Gwen's sisters for the day, but I got home and it's so quiet here. What are you up to?" she asked.

"I was going to make some pasta." He didn't know why but even with that humongous lunch he was hungry again.

"Oh," Elise sounded disappointed. In fact, he thought it was rather cute how transparent her sad little voice was.

"Why, what were you thinking?"

"I wondered if you wanted to come and watch a movie?"

"Sure. I can make us both some dinner."

"That would be great!" Elise perked up no end.

"See you soon."

Ethan hung up and went and gathered his ingredients. As he reached the bus stop a bus was coming. It wouldn't take him all the way to Elise's, but it would go near enough, and buses were free on Christmas day, so he jumped on. He rested his head against the glass as the bus rumbled and shook through town.

As he stepped off calling out thank you to the driver, he found the heat of the day was fading.

He sauntered up the empty streets and past the bucket fountain. The top bucket tipped and sent a cascade of water crashing down, sparkling in the sun.

Ethan went over to the edge and dipped his hand in the water and splashed some on his forehead before carrying on. Shortly he swung through the little blue gate, went up the zigzag path, made his way around the back of the house and sprinted up the stairs.

Elise had moved the mattress from her room onto the balcony and folded it up against the house like a couch, like he'd done the other week. She was sitting on it, her legs stretched out and her little orange sunglasses on, with a glass of coke sweating beside her casting a little pool of water on the wood of the balcony.

She had a bag of lollies in her lap.

"Hey," Ethan held up his bag of food and went inside to put it in the kitchen.

"There's some beer in the fridge" Elise called.

He came back out with one in his hand and slouched down on the mattress next to her. He put the unopened beer down and took off his shoes and socks and threw them into the shade which was creeping along the side of the house.

Then he held his forearm out palm down, clenched it into a fist, and twisted the beer top into his forearm, popping the cap off.

"Is that your party trick?" Elise laughed.

"Yeah, are you impressed?" he grinned at her and took a sip of beer.

"Did it hurt?" she reached out and held his arm. There was a mark where the screw cap had bitten in.

"No, I have arms of steel."

Actually, Ethan found out later that Elise thought he did have sexy forearms, and that was one of her favourite things about him. But she had decided it wasn't the time to tell him that.

They looked out at the view together. It wasn't much to look at, the concreted backyard and washing line. Above them, it was nothing but blue sky and the occasional cloud. So without discussing it, they both angled themselves to watch the sky.

"I brought you something" he leaned back and felt into his jeans pocket and pulled the joint out that Aria had given him earlier. "You need to get off your face at Christmas."

"I am already a bit am. This is half vodka," Elise said picking it up and taking a sip.

"Half vodka?" Ethan took the glass out of her hand, took a sip and almost spat it out. "Jesus, you're not joking. Maybe we can save this till later then. You're going to get completely wasted if you drink all of that."

"What makes you think I'm completely not wasted already?" Elise grinned.

"Well, now I'm not sure. What *did* you do today?"

"I stayed at Gwen's last night and then went to her sisters for Christmas brunch."

"Brunch?"

"Yeah, we had smoked salmon and scrambled eggs and champagne and ham and salads. It was really nice. Gwen's sister and her husband have this little house over the other side of town, and they have a lovely little garden."

Elise told him she'd then gone to Fran's who was having a late Christmas lunch with some of her cousins. They'd played mini golf in the back garden making holes up

151

that went around the pond or trees or under where people were sitting.

"So if you've been eating all day, are you even hungry?" Ethan said.

"Starving."

The shadows were starting to make their way towards them, so they climbed up and went into the kitchen. Elise watched Ethan cook. Later he would find out that she thought he was very good at chopping things and that when he was making the pasta sauce, she had been checking out his arse. His jeans had so many rips that she could see he was wearing tight grey boxer briefs.

But at the time he was oblivious and just kept on cooking.

*

They ate the spaghetti in Elise's room, each of them in one of the window seats.

"And what tunes will you be spinning this evening?" Ethan asked.

"Have I played you Pulp yet?" Elise put the CD in. "I'll play you my favourite song. It's called Something Changed."

They started eating and listened to Jarvis singing that waking up in the morning, he didn't know that a few hours later everything would change. Elise explained the concept of it. That a normal day could seem normal but then something would happen that would change the way you were going.

"I like it" Ethan nodded his mouth full of pasta.

"I never asked you what you did today" Elise took a huge forkful.

"Had a huge lunch at Aria's," Ethan said. "I don't know how I'm eating this." But both of them continued to scoff their bowls down until they were both finished. Empty bowls on the floor.

"What's for dessert?" he asked.

"Are you joking?"

"I'm deadly serious."

"Sure, follow me" Elise clicked off the stereo and they went into the lounge to watch bad TV.

"Look what Harriet's got" Elise reached under the couch and pulled out a giant container of sweets.

"Excellent, that's a brilliant dessert" Ethan pulled the lid off.

"We can't actually eat them!"

"This is a fucking great tub of sweets. She'll never know. Just make sure you eat a range of different ones" Ethan shook them up. They sat happily munching and making jokes about the bad movie that was on.

"So, what's the deal with you and Aria?" Elise asked at one point. Ethan looked over at her sharply but she was keeping her eyes on the TV.

"We're good friends. Just like you and me" he said.

She nodded but still didn't look at him.

Later still they were feeling very sick and sorry for themselves. Elise was now on the floor, propped up with cushions, rubbing her stomach.

"I ate too many sweeties" she moaned.

"You ate too many half an hour ago, yet you kept on going" Ethan was lying on the couch.

"Maybe I'll just have one more" Elise reached out and popped another one.

"Don't blame me for the consequences!" Ethan said.

*

"Alright, I have to go to bed" Elise had drunk far too much and was slurring her words. Ethan thought that was very funny and started laughing. Elise climbed up and stood with her hands on her hips.

"What is so funny please?" she said.

"What is so funny please" Ethan imitated her.

"Right!" she came over and leant over him and tried to pull him up off the couch. Ethan struggled against her. He was laughing too much to try and move and she ended up falling on top of him.

They lay like that for a moment.

Elise right on top of him looking down at him.

He looked at her.

Then she blinked and pushed herself up and away.

"You can sleep here in Blair's bed" Elise climbed off him.

Ethan wasn't sure what had just happened. Or maybe it was nothing. He had had a lot to drink too. Elise took his hand and pulled like she was in a tug of war, so he pushed himself up from the chair and let himself be led through into her room.

"Oh!" Elise cried. "I forgot the mattress is out on the deck".

"I'll just sleep with you," Ethan said and collapsed on her bed. He rolled over slightly and found a lump under the duvet against the wall.

"Is this crap still in your bed?" He started throwing clothes and books out from under the duvet. Then he lost focus and felt Elise putting something over him. A blanket? He tried to mumble to check she was okay. Then he knew nothing more.

Jack & the Beatles

Recommended listening: F.E.E.L.I.N.G.C.A.L.L.E.D.L.O.V.E

From the album Different Class by Pulp

Album released in October 1995, by Island Records.

This song was not released as a single.

Jack was mooching and he had to admit to himself that he was playing it up. It was another gloriously hot day, and he was wandering through town. Hands buried deep in the pocket of his favourite yellow shorts, shoulders hunched over, crumpling his 'don't worry, be happy' t-shirt.

Did he really expect someone to notice? He glanced furtively around Cuba Mall as he mooched past the bucket fountain, the chipped multi-coloured buckets creaking and ready to tip water on him. Perhaps he would get drenched. A drenching might be nice to cool him down.

But as he stood there, shifting from one foot to another, the buckets were wobbling but seemed determined not to spill on him.

He sighed. There weren't even many people out today. Most of the shops were shut for New Years and people had left the city for the beaches or somewhere other than here.

He straightened up. There was no point mooching if there was no audience.

He heard footsteps behind him running up the mall and turned to find Elise slowing to a halt, like she'd just run through the finish line.

"I thought it was you" she panted, a little red in the face and trying to catch her breath. She bent down and put her hands on her knees like she'd just run a marathon. She straightened up and rubbed her singlet across her forehead, for a moment exposing her semi-tanned stomach.

"Are you okay?" he asked, amused at how unfit she was. He was overweight and did no exercise and he was fitter than this.

"I ran all the way from the other end of town. There were no buses! I was supposed to be meeting someone here 15 minutes ago" she looked at her watch.

"Are they here?" Jack looked around. There was an old man asleep on a bench under the shade of one of the few trees in the mall and a couple of people in the distance standing looking a closed shop window.

"No, she never waits very long when I'm late" Elise seemed to have caught her breath now. She sounded annoyed.

"Her loss then. Did you have a good Christmas?"

"So so….." she shrugged. "Do you want to get a thick shake?"

As they walked towards McDonald's, knowing that even if nothing else was, the golden arches would be open, she asked how his Christmas had been.

"Not bad" he shrugged. "We went to my parents on the day, then Sarah's on boxing day and then a couple of nights camping." He paused and Elise looked at him as they rounded the corner and walked into the shade. Jack sort of had a grin on his face "And Sarah and I set the date. We're getting hitched."

"Hey, congratulations!" She punched him on the arm. "You're all grown up."

"I guess so."

"You don't sound so sure."

And he wasn't. He told Elise that it wasn't that he didn't love Sarah, but things worked well as they were now. He had thought they had both liked living together only and his philosophy was that you don't change something that isn't broke. As he pulled open the door to McD's, he stopped and looked at her.

"What do you think about this whole marriage gig?"

"I'm probably not the best person to ask" Elise took her sunglasses off.

"Why?" He was standing and blocking anyone from entering, not that anyone was around. But Elise shifted uncomfortably.

"I've barely even been in love let alone considered getting married. Come on let's go in."

Once they had their shakes, they went to sit upstairs by the window looking out at the mall. The one small tree that had been planted in that section of the sea of grey pavement, shook itself gently as a breeze rolled in from the harbour. Its leaves shone green in the sun but provided hardly any shade.

Elise took off the lid of her shake, stirred it with her straw then lifted the straw and licked the chocolate off it. Jack watched and smiled.

"You do know how a straw works?"

"Of course." Elise raised one eyebrow.

Jack had always wanted to be able to do that but couldn't get the right muscles to respond.

"Actually, I do need to ask your opinion. As a male of the species," Elise said.

"Sure. Being male is what I do well" Jack shrugged.

"Okay well, it's a bit complicated.'

"Try me" Jack drank some of his shake demonstrating how a straw worked. Elise was now dripping chocolate on the table.

"Well, I've got this friend. He's actually the ex-boyfriend of one of my best friends. They're still good friends but now I'm friends with him too. And the thing is we slept together once a few weeks ago."

"Uh oh," Jack could see where this was going.

"No, but we decided that it shouldn't happen again because I don't think my best friend would be very happy about it. And then on Christmas Day, he came over for dinner and we got drunk and there was this moment."

"Oh I know all about moments," Jack said.

"Well, now I kind of realise that I really like him. I'd like to go out with him. But he seems happy just being friends with me. So, what I want to know is how can I tell if he's interested in me. You know, in that way."

"You just kind of get a sign, don't you?" Jack said.

Elise was swirling the chocolate on the table into a flower shape. She looked up at him.

"I just don't know if this moment was a sign or not."

"Well, next time you have a 'moment' do something about it."

"You make it sound so easy."

"Just imagine you're in a movie" Jack shrugged.

"Yes, but in a movie, there's always music playing, and no one ever says anything really stupid. What I want to know is how come songs say things so much better than you ever can in real life? I mean you just add a song to a scene in a movie and you get all this emotion and messages that you could never say in the same way."

"I agree," Jack said. "When I first wanted to get together with Sarah, I put on 'I want to hold your hand' and she laughed and so I held out my hand, and she took it. Now if I'd tried to ask her out, I know I would have stuffed it up."

"That is so cute. I would have held your hand too." Elise blinked and looked out the window.

"You've got an idea I can tell," Jack said.

"Well, I'm just thinking if playing a song could be a way I could tell Ethan that I like him. I'm thinking Wonderwall. Except it's playing in so many places that maybe he wouldn't get it. And would Wonderwall be too obvious? Or not obvious enough? Or actually, there's this Pulp song that says something like 'what is this feeling called love?' I could play him that" she shrugged.

"And then raise your one eyebrow like that and he's sure to get it" Jack laughed.

*

"I need to ask you a question, as a female of the species," Jack said a while later. "What do you know about weddings?"

"Pretty much nothing. I don't even know anyone who is married."

"You've never been to a wedding?" Jack asked.

"Well, I went to a couple of weddings of university friends who got married to get their student loan payments but those were just parties. No one even got dressed up. One of the girls got married in jeans."

"Oh yeah, I went to one of those."

It had been a ridiculous law that students who were married got twice as much student allowance as when they were single. So there were lots of students who decided to get married to get the allowance. They'd changed the law now but there must be a whole load of people stuck in fake marriages. And New Zealand wasn't like the US. You couldn't get a quickie divorce, you had to go through a proper separation for 2 years before you could end it.

Of course, Jack knew that was not what Sarah was planning, an informal piss-up wearing jeans. She had said that she wanted the proper thing. Four Weddings and a Funeral style. In a church, with a non-meringue but beautiful dress and a big reception with lots and lots of people.

He wasn't sure if she realised what it would cost. Her parents would probably pay for some but he was going to have to pay too. On a good night if he made 4 sales he would be able to afford the layby payment on a veil. So it was going to be a lot of sales to afford a whole dress. Still, he was sure that Sarah would realise it was about the two of them saying their vows and then getting completely drunk and you didn't need lots of frills for that.

Jack hadn't planned on getting married anytime soon. He was having too much fun. But he loved Sarah and, in the end, he would rather marry her than lose her. They had lived together already for two years. How different could marriage be? He was just worried it would make them get all serious like their parents.

"But how do you know you love Sarah, and you'll love her for the rest of your life?" Elise asked. She was interested to know what a guy thought about this. She'd discussed it with enough girls.

"I can't guarantee it will last but Sarah and I have been together a long while. There's no light going off saying 'I love her' but I just can't imagine being without her." Jack shrugged.

"Aw, that's sweet. You should say that in your vows. Or do you just have to say that 'in sickness and in health stuff'?"

"So, you do know something about weddings," Jack said.

"Mawage" Elise said in her best imitation of the scene in Four Weddings "is an institution. Yeah, that's all I know really." She paused. "Does it freak you out that you'll only have sex with Sarah for the rest of your life though?"

"Wow. That came out of nowhere" Jack scratched his nose. "You know. I don't think it does."

"Okay." Elise didn't sound convinced.

"Why?"

Elise shrugged. "I mean, it's just that so many married men cheat. A friend of mine is having an affair with a guy who's married. They have sex a lot so I'm guessing he was really bored of sleeping with just his wife."

"I'm not going to cheat."

"That's good. Do you know, when my friend started going out with this married guy, she was really worried she wouldn't be good enough at giving him a blow job. Actually no, I won't tell you this story" Elise stopped and looked out the window.

"You HAVE to tell me this story" Jack grinned.

Elise sighed. "It's kind of embarrassing."

"I totally have no idea where this is heading." Jack leaned forward.

"Okay," Elise turned back to him. "So the only thing we could think of to learn how to do a good blow job was in this series of books called '*Clan of the Cave Bear*'. Basically, it's about cave man times and there's this blonde woman called Ayla and her and Jondalar have sex a lot in it."

"I've never heard of it," Jack said "It sounds like classic literature."

"It is highly enjoyable" Elise laughed. "So I went to the public library to find a copy, and to photocopy out the pages that have the blow job scene, so my friend could study it."

"Does she appreciate what a good friend you are?"

"Sometimes I wonder" Elise grinned. "The embarrassing part was that the only copy they had in the library was in the large format section, for people who can't see properly. The font was HUGE. And there's me, at the photocopier, making copies of these pages and there are people queuing behind me, and there's no way they can't see what's on the page."

Jack was laughing and laughing as Elise told this story. Even Elise started to smile. It was quite funny.

When they'd calmed down, Jack asked "Did she give him a good blow job? With her giant worded instruction manual?"

"She never told me!" Elise said and they started laughing again.

Later, they decided to walk back uptown. Coming out of McDonald's into the heat they decided perhaps it was time for a drink.

"Garden bar?" Jack asked, referring to the bar by their work.

"I'm jobless. I can't afford it." Elise had finally quit tele-marketing.

"I'm pretty sure we have some beer and vodka left at ours."

"Lead the way."

"With pleasure."

*

"Did you hear that the actors in Friends are asking for like a million dollars an episode?" Elise asked as they meandered through the city streets, trying to keep to the shade. "If they don't get paid it, I guess this will be the last series."

"Did you see that 'With or Without You' is back in the charts, for God's sake?" Jack said.

"I know. But it was sad. I want Rachel to forgive Ross."

"Yeah, but that was really dumb making a list."

"But we all do it in our heads. We just don't write it down."

"But that's exactly it! We don't write it down because then nothing can be proved." Jack said.

There are episodes of shows that define things. Friends was one of them. Melrose was another. But it was the X-Files that Elise, Ethan and sometimes Harriet got together to watch most weeks. Fox Mulder was hot in a kind of off-beat, chinless way although, of course, all the guys thought Scully was hot.

"Do you watch X-files?" Elise asked.

"Of course" Jack nodded.

"So what is hot about Scully?" Elise wanted to know.

"There's something about an uptight chick that makes you want to make a believer of her" Jack explained "And there's something about a woman who knows about science. Or sci-fi."

"I went for a job in that comic book shop in the market" Elise admitted.

"That would be a great job."

"Yeah, I kind of botched it up. They asked me what my favourite X-men character was, and I couldn't remember any of them. Harriet had an X-man comic once but I didn't read it properly so I really didn't have any idea."

"Oh my god. You are such a failed geek" Jack slapped his forehead. "You know one day they'll make X-men into a movie. That would rock."

"That would have helped me a lot. Because I probably shouldn't tell you, but it gets worse."

"How can it get worse?"

"Well after I realised I couldn't remember, then I said 'the wolf one' because I remembered one of them was a wolf."

"Oh god that is worse. The wolf one. It's Wolverine for God's sake."

"Yes, I know that now. If they'd asked me about sci-fi, I would have done better. I'm having a bit of a fad for that. Harry Harrison. Arthur C. Clarke."

"Yeah, but still, you gotta know your X-men."

"Only comic book geeks know X-men."

"Clearly" Jack laughed.

She punched him on the arm.

As they reached the top end of the city and turned up the hill towards Jack's, they heard Wonderwall playing somewhere. It always seemed to be playing somewhere.

"I read that Noel actually wrote this about his ex-girlfriend. But Liam doesn't feel weird singing about it" Elise said.

"Why would he? Everyone who listens to it will make it about them anyway. Don't we do that with most songs? We think about some situation and how the song applies to our life? That's why it kicks in and means something to us."

"Yeah, you're right. I'm thinking about how it could be about me and Ethan."

"See, I'm always right." Jack shrugged.

"Actually, you're wrong. Sympathy for the Devil I don't relate to myself – Gwen and I just love doing the 'woo woo' bit" Elise said. That was one of their favourite songs as they drove around the bays.

"Look how long you lasted before talking about the Stones" Jack laughed.

"Oh I haven't even gotten started" Elise warned.

*

Curled up in the corner of Jack's deck, a vodka and lemonade glistening in her hand, Elise had no-where else to be that afternoon.

"Listen, we've gone through Oasis, Blur and the Stones albums. It's time I educated you on the Beatles." Jack announced.

"Do I have to?" Elise pouted.

"Yes, you do. Your knowledge of the best, yes you know I'm going to say it, the best band ever, is ...... pathetic."

"Fine. Educate me."

And so he brought out his tape deck and as the sun drifted across the sky, Elise listened to Jack's Beatles collection and got educated.

Harriet
in the firelight

Recommended listening: Connection
From the album Elastica by Elastica.
Single released October 1994 and one of the few to chart in the US.
Album released in March 1995 and went into the UK charts at number 1. It was the fastest-selling debut album since Definitely Maybe, and held the record for 10 years, until the Arctic Monkeys.

Harriet opened the front door in a grump, and threw her suitcase onto the kitchen floor. Elise was in the kitchen heating up some porridge.

"Hey, you're back," she said "Just in time for New Year's!"

"I'm supposed to be driving to the beach to go camping right now" Harriet sat down on the steps that led up to the hallway. "The stupid woman at the travel agents booked my flights wrong and I didn't check them, so I had to come back today or pay some huge amount to change them."

"Well, I'm glad you're back. It's been lonely here." Elise hadn't been looking forward to Harriet being away as everyone else seemed to have suddenly disappeared too. She knew that Harriet still had heaps of university friends in

166

Christchurch and had been looking forward to going down for a week on holiday to visit her parents and then to go camping. But Elise had suddenly been contemplating New Years by herself and hadn't liked it. So while Elise was sorry Harriet was annoyed about being here, she was also kind of glad the travel agent had stuffed it up.

"Isn't Rosalie around?" Harriet looked down the hall. Rosalie's bedroom door was wide open.

"No, she's gone to friends for a few days."

"What are you making?" Harriet sniffed.

"I found some rolled oats in the back of the cupboard. It's the only thing we have to eat. Do you want some?"

"Okay," Harriet shrugged "All I had time for this morning was a cup of coffee."

Elise served the porridge and they took the steaming bowls out onto the balcony and sat down on the mattress.

"The last day of 1995" Elise ruminated "and we're eating like Oliver Twist."

"Did you get that for Christmas?" Harriet asked. While Elise was wearing her usual cream skirt, she had on an Oasis t-shirt instead of her usual singlet.

"Yeah, my sister sent it. What did you get?"

"Some money, a new bag, a sweater, some socks from my father. The usual" they were scraping their bowls out. "Oh, and that big tub of candy in the lounge."

"Yeah.... about that" Elise felt guilty. "I may have eaten a few. And Ethan may have eaten a few."

"Well, you're allowed to, you're my flattie. But Ethan is in deep, deep trouble." Harriet widened her eyes and shook her head, like she would actually do something to Ethan. Elise laughed.

"So what will you do tonight now you're back?" Elise took Harriet's bowl, stacked it in hers, and put them to one side. They leaned back and watched the sky. Today was a little cloudier although still golden warm.

"I've been invited to a beach party which I guess I'll go to now. How about you? Are you going to Gwen's?"

"No, she's going to some party at her sister's, but I'm not invited."

"What about Ethan?"

"I think they're having some flat thing" Elise sounded unsure because she didn't really know, but she wasn't going to ring him and find out. He'd mentioned something and it was clear that it didn't include her.

"Blair?"

"She's moved in with Zöe. I haven't talked to her for a while." Elise turned her head sideways to look at Harriet. She thought she could detect that Harriet might be slightly pleased by that, but Harriet's expression didn't change. Elise decided Harriet was trying to make sure she didn't show if she was pleased.

"So you were going to be all alone? You have to come with me then. It'll be fun" Harriet ran her hands through her hair and then pulled it back into a ponytail. "Is there anyone you want to bring?" she asked.

"Men wise?" Elise shrugged. "No."

"Poor Elise. You're not having much luck at the moment, are you?"

"Not really" Elise pouted.

"I know lots of guys I could set you up with."

"No, I'm fine. It'll happen when it happens" Elise shrugged.

"What sort of attitude is that? There will be lots of guys there tonight. You just tell me the one you think looks okay and I'll introduce you."

Elise shrugged. She supposed it was time to stop feeling sorry for herself. First about Scott and then thinking something had happened with Ethan. Obviously, it hadn't. Because he hadn't spoken to her for days.

"What about you?" Elise asked. She wasn't sure if Harriet was really seeing anyone at the moment.

"What about me?"

"You know. How's your life? Men-wise I mean."

"Men-wise? There's no-one serious."

"Can I ask you a personal question?" Elise asked.

"Sure."

"How many guys have you slept with?"

"Just a number or you want to whole Four Weddings and a Funeral style list?"

"Ooh, do the Four Weddings style!"

"Okay, but we need something to drink, to wash the porridge down." Harriet looked up at the sky. The sun was hidden by clouds now, but it was still clammy and warm.

"Hold on" Elise climbed up and went inside, and a few minutes later came back with some lemonade and vodkas. They both got comfortable and took a long sip.

"Okay, so here's my list" Harriet started. "The very first time I was sixteen, met him at a friend's party and went back to his parents. I bled and I was so mortified about it that I got up and walked home which took hours." Harriet sipped her vodka.

"That's awful," Elise said. "Did it put you off for ages?"

"No, the next time was better. That was in a field."

"Outside?"

"That's generally where fields are" Harriet laughed.

"I've never done it outside" Elise admitted. She was also still counting on one hand the number of guys she'd slept with, and they'd all been in a bed. Pretty conventional she would find as she listened to Harriet's list unfurl.

"Then there were a few while I was at university. My first serious one I actually lived with but he got nasty, and I moved up here for a while to get away from him."

Harriet continued with her list. As Elise drank her vodka lemonade, she reckoned Harriet was up to about 30.

"Then there was Ethan. That was nice, but we are so much better as friends. Jason was kind of arrogant. Then I've had a couple this summer…. one of which was fantastic." Harriet stopped. "Was I supposed to do numbers? I think I lost count."

"I don't think we need to tally it up. I think you're in the same ballpark as Andie McDowell's character. I don't think I'm even up to Hugh Grant's number." Elise knew she was nowhere near Hugh Grant's number. She didn't know why but it just never happened with her and guys.

"Well sometimes quality rather than quantity is nice" Harriet shrugged.

"That would be fine if they had all been quality" Elise pouted.

"Poor Elise. We'll find you someone quality tonight" Harriet promised.

*

"Do you think this will be okay to wear?" Elise came into Harriet's room in her daffodil dress.

"You'll definitely attract some quality in that" Harriet herself had put on a black skirt and a dark red t-shirt.

The two of them headed to the kitchen.

"I think we need to bring something to drink," Harriet said.

"There's a bit of vodka left" Elise had shrugged on an old battered flowery backpack that she'd found in the back of her wardrobe. She had stuffed in her wallet and a white sweater and now put in the three-quarters empty bottle.

Hurrying down the back stairs, the sun was setting above them, streaking the clouds orange and yellow. Harriet's VW was parked in the street around the corner. They climbed in and Harriet gunned the engine for a moment. Neither of them were sure if it would start. It never liked it when it was left for a few days without being driven.

But then it coughed into life, and they were off.

"The poor little beetle doesn't like hills," Harriet said as they chugged upwards.

"This isn't as bad as when we go to the supermarket" Elise laughed thinking about them crawling up the gorge road so slowly they could have got out and walked faster.

They were driving out to Makara for the party. It was a 20-minute drive through a winding valley before you came out on the coast. Makara was a small settlement perched right by the beach, just a few houses really. The main attraction was the track that led around the coast, past inlets and bays. It was on one of these bays that Harriet told her the plan was to light a big fire and have a party.

First, they went and picked up two guys that Harriet said she'd told she give a ride to. Elise ended up in the back with the one called Will. He was one of those very beautiful Indian boys with gorgeous thick black hair, dark flashing eyes and glowing skin. The other one Sean sat in the front with Harriet. He was kind of tall and gangly with light brown sticking-up hair.

Elise had had to keep her head almost out of the car window most of the trip, she was feeling so sick. She and Harriet had eaten dinner early, scraping enough money together to share a roast charcoal chicken meal with extra fries. Now Elise was wishing they hadn't.

It wasn't that Harriet was a bad driver normally. But on this road with its hairpin bends that often went downhill, the VW would speed up and then Harriet would have to break hard around the bend. The suspension not being up too much, it sometimes felt like they were going around the corner on two wheels.

"Are you okay?" Will, who Harriet had obviously assigned to Elise, had asked several times.

"I'm great" Elise had lied, not taking her face away from the window.

Will had actually leant forward and suggested to Harriet that she take things a little easier, but Elise didn't think Harriet actually knew how to. It was getting dark now and the VW's headlights weren't that strong so the braking got worse.

Once they'd parked, Elise was the first out of the car, breathing in the sea air. The moon was out and almost full, so it was bright enough to see. It felt like it should be cold, but the air was still warm. The sea was fairly placid but out here the beach was rocky and the coast line was rugged and wild.

There were huge gluts of seaweed washed up on the stony beach and waving in the sea.

"Have you been out here before?" Will asked her.

"A couple of times. I've done the walk up over the hill" Elise pointed to a track that led steeply up from the car park.

"There's some gun battlements up there or something isn't there?"

"Yep and once there was a dead cow."

"Nice" Will grinned. He was very good-looking Elise had to admit. Fairly quality so far.

"It was really gross actually." Elise hadn't thought about that cow for years. They'd seen it when they'd come out here on a school trip.

"What are you two talking about?" Harriet came over. She and Sean had got his bag of stuff out of the boot.

"Dead cows," Will said.

Harriet frowned.

"We're going to head around there" Sean came over and pointed around the headland. In the distance, they could see a glow. Whoever had arrived first must have lit a fire.

Sean led the way along the well-trodden path, with Harriet following, then Elise and Will bringing up the rear.

For a while, the path meandered through the grass above the beach, against the hill. But after a while that disappeared, and they had to climb down onto the beach. It was easier to walk near the water and they formed into pairs, crunching across the stones.

Ahead was a wall of rock with a large hole in it, like a doorway.

"Oh, I remember that" Elise pointed.

"If you walk around here at the wrong time, the sea blocks it and you're stuck" Sean called back to them.

"What time does the tide come in?" Elise asked. She could never really tell whether it was coming or going in the harbour.

"When it's coming in, every seventh wave will be a bigger one," Will said.

"Really?" Elise stopped and they stood and watched. All the waves were small.

"It's still going out then. We'll have a few hours before we get stuck."

They continued crunching along the beach, made their way through the hole in the rock, and then a couple of hundred metres further on came to a small, sheltered cove with a half-sandy, half-stony beach.

"Here we are" Sean declared.

There were about a dozen people who had already arrived. They'd built a fire and there was a portable CD player blaring Oasis. It was Shakermaker. Elise could see some people were sitting on logs near the fire, there were a few down by the water and a group of girls were dancing on a clear area of sand.

The four of them made their way past the fire and the dancing group.

"I think we should start another fire over here," Sean said.

They all set about collecting driftwood and piled it together. Harriet unpacked a couple of blankets from the bags and spread them out next to the fire pit.

"Me make fire" Sean beat his chest and they all laughed. He picked some smaller twigs and started to rub two of them together.

"Can you really make fire like that?" Elise asked. She had sat down next to Will.

"Of course!" Sean rubbed harder. "Actually.... I'm joking. Pass me the lighter?" he asked Harriet. She rummaged in the bag and handed it over. It took a few minutes but soon they had a fire going. They piled some of the larger pieces of driftwood on.

They sat around the fire warming their hands, even though it wasn't cold.

Elise loved fires. When they went out for dinner or somewhere with a candle, Elise would sit there making the flame bend or blowing it, so it melted the wax and made it run down the side. Or she ran her finger through the flame until her skin was sooty and black. Harriet was glad they didn't have any candles in the house.

Now they all seemed mesmerised by the fire. They watched the logs turning slowly black on the outside but orange inside like a flickering heart.

Sean had brought marshmallows, and they threaded them onto sticks and toasted them. Harriet's kept falling into the fire which they all found hilarious. Several other party goers had joined them by this time and when Elise looked over at the other fire, she saw lots of other people had arrived too, and were dancing at its edge. The other fire was bigger than theirs, but this fire was more laid back.

Will had brought a joint and they sat smoking and watching the clouds roll across the dark sky, lit by the moon. It felt like it was getting slightly cooler, and Elise put her sweater on.

The CD had been changed to Nirvana. So, they were moving backwards from Brit Pop now.

The mood at their fire remained the place to hang out when you needed a break from the dancing or the main fire. The group talked about movies and the summer weather, and other stuff that later Elise couldn't remember. They had drunk the vodka and were onto boxed wine cooler that someone had brought.

Elise saw Harriet and Sean stand up.

"We're going to go for a swim," Harriet said.

"Won't it be too cold?" Elise sat up.

"Nah, we're hard. We can handle it" Sean said.

"We're just going to go along there" Harriet pointed further around the beach.

"Don't go too far. You might get lost" Elise said.

"Come on" Sean was behind Harriet, lifted her off her feet and started carrying her off down the beach. Harriet shrieked with laughter. Elise watched them. She realised everything was black and white in the moonlight away from the fire. Why had she never noticed that before?

Will sat up too.

"Do you want to go for a swim too?" he asked.

"No, I'm happy here" Elise didn't fancy going into the seaweed. Not to mention the sea would be cold. Harriet and Sean were now just white blobs down on the sand. She couldn't quite make out what they were doing and then realised. They were undressing. They were going skinny dipping. They didn't seem to care about everyone else being around.

A moment later even above the sound of music and talking, there was the sound of a splash and a scream. Others turned to look and then there was a mass movement of people down to the water. Clothes were being pulled off and people were running into the water naked.

"I bet it's freezing in there," Elise said.

"Probably. They're screaming pretty loud."

She felt Will move over beside her and put his arm around her. She looked at the others sitting around them but they were all talking or kissing. Will leaned in and kissed her and Elise lay back on the blanket and kissed him back.

After a while she pulled away, wiggling out from him.

"What's wrong?" he asked.

"I'm still getting over someone," Elise said.

"Did he dump you?" Will asked. He stretched out on his side, propped up on his elbow, watching her. Elise just looked like what she hoped was sad.

"Well, he's an arsehole then," Will said. He patted the blanket next to him and after a moment Elise moved back over to lay next to him and he leaned down and kissed her again.

*

The next morning Elise knocked on Harriet's door.

"We're busy" Harriet called and Elise heard Sean's muffled grunt. She shook her head and went to the kitchen to make some toast.

Later Sean left and Harriet knocked on Elise's door.

"Come in" Elise called out. She was sitting in the window seat reading. Harriet came and took a seat next to her.

"How did it go with Will last night?" she asked.

"Okay." Elise shrugged.

"Don't be silly. Do you like him or not?" Harriet said.

"He was okay."

"I'm happy for me and Sean to come with you if you want to do a joint dinner or something" Harriet really was trying.

"I know I should. I'll think about it okay?"

"Are you feeling sorry for yourself about Scott again?"

"No not really." She was thinking about how it would have been better if last night had been with Ethan.

"Elise, nothing even happened with Scott."

"So? That doesn't mean I didn't feel something."

Harriet shrugged.

"I'm going out" Elise didn't want to talk about it anymore. She went and grabbed her bag and strode down the hall.

"Elise! Wait" Harriet called out, but Elise was already out the door and running down the steps. She didn't know where she was going until she realised she was heading over to Mt Vic. She got to Ethan's and went and knocked on the door.

Some girl with a short black bob answered.

"Hi is Ethan here?" Elise said.

"Non, I think he is out with Aria."

"Oh. Okay. Thanks."

Elise wasn't sure where to go next. She couldn't be bothered walking all the way over to Oriental Bay to see if Gwen was home, so she ended up going to the library to sit and stew for a while.

*

On Wednesday it was Ethan's birthday. Harriet came and told Elise that she was taking him out to dinner at Pizza Hutt and Elise could come too if she wanted. This was a strange way to put it as Elise felt she was probably closer with Ethan now than Harriet was.

Excluding the last couple of weeks since Christmas when she hadn't seen him much.

She'd always thought that having a long history together and being exes would mean you always knew that person better than others, but now she realised that didn't mean someone else could become closer.

That was what she had always been envious of with Greer that she had a much longer history with Gwen because they'd gone to primary school together. But then Greer had got caught up in her own life and hadn't seen as much of Gwen recently so Elise felt she had become the number one friend there too.

For Elise, she felt like her friends were kind of like a family. They were who she relied on. None of them really saw their actual families once they'd moved out of home. It was that she didn't like her parents, it was just she didn't have anything in common with them.

When Ethan arrived, they went into Elise's room. She had all the windows open and for once, there was a breeze.

Harriet made a great display of bringing out a pile of little presents all wrapped up in green tissue paper for Ethan. Elise thought she could have picked a different colour considering green was a bit Christmassy and with his birthday this near to Christmas surely Ethan appreciated not having things wrapped in those colours.

But Harriet seemed oblivious. She made Ethan open each present.

There was olive paste and toothpaste, and a book and a bookmark. Ethan said thanks for each one, but Elise wasn't sure he actually wanted any of it. Once he'd finished opening them all Harriet sat back self-satisfied.

"I got you something too" Elise went over to her wardrobe and brought out a large box wrapped in happy birthday paper with bears all over it. She handed it to Ethan and then sat back down on her bed. Ethan ripped the paper to shreds. He wasn't a conserver.

It was a large box of Liquorice All Sorts.

"I hope you like them, otherwise I'll eat them," Elise said.

"I love them!" Ethan sounded more enthusiastic than the twenty presents Harriet had brought him put together. He pulled the top open and broke into the wrapper. He offered them round. Harriet had her sour lemon face on.

"Leave some room for pizza," she said as Ethan stuffed liquorice in his mouth.

"Sure," he said, his mouth full.

Elise couldn't help laughing.

Later they walked to Pizza Hutt. Normally they wouldn't have been able to afford it, but Pizza Hutt had an 'all you can eat' night including pizza and desert for only $12.95, rather than the $30 they usually charged for just one pizza.

None of them had eaten lunch so they would be able to fit more in, but of course, Ethan was now full of liquorice. Elise found that once she'd had a couple of slices, even though she had thought she was starving, she then felt full.

"Wait till you get your second wind," Ethan said. He had piled six slices of pizza on his plate determined to get his money's worth.

"You've got to eat fast, or you start to feel full" he explained.

"It's too late for me. Go on without me." Elise said.

"You'll catch up. We can sit here all night if we have to" Ethan laughed.

"Actually, we can't. Our movie starts in an hour" Harriet huffed.

"What are we seeing?" Ethan asked.

"It's a film that was on at the film festival last year. It looked good" Harriet said.

"Have you seen Pulp Fiction?" Elise asked.

"Yes, me and Cèline went," Ethan said.

"Is that who I met the other week?" Elise pulled a piece of salami off her pizza and ate it. Perhaps she could manage more if she ate it in small pieces.

"When?"

"I came round but you weren't in. She's got a black bob, hasn't she?" Elise had assumed that was her. Ethan nodded.

"I met her too," Harriet said. "I bumped into Ethan when he was taking her flowers."

"I was meeting her for a drink" Ethan explained "But she saw me with Harriet and wanted to meet her."

"And I even spoke French with her," Harriet said.

Ethan choked on his water and started laughing.

"Your French was awful. Cèline asked me afterwards what language you'd been speaking."

"Don't be mean" Harriet was laughing too.

Elise remained silent. He'd brought flowers for Cèline? While Elise hadn't even realised that she liked flowers, now she felt jealous that someone else was getting them. But when she'd gone round, he'd been round at Aria's.

And he'd been there on Christmas Day too.

Which of them was he friends with? She wasn't sure. Was he friends with them like he was with her? Which meant that possibly he had slept with one or both of them? She wanted to ask but suddenly felt self-conscious, even though as his friend she should be able to.

Elise managed a couple more slices of pizza then they were onto dessert. Pizza Hutt had an ice cream machine and then bowls of sprinkles, coloured candy and chocolate buttons. Elise made a multi-layered sundae which she managed half of before feeling full again. Ethan leant over and mixed it around until it became sludge.

"Now you can drink it," he said.

"It looks revolting!"

"Look at mine" Harriet had sculpted hers into a pyramid and put buttons up the side.

When all the ice cream had melted and they couldn't eat another bite, they went to the movies. It was cold with the air conditioning which was kind of nice for a change.

"Thanks for the liquorice" Ethan whispered before the movie started and Elise smiled.

Gwen & the Flasher

Recommended listening: Married with Children
From the album Definitely Maybe by Oasis.
Album released in August 1994, by Creation Records.
Inspired by Noel's then-girlfriend, Louise Jones, who was being kept awake by Noel, while he was practising on his guitar

Gwen had had enough. Yes, it had been exciting and illicit to start with but now Brian was getting whiny and needy. She had been planning to spend the morning cleaning her room. This was a new year and she had decided it was time for a clear out. But then she'd heard a motorbike coming up the hill. She looked out and saw him skid to a halt in the parking bay at the bottom of their driveway.

She sighed dramatically.

She watched him stop the bike, take off his helmet and hang on it on the back. His hair was going more and more grey and suddenly it didn't make him look distinguished, it made him look old.

In fact, as he looked up, she stepped backwards so he didn't see her watching. She suddenly had the horrible image of him being an old man and once she'd thought it she couldn't stop. Is this what Elise had been talking about? And she really hadn't been able to see it? She had been so caught up in finding a way to catapult herself to being married, with children, in a nice house in the suburbs and finally catch up with where her brother and sister were, that she had been willing to do it with an old man?

She sat down on her bed feeling sick and suddenly icy cold. She knew this feeling. This was the feeling that came when things were ending. It was just her other loves had been taken away from her. She hadn't had to fall out of love with them.

She'd never realised it would be so sudden. How could you feel one way about a person and then have it change so completely?

She knew she would hear Brian coming up the stairs in a minute and she would have to compose herself. But she couldn't move. She didn't want to see him.

Could she be like Elise and just not answer the door? She'd never been able to do that before. She felt it was immature. But now she felt it would be more humane. Because if Brian saw her like this, surely he'd know.

Now she heard his steps on the stairs and her heart quickened. She held onto her duvet like it would anchor her and stop her from going to the door. And for a moment it did. He knocked, and she just sat there swallowing noisily and trying to breathe. He knocked again, a little louder.

And then she heard her flatmate's door open.

Her eyes widened. They would let him in! She leapt up and as quietly as possible opened her door. Ben was halfway down the hall to the door.

"Shhh!" she hissed and then made frantic hand signals for him not to answer the door. He looked at her amused, shrugged and turned and went back to his room.

Brian knocked again and this time called out if anyone was there. Gwen was standing centimetres away – with just a door between them. She felt sure he would be able to hear her heart pounding. But she stood her ground and finally, after the longest time, she heard his steps retreating.

She walked down the hall on wobbly legs to the lounge and collapsing on the bean bag, picked up the phone and called Elise.

Then it was a matter of pacing her room for half an hour until Elise arrived, hot and sweaty from a frantic walk across town.

"I'm here" Elise was panting.

"You took long enough."

"I walked. You may not have noticed but your hill is steep" Elise followed Gwen into her bedroom and slouched down onto the couch by the open window. Gwen threw herself face first on the bed dramatically, her arms straight like she was dead.

"I'm fucked" she moaned into her pillow.

"I thought you said you didn't let Brian in," Elise was trying to be sarcastic and funny and Gwen didn't appreciate it and ignored it.

She sat up. "I didn't let him in. That's just the point. I didn't want him to be here. I don't want to see him anymore."

"When? When did this happen?" Elise seemed confused.

"This morning. I saw him and realised everything had changed. I've never fallen out of love like this."

Up to just now, Gwen had been enjoying the thrill of being with Brian, enjoying the secrecy that nobody knew what they were doing, enjoying that she was experienced at this and could instruct Elise.

And now it was like everything had changed.

Not that she'd enjoyed losing her first boyfriend but when he decided to go overseas when he was 18, they'd both known that it had kind of seen its course. And ending it like that left it as a perfect first love. Untarnished. Nothing turning sour.

Her third boyfriend who she'd also fallen for had got into a university programme down south. They both knew he had to go, or he'd regret it forever. They were both happy to believe that if the love was strong enough, he could come back during holidays and when he graduated, and if they were meant to be together, they would still be in love.

They found that they drifted apart fairly quickly. But again it had been a mutual thing that they'd both moved on.

And then there had been Hugh who had devastated Gwen and broken her heart. That had been especially hard as she never got to actually be with him.

So this was the first time that she'd actually wanted to end it. When she'd actually found she didn't want to be with someone anymore.

"Don't you have to go back to work tomorrow? What are you going to do?" Elise moved to sitting up on the arm of the couch, by the windowsill, so she could get some of the cooler air coming in the window.

They had both agreed that was the good thing about Gwen's flat being buried in the bush where it was shady and cool. Normally that meant a dripping and damp house, but this summer it had been the next best thing to having air conditioning.

"I'll have to go back to work and find some way to end it." Gwen wrapped her arms around herself.

"You could be really nasty to him. You know just make some really cutting remarks and he might get the message."

"Or it could go horribly wrong and backfire."

"What about uglifying yourself?"

Gwen shook her head. Why had she thought Elise would be any use at this? This was serious and Elise was being completely immature about it. Gwen didn't want to lose her job. She wasn't in a position to lose her job. She was going to have to play this carefully. But she didn't have anyone else she could talk about it with. She hadn't told her family because they would be mortified. Even Greer didn't know that it was a proper affair; she thought there was just flirting going on. Maybe it was time that she told Greer about it. Properly. At least Greer knew how to have an adult relationship. Unlike Elise.

But then Greer would judge her. She would purse her lips in that way she had when Gwen knew whatever she'd done wasn't approved of. Perhaps that was why she'd only told Elise. For all her faults, Elise hadn't judged her. Hadn't told her it was the wrong thing to do.

Elise had been awed, let's face it, by the whole thing.

"Let's go for a walk. I'll figure something out. I don't want to think about it anymore" Gwen grabbed her bag and they decided to go down to Oriental Bay and have an ice cream.

*

The next day back Gwen found she was on edge all day. Brian and Samira had come back from the Christmas/New Year break, and they'd thrown a big morning tea for everyone to talk about their holidays. Gwen had hardly been able to speak and hoped her colleagues would just put it down to her being bummed about having to be back at work.

It wasn't until the day after, when Brian had come into her darkroom. Gwen had been dreading it. She'd decided that she would just kind of try and cool it down a bit with him as she couldn't face telling him it was over. Suddenly she found she couldn't flirt with him like she used to. She couldn't even force herself to.

"What's wrong?" Brian had been kissing her but must have felt her pulling away.

185

"I'm turning on the light" Gwen reached over and flicked it on. She didn't care about the few sheets of photo paper that would be ruined. She realised that Plan A was not going to work. She had felt physically sick when he'd stuck his hand down her pants. Brian didn't even seem to be aware of what was going on.

Still, she would have to get used to this, have to get used to breaking up with someone. Surely there would be other men who fell for her that she didn't feel the same way about. She decided to bite the bullet.

"This isn't working," she said.

"What isn't working?"

"Us." She couldn't expand. She hoped he'd just get it.

"Look don't worry about Samira finding out. She's got no idea."

"I'm not worried about that" although suddenly she realised what she was playing with here. Not just his marriage but he was a father. He had two children. "I want to be with someone who isn't married. Who doesn't have children."

"Gwen, love" he stroked her cheek "I'm going to leave them. I love you. But the timing is wrong at the moment. I thought you understood that?"

"I don't want you to leave them!" her voice was rising.

"Okay, let's talk about this tomorrow morning. We'll have breakfast. In our usual place?" his tone was placating like she was a child. She wasn't a child.

"Fine whatever," she said pleased that at least this would get him to leave.

But it just postponed and extended the conversation. Over the next few days every morning, they would meet for breakfast and Brian would whine that he loved her, and he needed her, and she would say that she couldn't see him anymore.

He turned up on his bike late at night, and he came into her darkroom during the day. If it went on much longer, she didn't know how she was going to cope.

Elise didn't seem to have much sympathy.

"You said you knew what you were getting into," she said throwing Gwen's own words back in her face.

"Well, it's got more complicated. You wouldn't understand."

"If I wouldn't understand, why do you bother talking to me about it?"

They were at a party that Gwen's flatmate Gareth had invited her and Elise to. Gwen regarded Elise. She wasn't used to her talking back. Ever since their school days, Elise had been the one following behind Gwen. Gwen had been the one in the spotlight and Elise had been the one there supporting her. Because Elise didn't need the spotlight or have anything going on that needed a spotlight shone on her. Whereas Gwen was going to be a famous photographer.

In fact, in school, both of them had entirely different circles of friends. Gwen hardly knew the girls that Elise hung out with and vice versa. Most of Gwen's friends hadn't even known that Elise was her friend too.

And if they knew what she and Elise got up to, they wouldn't have understood. For Gwen and Elise did things, stupid dumb teenage girl things that she didn't do with her other friends. She and Elise rented Mel Gibson movies and watched them salivating at how good-looking he was. Everyone knew about Mad Max and Lethal Weapon, but they had found some really strange films that Mel had done when he was younger like Mrs Soffel and Tim and they watched them and groaned at his blue eyes.

Elise never seemed remotely embarrassed about having these girly weekends with trashy movies, whereas Gwen's proper circle of friends would have frowned. They spent weekends at one of their parent's beach houses, talking about art, or literature. Not acting out scenes from Top Gun with each other and laughing so hard their sides hurt.

Now Elise seemed to be throwing the spotlight back in Gwen's face and she didn't like it. Elise might not really be able to help with the Brian situation, but she could just be there for Gwen.

"I'm going to get a drink," Elise said and pushed into the crowd.

Gwen turned and headed into the front room and to her horror saw Brian coming through the front door. She turned away and tried to stand behind a couple talking. What was he doing here? There was no way he knew anyone that would have invited him.

She realised that she had mentioned at work yesterday that she was coming to this party when they'd all been talking about what they were doing for the weekend. And she'd mentioned the house that the party was at, simply because she'd always been interested in it. It was a strange house, set off the road, with these turrets that reminded her of the Psycho house. Had Brian actually listened in, and then decided to gate-crash?

She stealthily wound her way around the edge of the party, peering through gaps to see where he was. For a while she lost him and decided perhaps if he hadn't seen her, he might have decided to leave.

She worked her way through the party to the kitchen to get another drink and found Brian there regaling a group with a story of how he'd once crashed his motorbike.

"What are you doing here?" she asked pulling him to one side once he'd finished his story. Brian put his arm around her and led them deeper into the corner of the kitchen.

"Samira's visiting her sister with the kids so I thought I'd come. It didn't sound like anyone would be bothered."

"But that's not the point. You weren't invited." She ducked out from under his arm. Now he was becoming like a stalker. She strode off. But over the next couple of hours, everywhere she went and everyone she started talking to, she would feel Brian hanging out behind her and at some point, he would break into the conversation and stand next to her.

She realised she was going to have to get out so went looking for Elise. She found her snuggled up in a window bay with Matt, a friend of Gareth's. They were talking intently and as Gwen watched, Elise got up and put her drink down, and Matt put his arm around her shoulder and led her towards the door.

Gwen pushed her way through the party and managed to cut them off at the door.

"Hey, where are you going?" she asked.

"We were just going to get a drink somewhere a bit quieter," Elise said raising her eyebrows at Gwen. Gwen knew what it meant but ignored it. Matt had broken up with his girlfriend a few weeks ago and ever since he had been coming over to the flat and had turned into a complete sleaze. Gwen wasn't having Elise getting involved with him in any way.

"I'll come with you. I need to get out of here" Gwen said, linking her arm with Elise.

"I can look after her," Matt said.

"I know you can" Gwen stared at him. A couple of weeks ago Gwen had been home alone watching TV and Basic Instinct had come on. Gwen had started watching it. She suddenly looked up to find Matt was standing in the doorway watching it too. He was staying in Gareth's room while Gareth was away.

"This scene is a killer," he said, and Gwen realised they had reached the scene where Sharon Stone was crossing and uncrossing her legs, wearing a very short white dress, and it implied she was wearing no underwear.

Matt came in and sat down next to her. He looked down at her lap. Gwen was wearing a skirt that day and she could almost read what he was thinking.

"I'm going to bed" she had said, uncrossing her legs and feeling like she wanted to hold her skirt down as she did it, even though nothing was going to show.

"Fancy any company?" Matt had leered.

"No, I'm fine" Gwen had hurried off down the hall. But now she tried to avoid being alone with Matt. And she certainly wasn't going to let Matt take Elise home.

*

They were halfway around Oriental Bay parade. Below them, lapping at the sea wall, the water was dark and oily. There were still cars parked along the parade, and the trees still had their Christmas lights strung up in them. It could have been a very romantic walk.

Matt had tried to talk to Elise and Elise had tried to answer, but Gwen had started singing and pulling Elise into little dances. When Matt had tried to ask her about what she did, Gwen had said 'she doesn't do you - that's for sure!'

She'd then started whispering loudly to Elise that she mustn't go home with Matt. That Matt had a small cock and Elise liked Ethan so she mustn't do it with Matt instead. Elise was trying to shh her but failing miserably.

Matt seemed to have finally had enough.

"Listen Gwen, Elise and I are going to get a coffee. Perhaps you should carry on home."

"Oh no, no you don't!" Gwen fumbled in her bag and brought out her flash. She flicked it on, and they heard the strange electronic hum it made as it warmed up. Then Gwen held it up in Matt's face and pressed the shutter.

Matt was blinded and reeled away.

"Off you fucker! The light has shown the way!" Gwen shouted, realising she must be a little more drunk than she realised. She fired up the flash and held it up again. Matt put his hands up in front of his face.

"Don't make me do it!" Gwen shouted.

Several people walking past had slowed down to watch the spectacle.

"Elise don't do it. Don't go home with him. Come home with me" Gwen whispered again, waving the flash around. Elise was laughing despite herself.

"Okay," she said, "I'll come home with you."

"Perhaps I'll see you later" Matt put his hands down and nodded to Elise.

"Off fiend!" Gwen pressed the flash and blinded him again. Matt swore, turned, and stumbled off. Several people clapped and cheered, and Gwen took a bow.

"Alright put it away now Clint Eastwood!" Elise pulled the flash out of her friend's hands and put it back in her bag.

"Run loser run!" Gwen shouted after Matt who they couldn't actually even see anymore.

"You need to sober up" Elise laughed. Together they made their way back to Gwen's flat climbed into bed and fell asleep.

Gwen woke early. The sun had come up, but it was still before 8 am. She found Elise had already gone, leaving a note. It took a moment lying there looking at the morning light pushing at the curtains for Gwen to remember what she'd done. And once she did, she headed to hide out at Greer's for the rest of the weekend.

*

It was Monday afternoon when he came into the dark room. "I lost you on Saturday night," he said.

"That's because I left." She wanted to say 'with someone' but she had a gut feeling that might throw him into a rage. She needed him to stop but she needed him to stop without hating her. She flicked the light on. She was crying.

191

"Hey, it's okay" Brian hugged her, and she let him hold her against him. Then she had an idea and pulled away.

"It's not okay. I can't be with you and I don't know what to do to make you understand that. Do I have to tell Samira what happened?" It was a desperate move.

"I don't want you to do that" Brian's jaw hardened.

"I can't be with you anymore."

"If you feel that way, maybe you shouldn't work here anymore," Brian said.

Gwen supposed it was meant to scare her into realising she couldn't be without Brian. He still wasn't getting that she could be without him and wanted to be without him. She wanted to be with someone that she could take to family events. If she was part of breaking up Brian's marriage, she didn't think she would ever be able to introduce him to her parents.

She had also realised that the getting married and settling down wasn't all it was cracked up to be and perhaps she should enjoy the journey more.

Both her siblings had told her that marriage and long-term relationships weren't all plain sailing. It wasn't all happy ever after. But Gwen's parents had always seemed so happy together and had been together a long time, she just kind of figured once you found the man to marry it was easy. After all, that's where every movie ended.

"If you think that's best," she said "but I don't have another job to go to yet. I need to be able to pay my rent" she suddenly worried Brian was going to fire her. She wouldn't really have any grounds to complain.

"Don't worry I'll talk to a couple of friends and see if I can set something up" he turned and left her there in her darkroom. And even though that was exactly what she had wanted, it didn't feel good.

France
by the sea

Recommended listening: Disco 2000
*Based on a crush Jarvis Cocker had on a girl called Deborah he went
to school with, but he couldn't find a way to impress her*
Single released November 1995 and reached No 7 in the UK charts.
From the album, Different Class by Pulp, released by Island Records

Ethan and Céline had been to the movies. Ethan should have known better. When he'd taken her to see Pulp Fiction, they'd been watching the scene when John Travolta tells the joke about ketchup. Suddenly Céline had grabbed his arm and said loudly 'Oh now I get it! When I saw this in French it made no sense. But the little tomato must catch up – this is funny, no?'

Ethan had nodded. Normally he didn't like it when people talked in movies. Harriet always did it, pointing out the obvious 'Look, it's that Russian guy' or 'He's the assassin'. There was never anything to say to her completely obvious observations and so he had stopped going to the movies with her. But he had to admit that Céline was kind of just amusing.

So he had given Céline a second chance and this time they had gone to see French Kiss, a terrible Meg Ryan movie set in Cannes.

Everything had been going quietly until Meg arrived in the town and started walking about. Céline had almost leapt out of her seat.

"Oooh that is just near where I grew up! I used to walk to school along these street!" she was pointing and spilling popcorn. For a moment Ethan thought about telling her to shush, but then as she gripped his arm harder and pointed again excitedly, he had to grin.

In fact, over the next half an hour it became quite funny as Céline enthusiastically treated the whole movie theatre to her thoughts about Cannes.

"That store would not let me in once and I wanted to buy something!'

"My mother's boutique was down that street, look can you see the little yellow veranda?"

"Oooh ooh, I had my first kiss in that doorway!"

It actually had made the whole movie better. When the film finished and Ethan and Céline had stood up, everyone had burst into applause. Céline had only taken a moment to realise what was happening and then she had taken a bow.

As they flowed with the stream of people making their way back out onto the street, Céline wrapped her arm in Ethan's.

"I have to go and pick up some photos. You will come with me?"

"Sure" Ethan shrugged, although it didn't really feel like it was a question. Did all French people do that, or just Céline?

It was warm outside, and they broke away from the pack of people leaving the movie theatre and headed up through town towards the photo shop.

"I feel very, how do you say? Nostalgia?"

"Nostalgic. Why? Have you been to Cannes before?" Ethan asked.

"What do you mean?" she asked frowning and then when she understood, she laughed and squeezed his arm. "You are too funny!"

In the photo shop when she asked for her photos, the guy behind the counter gave Céline a strange look. Ethan couldn't pick it until Céline ripped open the package and started flicking through the photos right there at the counter.

"This is my holiday" she explained holding up photos for Ethan to see. Many of them were of Céline and her mother on the beach, both topless. Ethan couldn't help but look, to not look would be rude, but he tried not to be too engrossed. Now he knew what the photo shop guy was leering about.

"Oooh this beach was beautiful" Céline held a photo up close to his face. The beach might have been beautiful, but it was hard to focus on it when Céline's mother's nipple was in half the shot.

"Great" Ethan managed.

Céline shoved the photos back into the package and then rummaged in her handbag for her wallet, and took some coins and notes out to count. A pair of black lacy knickers fell out onto the counter. Céline didn't seem to notice and both Ethan and the photo shop guy looked at them, then at each other, then back at the knickers.

"Aha!" Céline finished counting her money and noticed the underwear. She picked them up gingerly and dropped them back in her bag. "Those are from last night. I met a very nice man" she smiled at Ethan while giving the photo man her cash.

"So, they're not a spare?"

"No, no, they are dirty. I forgot to carry a spare."

She hooked his arm in his again as they left the shop.

"Are you coming to Aria's to say goodbye?" she asked.

"Why, where's she going?"

"She got selected for the Olympic rowing team. She is off to go training. I thought she had told you."

"No" Actually Ethan hadn't seen Aria since Christmas. It was only a couple of weeks ago but seemed like longer.

"Well, you must come say goodbye then."

That seemed to finalise it and they walked together through town, Céline as usual sharing her thoughts on the world and Ethan happy to listen. Sometimes it wasn't worth trying to interject or argue.

They headed around the waterfront, and as they passed the building site where the new museum was going, Ethan saw Elise approaching from the other direction. A wind had sprung up from the harbour and Céline suddenly stopped in her tracks, pulling him to a halt, and stood with her eyes closed facing the water, the wind blowing her hair.

"I can smell the sea. Can you smell it?"

"Sure" Ethan shrugged. They were standing right next to the sea wall and the wind was blowing the spray towards them. You could smell nothing else.

For some reason that made him think of Christchurch. Not the smell of the sea because the city centre was miles in land, and he and Harriet had only been out to the beach once. But in summer in Christchurch, there were a few weeks when a strange hot wind blew in, from the north. It was usually when the city was already baking and dry and that hot wind drove people mad.

He remembered getting home one day to the flat and Harriet pulling shut all the windows, swearing and complaining and even waving her fists at it starting to howl around the house.

"I don't think waving your fists will do anything" he'd laughed, not yet aware of how much it infuriated her.

"I hate it!" she had turned to him and stamped her foot. "It makes me feel itchy."

"I couldn't feel it by the river." Ethan had been sitting under a tree on the riverbank reading a book.

"Right, we're going there then!" As they had hurried back to the park, and around the curve of the river Ethan liked, the wind had been itchy against his skin. Harriet had been right. It had been like walking in a fan bake oven.

But then they'd sat by the river, and it was sheltered from the wind and somehow that feeling reminded him of right now.

A freak wave broke at their feet and sent a white plume into the air, gently showering them with salty foam and breaking Ethan out of his reverie.

"Merde!" Céline jumped backwards.

"You can smell the sea now" Ethan grinned, wiping his face with his t-shirt.

"Did you get wet?" Elise had seen it happen and came hurrying up to them.

"Hey, no not too badly," Ethan said as they backed away from the harbour towards the city.

"Where are you guys heading?" Elise asked. Ethan noticed she and Céline were eyeing each other up from the corner of their eyes. Which made him completely forget to introduce them to each other.

"We're going to Aria's. What about you?" he asked her.

"I'm just going to meet Harriet for a coffee". Elise looked at her wrist. She wasn't wearing a watch. "I better get going. See you." She turned and walked away towards town.

"What is up with her?" Céline asked, hooking her arm in his again as they continued around the waterfront, weaving through a car park rather than risk getting sprayed again.

"Nothing" Ethan frowned.

"This is Elise is it not?" Ethan realised that Céline hadn't actually met her.

"Yes, sorry" Ethan turned to watch her go. He saw her crossing the road in the distance. Had something been up?

"Or maybe something is up with you?" Céline replied, and Ethan hadn't realised he'd spoken out loud. She narrowed her eyes at him. Ethan narrowed his eyes back.

"Nothing is up with me."

They continued round the waterfront.

"I need to stop and get Aria some flowers" Ethan realised out loud as they left the waterfront and headed up through the villas on the lower streets heading up Mt Victoria. They stopped at a flower shop and Ethan got a large bunch of gerberas and roses.

"Beautiful," Celine said.

They took the last part of the walk slowly, both tired and thirsty. Finally, they were heading though the little front garden, and Celine was banging on the front door. It took Aria a minute to come and open it.

"Hey," she grinned seeing them both.

"We brought you flowers," Celine said taking them out of Ethan's hands and giving them to her friend.

"Thanks Ethan. They're lovely" Aria leaned over and kissed him on the cheek while hugging Celine.

"They are from me too" Celine lied.

"I sincerely doubt that" Aria laughed. She took Ethan's hand.

"Come on through, the parties in the back yard."

And Ethan kicked the front door shut behind them.

Blair Stretches out

Recommended listening: Fake Plastic Trees
Single released May 1995 and charted in the UK, NZ and Canada.
From Radiohead's second album The Bends.
Thom Yorke said this song was the product of a joke that wasn't
really a joke, a very lonely, drunken evening and, well, a sort of
breakdown.

Blair was sitting in the small garden at the back of Zöe's house. The French doors from the kitchen led onto a brick patio which was scattered with old rickety wooden furniture. Beyond the patio, a small patch of lawn surrendered to the overgrown mess that went several metres to the back fence.

Blair was sitting cross-legged on a mismatched bench that had been there before any of them had moved in. She had a half-finished spirulina smoothie on the table and was attempting the weekend crossword puzzle.

She looked up at the blue sky, chewing on her pencil. It was going to be a lovely day again. This was normal summer weather that you got in January, and they'd already had two months of it.

The sun was climbing over the tree line and the top of the house was shining with light. Zöe opened one of the French doors.

"Feel like some company?" she asked.

"I'm stuck on four across" Blair put the paper down and picked up her smoothie. Zöe padded outside in her pj's with a cup of coffee. She sat down on the bench next to her friend and folded one leg underneath her. She peered at the paper.

"Succubus," she said.

"Brilliant" Blair sucked down the rest of her green goo and then wrote the answer in.

"Morning" Bowie came out with his cup of coffee, kissed Zöe on the cheek and took the blue deck chair. "What are you two lovelies up to today?"

"I've got to get some costumes for the play. Blair?"

"Yeah, I can help with that."

Blair had read the script for the play that Zöe, Bowie, and a few of their actor friends were putting on. Blair had been tempted to be in it herself but they'd already cast it last year before she was back, and she guessed it wasn't really fair to kick someone off the cast just because she wanted the part.

It was set in the mid-1800s and they were going to use the front garden as their theatre. The front porch of the house would be the stage, and they would set chairs up each side of the garden path. Thankfully out the front, the plant life was under control, with just a thinning lawn and a couple of scraggly bushes.

"Do we need to go to a costume shop?" Blair asked.

"No, we can't afford it. I thought we could find some vintage dresses and suits and then I could sew them to make them look Victorian" one of the girls living in the flat had a sewing machine and Zöe had always been good with making her own clothing. "We might have to find some out-of-the-way second-hand shops though. I've already looked in the two in town and they have nothing.

Bowie got up and went back into the house and came out with the Yellow Pages. They found there were a few places they could try.

"I'll have to go and borrow Zac's car," Blair said. He was now living at the other end of town. He didn't use his car a lot and they all tended to borrow it when they needed it.

The shade was gradually shrinking, and the sun was now blazing across the patio. Blair left Zöe to finish her coffee and went inside to get dressed. She had liked living at Elise's, but she had wanted her own space.

When Zöe had said that one of the rooms in the house she was living in was coming free, Blair had jumped at the chance. She hadn't realised just how many people were living with them.

Zöe and Bowie had the only double-sized bedroom which being a couple was kind of understandable. The other six bedrooms were all tiny. They used to be bigger, but someone had put in makeshift walls down the middle of one room to make each into two.

As well as every room being full, there was even a guy living under the stairs. Blair still hadn't managed to have an actual conversation with him weeks later. He drifted around in a haze of weed, occasionally coming and looking in the fridge to see if there was anything to eat.

While none of them owned much, the house was full of things the previous tenants had left behind. There were books, suitcases, broken TVs and an assortment of hats piled in corners and on the stairs. In the large open-plan kitchen, which may at one time may have also been a lounge, there were 3 broken ovens, and several dressers filled with different plates and an assortment of forks and saucepans.

Blair hurried through the mess and picked her up the stairs. After showering and changing, she came back out into the garden.

"Are you going to get up and come with me?" she asked. Zöe and Bowie were now snuggled on the bench together reading the paper. Like an old married couple. Blair was used to it. Zöe had started going out with Bowie while they were still at high school, so he felt like a brother-in-law already.

"Can't you go and get the car and pick me up in a while?" Zöe pouted.

"You'll owe me."

"Sure" Zöe nodded. Blair knew what Zöe was doing. She'd overheard her friend telling Bowie that she could manage Blair. That if you didn't make her do some thing's herself, she'd do nothing. Blair didn't think it was true at all, but she let Zöe have her theories.

Half an hour later Blair was back to pick Zöe up who had only just finished getting ready. They ended up having to visit all of the shops that Bowie had found in the Yellow Pages, but by late afternoon they had a number of goodies that Zöe thought would be perfect. They'd even managed to bargain the shop owners down on most of the stuff.

They found a car park up the road and lugged the bags into the house.

"Success I see" Bowie was sitting on the front porch now the sun had moved around.

"We got lots and lots" Zöe dropped the bags down. "I'll be sewing frantically though to get it done."

"I'm sore" Blair was also tired from the day of driving. And she still had to drop the car back. "I'm going to go to yoga. Come with?"

"No, I don't really feel like it" Zöe was busy laying out the dresses.

"Come on, it'll be relaxing."

"You go."

Blair went upstairs and came back down with both her track pants and a pair of Zöe's. She held them up and then put them into her bag.

"Come on, I've got your stuff for you."

"Seriously you go" Zöe came over and hugged her. "Thanks for driving me today. Go yoga."

*

Blair dropped the car off and walked down the hill heading into the city centre when she saw Elise coming down another street towards her. They met at the bottom.

"Hey stranger, fancy seeing you here!" Blair said as they hugged. Elise looked good, happy. Perhaps she wasn't torturing herself about men anymore.

"Where are you off too?" Elise asked.

"I'm going to yoga. Do you want to come?"

"I've never tried yoga," Elise said. "Is it hard?"

"No, you just stretch a lot. Come on, I've got a spare pair of track pants." Blair realised she'd still got Zöe's stuff in her bag. "It's a gold coin donation for the Buddhist's but then you get dinner too."

"Sure" Elise shrugged.

They weaved their way through the city streets.

"So how are you? Still in love with that guy?"

"Scott? No, I'm completely over that" Elise said. "Why didn't you tell me what an arsehole he was."

"Um, I think I did."

"Yeah, you probably did. I just couldn't see it. I'm kind of in a weird place at the moment."

"Tell me everything" Blair linked her arm with Elise's.

"Do you want the long story?"

"Hit me."

"Well at Christmas I went to Gwen's sisters for most of the day but then Ethan came round that night. We kind of had this moment when I thought something might have happened. But then nothing did. He did sleep in my room that night but pretty much passed out. Now I realise I like him, but he doesn't seem to think of me as anything but a friend."

"Are you sure? Guys can be pretty crap at showing their feelings."

"Well, we did this quiz in a magazine about whether you were better as friends or lovers. We came out that we had the potential to be lovers, but he seemed to lose interest. And then we went and got Chinese takeaway."

"Chinese takeaway?"

"Sorry, that didn't really have anything to do with it. Then the other night he came round as we always watch the X-Files together. But it was early, and we had a tape of Friends, so we watched that first. And you know how Ross and Rachel got together? Well, I looked at him while we were watching….. but there was nothing. So yet again I think it's just one way. Just me liking someone who doesn't like me back."

"He does like you. If you keep hanging out, I'm sure he'll see you in a different light" Blair said.

Elise didn't look convinced.

"Where is this yoga anyway?" she asked.

"In the Buddhist centre."

"Right," Elise nodded but clearly didn't know where it was. "What about you anyway? How's your new flat?"

"It's fine. We have a guy living under the stairs."

"Fancy."

"Anyway, I've decided to go back to Sydney."

"When?" Elise let go of her arm.

"Next week. I need to be back in time for drama school starting. If I get in. And if I don't then I'll probably do some other course and get a job. There's so much more to do in Sydney. I didn't really realise it until I came back here."

"When were you going to tell me?" Elise was looking at the ground.

"I only just decided the other day," Blair said. All she'd done so far to organise it was booking some flights. The rest would work itself out. She didn't know why Elise was suddenly sounding so betrayed.

"I thought you said drama school was a lot of rubbish, breaking you down and all that," Elise said.

"I know but maybe I can convince them there's a better way" Blair shrugged. "Oh, we have to go up here" she pulled Elise down a side street and opened a door in the side of a large grey building. She heard Elise following her up the stairs. They paid their donation and went into the changing rooms.

Women were walking around in various stages of undress. She gave Elise her extra pair of track pants and when they'd changed, they went into a large, darkened room with mats spread out on the floor. Blair sat down, crossed her legs, laid her hands palms down on her knee, and closed her eyes. On the next mat, Elise copied her.

*

Afterwards, the instructor told them to lie quietly with their eyes closed until they felt ready to come back into the world. Then they could quietly leave and meet in the kitchen. Blair always felt incredibly relaxed after yoga. She could feel her body humming slightly and she concentrated on feeling her breaths in and out, in and out.

When she woke a few minutes later she found she was one of the last ones in the room. She stretched and yawned and climbed up. She went back to the changing room to get a sweater and found Elise standing in the corridor looking uncomfortable.

"Hey, why didn't you go and get something to eat?" Blair asked.

"I was waiting for you," Elise said.

They went into the canteen area. The food was a choice of lentil curry or a green vegetable curry and rice. Elise didn't seem to take a very big plate.

"Aren't you hungry? I'm starving" Blair piled her plate high.

Blair took a seat at a table of other women and chatted happily away about the food and visiting India or Tibet someday. She didn't notice that Elise said nothing. When they finished eating, they changed, and Elise gave her back her track pants. Back out on the street, Blair stretched again.

"Thanks. That was great" Elise said.

"It was. I'm going to go home and veg out" Blair said. She hugged Elise. "See you later?" she said.

"Sure," said Elise "See you later."

But she sounded unsure.

Gwen decides

Recommended listening: Bittersweet Symphony
Single released in June 1997 by Hut Recordings and Virgin Records.
From the album Urban Hymns, by The Verve.
Please note: This was well after Brit Pop Summer but the Verve are
part of Britpop and must be included. And it suits this chapter well.
Based on a sample from a Rolling Stones song.
This caused a furore and court battle.

Brian was true to his word and found Gwen another job. Within a week of having their last conversation, Gwen found herself on her first day at a new job in a small photo lab run by a guy called Simon who knew Brian. Simon had been thinking he needed some help and Brian had talked him into it.

The pace was slow.

Very slow.

Simon showed her the machines, which were far less complicated than the ones Gwen had been using. There were far less photos that needed developing too. Simon gave her some processing to do, and she got through it way too quickly and then had to fart around pretending to be busy. She didn't want to bother him sooner than he'd said she should be finished, because she knew that would set the wrong precedent.

She rang Elise.

As usual, she didn't answer. Annoyed Gwen left a message.

A few minutes later she called again, and this time Elise answered.

"What are you doing?" Gwen asked.

"I just woke up," Elise said sounding sleepy.

"It's 11:30!"

"I was watching some awful movie last night with Harriet and then I started reading this book that Ethan lent me," Elise said. Gwen narrowed her eyes. Ethan was having far too much influence on Elise. Elise used to be able to find her own books. In fact, she'd recommended a couple of her favourite books to Gwen, who had then read them and also given them to her family to read and they all thought Elise was some kind of marvel at finding wonderful books. The first one had been 'The Secret History' by Donna Tartt and then a few weeks ago one called 'Knowledge of Angels' by Jill Patton Walsh. Elise didn't need Ethan to lend her books.

"Can you get ready and have lunch with me in half an hour?" Gwen was going to go out of her mind if she didn't talk to someone.

"Yeah okay."

"See you soon" Gwen hung up and spent the 30 minutes reorganising the dark room which was a mess. At exactly midday, she breezed out and went over to Simon's office.

"I've finished. Do you mind if I go and have some lunch?"

"No problem. See you in an hour?"

Gwen and Elise had lunch at McDonald's. As usual, they were sitting up on the second floor looking out at the people below. Now the year was properly underway the city had come to life again.

You could tell the students from those that had a job. The students wandered about and got in the way of the ones who thought they were so important in their business clothes, rushing through town on their lunch break. Elise always said she couldn't understand their hurry. But then Elise had never had a proper office job like Gwen had. Well, photo labs weren't quite offices, but she'd still had to deal with only having a short time for lunch. Elise barely even started work before lunch time.

"So, how's the new job?" Elise said biting into her cheeseburger combo. It was the best lunch you could get for $2 although there had been a rumour that Georgie Pie was going to open a new outlet right in town in the site across from McDonald's. Gwen hoped it happened. The nearest Georgie Pie was down the other end of town and just always seemed a little too far to go. But their pies were only $1. You couldn't get better value than that.

"It's really slow. And it's just me and Simon. He seems fine but he's ancient so we're not going to have anything to talk about."

"You could have an affair with him?" Elise said, her mouth full of burger.

"He's about 70!" Gwen said sharply "And I don't have an affair with everyone I work for. God!" She thought about her first boss who was so hideously ugly that she pulled a face.

"I know. Sorry," Elise shovelled some fries into her mouth.

"Could you eat any more quickly?" Gwen asked.

"Sorry, starving."

"Hasn't Blair made you any more salads?" Gwen didn't like the sound of Blair. She hadn't met her and didn't plan to.

"Blair moved out," Elise told her that Blair had decided a few days before Christmas to go and stay with her other friend Zoë. Zoë lived in a house with about twenty flatmates and over Christmas one of them had moved out, so Blair wasn't going to need to come back to Elise.

"Oh, well at least you have your room to yourself again."

"I know. But now we're completely out of food."

"I don't know why you don't do a flat kitty like we do" Gwen and her flatmates dealt with their own meals, but they did put some money each week into a kitty and go and do a shop for some shared supplies. It meant at least there was always something to eat.

"Because we've actually managed the impossible. We have a flat without a pendant-a-ray." Elise had told Gwen before about her theory that someone always took on the flat leader role, and then got all snitty about people doing their chores and paying the bills. They go all pedantic about it. Ethan had apparently told Elise that he called one of Harriet's pedantic friends the pedant-a-ray and Elise had loved the term. That's what the flat leader became. A pendant-a-ray.

Except that Elise felt that she, Harriet and Rosalie had worked out a system that was not really a system at all, and it was working well.

"But you also have nothing to eat!" Gwen was annoyed. It was not a system.

"Harriet gets back tomorrow so we'll go and do a shop together" Elise had finished her cheeseburger and licked her fingers. She eyed Gwen's unfinished fries.

"Good because you eat far too much charcoal chicken."

"It's healthy. Sort of."

"Anyway, I don't think I'm going to last at this job long." Gwen brought the conversation swiftly back around to the main topic. "So…. I'm thinking about going to live in London for a year. Everyone else has done it."

"I thought you weren't caught up in that everyone else has done it thing."

"I'm not. But Wellington is so small. I know I'm going to keep seeing Brian everywhere. So, I think I need to get away completely. And Greer is thinking of going too."

"Oh," Elise said quietly.

"You could come?"

"No, I couldn't. Going back last time almost bankrupted me. I'm not going to be able to afford it again for years. When are you thinking of going?"

"In a couple of months. Once summer's over and it's starting to get warmer in England. I'll need to save up though so I'm probably going to have to move into a smaller flat" Gwen loved her flat, but it was more than other parts of Wellington because of where it was. "And I'm going to try and get a part-time job in a sandwich shop or bakery like you did, so I can get some free food."

"How will you do that with the photo job too?"

"There's not going to be enough work for full time so I'll see if I can fit both in."

"I don't want you to go," Elise said.

"I know. I'll miss you but you've got lots of other friends" In fact Gwen thought, Elise seemed to have more and more friends all the time that Gwen didn't know or like. "You and Ethan see each other all the time. He'll keep you company."

"I'm thinking of making the moves on him. Properly." Elise was fiddling with the straw in her drink.

"WHAT? When did you decide?" Gwen put down her burger which she'd only half eaten and leant across the table. "I thought you were only friends?"

"Yes, but I told you I liked him."

"You also said that you're not going to do anything about it."

"Well I've changed my mind. But I need a plan."

"You will need a plan" Gwen knew this would need some thought. Elise wasn't sure if Ethan liked her, and Gwen didn't want Elise doing something that would put it out there and be too far to go back if Ethan clearly wasn't thinking along those lines. It was always a dangerous game. "What are you going to do about a job?"

"Oh, that's sorted itself out" Elise started to eat Gwen's fries.

"How?"

"I got offered another telemarketing job to sell insurance. It sounds okay and its double minimum wage, so I'll actually have some money to burn."

Gwen narrowed her eyes. That was more than she was earning, and she was a skilled photographer. She was glad for Elise because she'd been worried when she'd thrown the job selling TV, but she wasn't supposed to land on her feet quite so easily.

"When do you start?"

"Tomorrow. I went out there the other day so I could meet the two guys that run it. It's a bit weird because they run the company from one of their houses, but it will be me and this other girl, and we're working in this big room that's set up like an office, and we each have a desk and a divider."

"That sounds weird."

Elise shrugged.

"Is he an okay guy?" Gwen asked.

"Sure. He's got a girlfriend and everything and he's not sleazy like the bakers" When Gwen and Elise had first lived together; Elise had been working at a Dutch bakery and was regularly sexually harassed by the bakers working there. They were constantly making cracks about sex. They also regularly whipped Elise's and the other shop girl's bottoms with wet towels. Gwen had thought it sounded awful and told Elise that she should tell them where to get off, but Elise didn't seem that bothered by it.

"Well just be careful" Gwen wasn't sure that Elise could defend herself. She knew from experience how hard it was to get a guy off you. One night when Brian had been drunk, he'd been making the moves on Gwen. She hadn't really been in the mood but once they were lying on the couch and Brian was on top of her, she basically couldn't get him off her. He had then passed out before he could get her skirt off and she'd had to lie there for ages before she could move her leg and get leverage to tip him off her. Her arm and leg had gone to sleep. Brian hadn't even woken up when he'd hit the floor, so she'd left him there for Samira to find the next morning.

She didn't like these memories. She wanted a new set and that was why London appealed. Elise had finished her fries and was now staring out at the mall, looking desolate.

"I can send you back magazines so you'll be able to read about what's happening with Blur and Oasis within weeks of it actually happening" Gwen tried to find some positives.

"I guess so," Elise said sullenly.

*

It was three days later when Brian showed up. He was just 'dropping off' something for Simon. Gwen came out into the reception area and found the two of them talking. She turned quickly to go and hide, but it was too late, Brian had seen her because, of course, Brian had been watching out for her.

"Gwen!" Brian called.

"Yes," she turned back and came out towards them.

"Simon says you've been going well."

"She has" Simon agreed.

"That's great" Brian smiled. There was an uncomfortable silence.

"I'll just take these through to my office" Simon put the box of photos Brian had brought over under his arm and headed off down the corridor. Gwen wished she could follow but obviously Brian had something to say.

"Do you fancy lunch?" he asked.

She frowned. What part of she didn't want to see him anymore, she couldn't be with him anymore didn't he understand?

"There's no problem with us getting caught now."

"I was never worried about us getting caught" Well actually, she had been, but that wasn't the issue here. Although Brian possibly thought it was.

"Well, this is much better. I can pop over now you've settled in and Samira will never know."

Gwen decided she was going to have to do something drastic here. Now there was no risk of her being fired.

"Brian, I'm going out with someone else now." She folded her arms and set her face. She was not going to break.

He blinked and swallowed.

Time seemed to slow down. Gwen could hear herself breathing. She could hear him breathing. She could almost hear the potted plant breathing.

"You really want me to leave her, don't you?" he stepped backwards and took a seat, and put his head in his hands. Gwen felt her heart pounding in her chest. If she was seeing someone, that made him figure he was going to leave Samira. What the hell was going on?

She came over and sat down next to him.

"No, I don't want you to leave her. I don't love you anymore. I don't want to see you anymore because I'm moving on." This was horrible. She could see she was hurting him. His shoulders were sinking lower and lower.

He must have loved Samira once but now he just seemed so lost. Had she become his life raft to survive in a marriage that wasn't great? Is that why he was so scared of letting go?

She wasn't the person for him. Why couldn't he see that?

"I'm sorry" she grabbed his arm suddenly. She was sorry. She shouldn't have gotten into this.

He shrugged her arm off, stood up, and went over the lift. She could see his shoulders shaking. He banged the lift button. There was a clunk from somewhere above them. Please don't let the lift break down now. Gwen could hear her breathing was more ragged now. Like she'd been running. She reached up and rubbed her eyes and found she was crying.

It had been that time in the lift when she should have said no. When he kissed her in the corner. But it had been exciting. Well from now on she was going to think about what she was getting into.

The lift pinged open, and he got in and stood to one side, so she couldn't see his face. The lift doors closed, and she took a deep breath and collapsed back. She had been sitting so upright that her neck hurt.

After a little while she got up and rang Elise. There was no answer and Gwen realised she would be at her new telemarketing job and she didn't know the number there. Gwen banged her forehead gently against the wall. She paused and then rang Greer.

*

Whoever thought meeting in public places to have emotional conversations was a good idea was completely wrong. Greer had agreed to urgently meet her, and Gwen had told Simon she was sick and going home.

They were in the library café, and Gwen was crying and hideously embarrassed that everyone was wondering what was going on. Greer was handing her tissues and trying to block her from the view of everyone else.

"You needed to end it. You know that."

"But I hadn't really seen his face. He needs me."

"Craig needed me, but I couldn't be with him. You can't be with someone you don't love" Greer had been through all of Gwen's break ups, sometimes as first choice and sometimes as second choice.

"Remember how easy it was with Dougal and Tom?" Greer said.

"We were just playing at being grown up" Gwen shook her head. Dougal and Tom had been their first boyfriends when they were sixteen. Both relationships had lasted a few weeks and then Greer and Gwen had both decided to break up. They had prepared together, gone and done the deed, then ran home to Gwen's to talk about how it went. They had both felt like they were women of the world. Little did they know how simple and innocent things had been. When wives and children came into it, it started to get nasty.

"What advice did we give ourselves then?"

"We said that they would get over it."

"And they did. I saw Dougal the other day. He's a cycle courier now."

"God, he was obsessed with cycling everywhere" Gwen remembered and took a sip of her orange juice. She didn't notice that she'd now stopped crying.

"I waved at him and he almost rode into a wall" Greer grinned. "I think he was trying to figure out who I was."

"Did you tell him?"

"No, I was late for work. He's probably still wondering who this idiot waving frantically at him was."

"You're not an idiot."

"Nor are you. And Brian will survive. It'll be hard because you're pretty fucking fabulous. But he will."

"I know. Thanks" Gwen finished drinking her oj. "Are you going to get into trouble sneaking out of work?"

"They probably won't even notice I'm gone, unless someone wants a coffee, or their filing done."

"Oh no, they're not still treating you like shit?"

Greer was working in a small advertising agency. She had been told that within three months she would be promoted from the Office Manager to taking on some copy writing work. But that hadn't happened. She was probably too indispensable at doing all the crappy stuff they gave her.

"I'm going to give it another couple of months then I'll raise it with them," Greer said. The problem was that there weren't many other jobs out there and she didn't really have enough experience yet. No-one had told them at university that a BA would qualify them for bugger all.

"Make sure you do," Gwen said.

"I should actually get back" Greer could see the tempest had passed "Are you going to take the rest of the day off?"

"Yes, I think so. I don't really have anything to do anyway. Simon is finding me stuff and it should tide me over but it's pretty boring. I told Elise that we were going to London though. She got all shitty about it."

"She's just jealous. Why don't you go and talk to a travel agent? See if there are any good deals at the moment. We should really lock in a date."

"Are you sure you want to come?"

"I'm sure" Greer grinned.

So Gwen headed off to look at booking them flights.

Elise
is evicted

Recommended listening: Alright
From the album I should Coco by Supergrass.
Single released July 1995.
Album released in July 1995 by Parlophone.
Lead singer Gaz said it wasn't supposed to be a rallying cry for GenX.
It's really about being 13 or 14 and just discovering girls and drinking."

"Did you see that we've been evicted?" Elise called up from the garden to Harriet, who was out on the balcony with a cup of tea. Elise had found the letter that morning under their door. The lawyer guy must have dropped it around but not wanting a scene, didn't knock and actually tell them to their face.

"I saw it" Harriet moved over on the mattress, and Elise arrived at the top of the stairs and took a seat next to her. She opened her backpack and pulled out a piece of fax paper.

"Look what Ethan faxed me," she said. It was a picture of an eviction sheep. Harriet smiled.

"He used to draw me sheep," she said.

Elise felt her back straighten. Did this mean that Harriet wouldn't mind if Elise made the moves on Ethan? That she recognised that something was happening?

"Before we got together," Harriet said, "Then he stopped."

Elise sagged. Damn.

She leaned back against the house. She'd worked late as she had seemed to be a roll. Selling insurance was far easier than selling satellite TV.

Now she realised it was actually getting nicely cool after the heat of the day. The sky was still blue above them but there was a breeze pushing the clouds along, reluctantly.

"Do you want to look for another flat together?" Harriet asked.

"Yes, I like us being flatties" Elise probably wouldn't even see Harriet that much if they weren't living together. They always seemed to be out with different sets of friends.

"If we get the paper on Wednesday, we can see what's out there. I didn't really want the hassle of moving again."

"We've got 3 weeks though. That should be enough time" Elise heard her stomach grumble. "Have you had dinner? I think I've got enough for some charcoal chicken. We could share?"

And Elise got up and went to scrabble together enough for them to eat.

*

Wednesday Elise called in and said she couldn't work. She got up early and went and got the newspaper.

She and Harriet spread it out on the floor in the lounge. There were not many listings and only four that were around the CBD. Once they had circled them in red pen, Elise rang and managed to set them up so they could visit each other over the course of a morning.

After some toast and a cup of tea, the two of them walked around the corner to where Harriet parked her car. Elise had always been good at navigating and without even having to look at the map, directed them as Harriet barrelled down the city streets.

"People always give way for the VW" Elise pondered as the little pink car cut in front of someone who waved them through. Just as well really as Harriet didn't pay much attention to others when she was driving.

The first house was fairly easy to find and they parked right outside. It was an old villa but didn't look in too bad condition.

A butch woman answered the door.

"Are you two a couple?" she asked once Elise had said who she was.

"No!" Elise laughed. But the woman scowled. She took them through to the kitchen.

"Do either of you eat meat?" she said sternly. Elise and Harriet looked at each other and decided to both shake their head meekly. "Good, we don't allow meat to be cooked here. We're all vegetarian and we can't have the smell of it in the house."

She then showed them her girlfriend's room and then the garden. They walked down the end of the path and at that point, Harriet whispered "We should have pretended we were a couple." It was clear that anyone straight was not going to be welcome.

The next flat was up near the monastery. Harriet parked in the monastery car park in a tow-away zone.

"I don't know if I could face walking up here all the time," Elise said.

"Fran does it and says it's not too bad. And there's a bus that comes right past here."

"I suppose so," Elise said.

They climbed up the 100 steps to the house.

"It'll have a good view," Harriet said.

But there was actually only one room for rent, and it was a tiny single which looked out at the wall of the house next door. Elise stayed for a few minutes and chatted with the young couple who were looking for a flatmate. Harriet went back to check her car was still there.

Elise didn't like the tiny room, but the lounge was great. Then they told her that that was really their zone and they weren't looking for someone who was home a lot and would want to hang out there. They showed her the kitchen. On the wall were three noise control notices.

"Those are from some of our best parties," Shavaughn said proudly. They had a speaker wired up into the kitchen. There wasn't going to be anywhere to escape if they did have a party. Elise knew in her heart this wasn't really her scene.

"We'll let you know. We've got a few people who are coming" Shavaughn said.

"Well, I didn't get that one," Elise said as she arrived back at the car. "And it didn't have a room for you anyway."

The third one was across town. One of the rooms was actually okay but the other one was basically a large hallway through which everyone else in the flat walked through to get to the kitchen.

"You can just put up a curtain around your bed if you want some privacy," the woman showing them the flat said.

"Sure" Elise couldn't believe these were the options.

"What do you do anyway?" the woman asked. Elise knew she would not be moving in here.

"I write Mills and Boons," she said. She had seen a stack of them under the stairs in the hallway.

"Really? I love them!" the woman said. "Do you write under your own name?"

"Oh no I have an alias" Elise said mysteriously.

They'd had to leave soon after as Harriet had been trying to stop herself laughing and had snorted. As they headed back to the car, Elise sighed.

"I don't know if I can take anymore today."

"We've only got one more. Maybe it'll be the one". But when they arrived, they found a note on the door saying that the person had already rented it out.

"Let's go and get some lunch" Harriet suggested. "There's a great little café out near the airport."

They climbed back into the pink beetle for the fourth time and drove through the suburbs the back way to come out at the coast near the airport. Elise liked it around here. While the inner harbour was fairly calm, the outer harbour was part of Cook Straight that ran between the Tasman Sea and the Pacific. It was grey and choppy and rocky. It would suit her mood.

But today with the sun out, and the sky blue, the sea was lapping gently, thwarting her bad mood. Elise scowled to herself anyway.

*

The next couple of weeks she was diligent. Checking the newspaper. Asking if anyone knew anyone who had a flatmate moving out. But there didn't seem to be anything with two rooms available, and hardly anything even with one room.

It was a a Sunday night, and Elise was in the lounge, just finishing watching Melrose Place, when Rosalie arrived home. Elise tossed up whether she should turn off and run to her room to escape, but she really wanted to see what happened next week. Also, if Rosalie wanted to talk, she would probably just follow Elise into her bedroom, and then the bad smell would linger in there for hours.

So she called out hello but leaned forward to show Rosalie she was concentrating on what Amanda was going to do with Billy.

Rosalie called out hello but didn't come through. Elise wondered if she should be worried about what was going on, but at least it meant she could finish Melrose uninterrupted. When it finished, she stood up, stretched, and went and turned the TV off. One of these days she would have to remember to get more batteries for the remote.

As she turned, Rosalie stepped into the corridor and Elise wrinkled her nose. The smell of the shoes was still bad.

"Look what was in the rubbish" Rosalie held up the empty takeaway carton that Harriet had eaten earlier. "Did you throw this away?"

"No, it was Harriet's" Elise was pretty sure Harriet had eaten it all, but now as Rosalie came towards her, she held the carton open.

"There's a lot left. Do you want any?"

There were some greasy noodles in the bottom and some fatty sauce. Elise shook her head. Rosalie sat down and started eating.

"Oh, by the way," she said looking up suddenly "A friend of mine is moving out of his flat. It's a two-bedroom. I thought I'd go and have a look tomorrow. Do you want to come?"

"Sure." At this stage, Elise realised that beggars couldn't be choosers. She needed somewhere. "For you and me to share?" she asked.

"Possibly. I'm tossing up whether I go and stay with my mother instead" Rosalie shrugged. Elise couldn't understand the woman. Rosalie was in her early thirties and still a perpetual student. Elise knew from experience that meant she didn't have much money for rent, but frankly, Elise would rather live on nothing than move home. She loved being independent. She loved knowing that she was making her way in the world and doing it on her terms. But Rosalie didn't seem to have any qualms about popping to her mother's for a few nights if she was hungry or wanted to get away from her broken, banging window which had smashed weeks ago, and she still hadn't called the landlord to come and get fixed.

"I have to work tomorrow. What time do you want to meet?" Elise asked.

"I have some lectures in the morning. What about 3?"

"Sure."

Rosalie told her where the flat was. It was right around the corner from Ethan's.

Elise stood up. "Alright, I'll see you there tomorrow then. I'm really tired, I'm going to go to bed."

"Sleep well!" Rosalie waved with greasy fingers. She appeared to be lapping up every dreg and Elise realised it was making her queasy watching.

*

She didn't make many sales the next day so wasn't in the best mood for meeting Rosalie. She caught the bus and got off at the bottom of the hill. She could see Rosalie lurking halfway up the street, waving.

When she reached her, Rosalie pointed up a row of 100 or so steps to a small blue villa.

"It's that one up there."

"Oh goody" Elise had forgotten to bring water and was hot and bothered. The smell of Rosalie's shoes wasn't helping. They trekked up the steps. Why were there so many of them?

Finally, at the top, Rosalie went up to the door and knocked. No-one answered. Elise narrowed her eyes. If they'd just come all this way and no-one was home, she was going to be most annoyed. Rosalie hammered on the door, but it didn't help.

"Oh well, I know where the spare key is!" Rosalie went into the little shed off to the side of the house where the laundry was. Elise came and stood in the doorway.

"It's hidden in here somewhere."

"But you don't know where? Who is this friend anyway?" Elise asked.

"Oh, I went to uni with him. He's been in a detox clinic for a while. He won't mind if we just go in."

"Is this the guy with anger management problems?" Elise seemed to recall Rosalie regaling them with stories when Ethan had cooked them all dinner.

"He's much better now." Rosalie was peering behind the pipe that came out of the back of the washing machine. "Oh, here it is!" she pulled it off the glob of blue tack it was stuck to. She led them back to the front door and opened it.

"Come on," she said.

Elise was holding back. She didn't feel entirely comfortable with this. She stepped sideways and looked down the flight of stairs. What if this guy arrived home and found them inside? He might genuinely think they were intruders or thieves. She turned to find Rosalie had already gone in and biting her lip, she followed her.

The flat was okay. There was a largish lounge, a tiny kitchen and bathroom and two long dark bedrooms. It was then that Elise noticed above the bed on the wall in one of the bedrooms, was an axe.

"Okay, I'm getting out of here," she said.

"What do you think? You can kind of get a view out of this window" Rosalie was in the corner of the lounge looking out of a small many-paned window.

"Let's go" Elise wanted out now. She thought she could hear someone coming up the steps outside.

"Oh look, he's got a coffee grinder. We had one of these when I lived in Italy." Rosalie went into the kitchen and started grinding, then opened the cupboards. What was she doing? Looking for coffee? They were not going to make a coffee while they were here.

"Listen….. I have to go. I'll take the flat if he is moving out. I'll see you at home." Elise turned and hastily clattered down the steps. She found she was breathing hard. She turned to head down the street and saw a large man coming up the street towards her. He had on a black leather jacket.

He looked dangerous and Elise looked back up the steps. She didn't want Rosalie to get into trouble, but there was only so much crazy she could take. The man came up nearer and nearer and then seemed to pause at the bottom of the steps next to her. Elise pretended to look at her watch. Then he carried on up the street.

That was enough. Elise headed down the street, turned at the corner soon found herself at Ethan's. She knocked. No-one was home and Elise sighed. She didn't want to go home yet, especially if Rosalie was there, so she decided to walk around the waterfront.

She was walking past the museum building site when she saw Ethan walking towards her. For once he wasn't with anyone and she grinned as she hurried up to him.

"I just went to see if you were home," she said.

"I just finished work," he said. He was in a suit and tie and Elise realised she'd never seen him in anything other than jeans. He looked good. Business like.

"I'm really thirsty" Elise realised out loud.

"Do you want to go to McD's?" he nodded back over towards town. She nodded and she took his arm without thinking about it. Then realised she couldn't let go easily without it looking obvious. It was a tense few minutes as she wondered if he was feeling what she was feeling. But he seemed to be unaware of her hand there on his shirt sleeve. As they crossed over towards Manners Mall, they passed through the stream of people hurrying to get somewhere and it was the chance Elise had needed to let go of him.

She got a chocolate shake and some water, and they went upstairs and sat by the window, looking down on the street below. A bus drove by with the Salvation Army number painted on the top.

"What's the point of that? No-one will see it" Elise said.

"Except for people about to jump off a building," Ethan shrugged.

"Oh my god. That's clever!!" Elise grinned. She was feeling better with some liquid chocolate inside her. She took the lid off the cup and mixed it up with her straw.

"Bad day?" Ethan asked.

"Just a little B&E," she said, concentrating on her shake.

"B&E?"

"Breaking and entering," Elise looked up at him. "Rosalie just made us break into some friend of a friend's flat and he had an axe on the wall."

"Sounds a little Stephen King."

"That's what I thought. I left her there. Hopefully, he doesn't come home and go on a killing spree. Actually, I hope she is okay."

"She'll be fine. If she was wearing those shoes then just the smell would have scared him away."

"Oh god," Elise groaned "If I do have to move in there, I'll still smell those shoes."

"Haven't you found anywhere yet?"

"Nothing I can afford. And nothing with two rooms for me and Harriet."

"Well, if you get to eviction day and you've got no-where to go, you can come and stay with me for a few days. I can fit your stuff in at mine." Ethan was peering out at the street, not looking at her, so she couldn't read whether this was something more than it was. Probably it wasn't. She wasn't getting any signs from him that any of this was anything more than him being a good friend.

"Thanks. I might have to take you up on that. Oh look, there's Fran!" Elise could see her on the other side of the street, hurrying somewhere.

"Mrs Frumpy," Ethan said.

"What?"

"She's a frump" Ethan paused and then sang a little ditty. "Living on frump street, where the people are so frumpy". There was even a little tune!

Elise had to laugh. Fran was a bit frumpy. She was probably trying to look chic, but she was just a little bit too short and not quite slim enough. Elise had never been able to figure out how the French and Italian women always looked so elegant, but they did.

When Elise had visited Paris, the crowning moment of her visit had been when someone had come up to her and asked her something in French. Elise had just smiled and told them 'Je ne sai pas'. But what she'd meant was 'yes! You thought I was French? I must look a little bit chic'.

"I'll send you a frump fax tomorrow," Ethan said.

"You got me in trouble today with your fax waster" Elise scolded. Ethan had been faxing her cute pictures of sheep, but it was normally one fax a day. Today Ethan had sent through a fax that had included several blank pages after the heading page that said Fax Waster in giant letters.

"That was my patented fax waster" he laughed.

"Yes, but as about 400 metres of blank fax paper came out, Alan got really annoyed with me and told me that you would have to stop faxing me. Those fax rolls are really expensive."

"He can afford it" Ethan shrugged.

"Please don't get me fired. Then I'll have no job and nowhere to live. I'll be a homeless bum."

"You won't be a homeless bum. You'll be a dosser living on my floor" Ethan joked. Elise almost flicked the last dregs of her shake at him, but she knew he only had one tie and she didn't want to get chocolate on it.

"Anyway after the fax waster incident, Alan had to go into town for a meeting, so he left me in charge. So I went and played minesweeper on his computer, but then I thought I should use the web. So I opened Alta Vista like you told me, even though Alan said that Lycos was better, and then I realised that I didn't really know what to look up."

"We've just got world wide web access too," Ethan said "at work. The only thing I've used it for is to order some t-shirts from America and to look on eBay. But there's no eBay for New Zealand so you can't really buy anything unless they'll ship it."

"Well, the only thing I could think of to look up was Friends. There were a few websites that came up. But they didn't really have any stuff about the actors. I just wanted to see how old Jennifer Aniston was but the ones I looked at didn't say."

"I'm glad you never got the Rachel cut," Ethan said.

"I did think about growing it out" Elise sometimes thought about when she'd had longer hair but realised she didn't really miss it. She loved the freedom of very short hair. It took a minute to wash and about two minutes to dry and this summer it had been brilliant with no hair hanging around your neck.

In Wellington having long hair was a disaster anyway. It was mostly whipping around your head and in your eyes. Harriet wore her hair up all the time as did Blair. So what was the point of it?

"You should keep it short," Ethan said, sipping some water. "What are you doing tonight?"

"Going to the movies with Gwen. Do you want to come?"

"No, there's a thing I have to go to" he looked at his watch. "I suppose I better head home."

"I'll walk with you." Elise was meeting Gwen at the movies so she could walk with Ethan for a while. She refused to ask Ethan what thing he had to go to and who with.

Harriet's New House

Recommended listening: Country House

From the album The Great Escape by Blur.

Single released on 14 August 1995, the same day as Oasis released 'Roll with It'. The media dubbed it the 'battle of Britpop'. Blur won in this instance, with the single reaching number 1.

It's about a man living in a bloody big house in the country.

The video was directed by Damien Hirst and was nominated for best video at the 1996 BRIT Awards.

Harriet made herself and Elise a cup of tea and they went and sat out on the back deck on the mattress that yes, was still there. It was another glorious day although there were some wisps of clouds very high in the sky, barrelling across at an alarming rate. Harriet looked up at them. From somewhere she recalled they were called cirrus. Why was that even useful to know? It must be windy up there. But down here it was still.

It was becoming eerie the lack of wind this summer. Normally even when it was a nice day, there was still a strong breeze to chill you. But it was hot again.

Harriet put her cup of tea down and leaned back against the house. Elise had sat down cross-legged near the edge of the mattress, possibly trying to get a little cross wind that usually swept across their back yard. But she was having no luck.

"Do you want to look at more flats tomorrow?" Elise asked. Tomorrow was Wednesday which was flat night in the evening paper.

"Well actually" Harriet picked up her mug and took a sip of her tea "I've decided I've had enough of flatting. I'm going to buy a house."

Elise choked on her tea and had a coughing fit. She put her mug down and after recovering said "You're going to buy a house? How? You've got no money."

Harriet was currently finishing her master's degree and working part-time at the University for a pittance. She could barely cover her rent, let alone have enough for a deposit on a house. And Elise had no idea how much houses even cost but they were a lot.

"I'm only a few weeks away from finishing my master's so I can get a real job and apply for a mortgage. And my father is going to lend me the money for the deposit and only charge me a bit more interest than the banks would for me to pay it back to him over the next few years. I'll just flat somewhere for a few weeks until I find the right place. But it means you can just look for someone with one room for you."

"What sort of job will you get?" Elise asked. Harriet's master's was in Classics. What job did that qualify you for?

"I'm not sure yet" Harriet shrugged.

"But ... how much does a house cost?"

"Well I'm only going to be able to afford something small and cheap," Harriet said. She had started looking at the property pages of the paper. Most of it was out of her price range but if she could find a small townhouse in somewhere like Newtown, you could get one for around $100,000. It was daunting. All she'd owned up until then was her car. She also had her runaway fund but that was only a couple of thousand dollars.

Ethan had teased her about that fund when he'd found out about it. She guessed he might have felt a bit miffed that she had money to run away if she'd needed to but she'd had a couple of exes who were abusive and she had had to escape fast when they'd gone out. She wasn't going to have to rely on anyone else if that happened again.

She'd never told Elise about the fund. Elise didn't have to worry about stuff like that. Even though Harriet worried that men would take advantage of Elise, they didn't seem to. Unlike Harriet who felt that she'd had her fair share of men who pushed too far.

"Is it my fault because I haven't found us a flat?" Elise asked.

"No. I'd love to flat with you but it's just time for me to buy. I can still help you look for a place though" Harriet offered. She didn't mind driving Elise around and there was now only a week before they had to move out.

*

Harriet didn't feel Elise would be very helpful looking at houses to buy. Neither of them had any idea how the whole process worked, so Harriet rang her friends Kitty and Greg. She hadn't seen them for a while as they had moved up the coast and had had a child. Harriet wasn't much good with children, so they'd sort of fallen out of touch.

But they had brought a house before and she felt it was the right time to get in touch. She drove up the coast to pick Kitty up to come and stay with her for a night and look at some houses.

Elise had told her that she would live with her if Harriet got a place in town, but Harriet knew she couldn't afford town. She'd found a couple of places to look at in the outer city suburbs. While it was a fairly grungy and run-down area, there was a supermarket and a few good Indian takeaway places. The other house Harriet was going to look at was up in the Wadestown hills to the west of the city centre. She had a bit of an aversion to Wadestown because of the fiasco when she and Ethan had moved to Wellington, but it was in a completely different area so should be fine.

She and Kitty went to look. The first house was the bottom half of a small townhouse, in a block of four. It was the second from the left. It needed doing up but had two bedrooms, a bathroom, and then a large room that was completely open-plan with a lounge and kitchen. There was a small garden outside. Harriet quite liked it.

The other house was an apartment. Harriet didn't like the idea of an apartment. She wanted to have a bit of a garden. She'd decided that perhaps she would find gardening relaxing.

Making the offer was terrifying. She was signing her name on a piece of paper that said she would be paying tens and tens of thousands of dollars. This would make her a proper person. Elise could go on renting, but Harriet was going to start being an adult.

Fran had thought it was a great idea and was all for it.

Even Ethan had said that it was a good way to make her save. Because apart from her runaway fund she'd never been good at saving. Yet she'd always paid her rent.

This would just be like paying a little more rent.

It just felt very serious sitting with her father's lawyer writing her name on the dotted line.

*

"I've made an offer," Harriet told Elise three days later. They were in the lounge, relaxing after eating a roast charcoal chicken meal.

"On a house?"

"Yes, on a house."

"When? I thought you were going to take me with you to look." Elise said.

"Sorry, I took Kitty and Greg because they know about buying houses."

"When do you hear if they accept it?"

"The Real Estate woman said she'd ring me this evening," Harriet said. The phone rang right then and they both jumped. Harriet looked at Elise and pulled a face.

"You better answer it," Elise said.

"I don't know if I can. What if they say no?"

"What if they say yes?" Elise got up and went and answered the phone. It was the Real Estate woman asking for Harriet. Elise held out the phone, and Harriet nervously got up and took it. The conversation was short and Harriet's shoulders slumped.

"Okay thank you," she said and hung up. She turned to Elise. "They declined it. I'm thousands lower than they want apparently."

"Perhaps it wasn't meant to be for a reason?"

"Perhaps." Harriet went into her room. Elise came to the door.

"Will you be okay?"

"I'll be fine" Harriet decided an early night, tucked up with a good book was just what she needed.

*

Harriet and Elise came home from the supermarket the next day to find Ethan had stuck a picture of an eviction sheep on their door.

"That's so cute" Elise loved the silly pictures that Ethan drew.

"Yes, cute until we actually have to leave and don't have anywhere else to live."

"It would have been pretty amazing if you'd got the first house that you made an offer on. But the next one might be even more perfect" Elise said as they went into the kitchen and unpacked their last few groceries to last them final few days.

Harriet went and sat down by the phone in the hallway. She hadn't told Kitty yet that the offer had been turned down so now she called her.

"Well, are you going to counter?" Kitty said.

"No that was as much as I could afford?"

"Harriet – you never offer your best offer the first time. Can't you even afford to go back with a thousand more? You might find that they'll come down if they know that's all you can afford but you've moved up slightly."

"I didn't know that."

"Of course you didn't. You haven't done this before."

"I'll talk to the lawyer and see what he says."

"Do that" Kitty said.

Harriet wasn't good at listening to people that she didn't agree with. She'd been seeing a range of counsellors over the years to talk to about the men in her life. The counsellors she liked were the ones who didn't make her do anything very challenging about her problems, or so Ethan had told her.

Once her counsellor had been a nun. Ethan had told her that a nun was not the right person to talk to, but Harriet liked the nun. She saw things from a purer and simpler place. She wasn't made subjective by being involved with men. Ethan didn't seem to understand that.

But she agreed with what her father's lawyer said, and so after talking to him, Harriet found she was making a counteroffer.

She signed again and felt like this time she knew the drill. Now she'd just have to wait again to hear back and this time it would be a few days as the house owners were away.

She got back home again to find Elise had gone out. Rosalie's door was shut, and the smell of old shoes was stronger, so Rosalie was probably home.

Harriet decided she might go up and stay with Kitty and Greg for the night. She would take them some takeaways to say thank you for helping with the house hunt.

As she hung up the phone, Rosalie opened her door and came out, leaning in the door frame suggestively.

"Are you going away for the weekend? Do you need any company?" she asked.

Harriet considered. She did feel kind of out of her depth on this. "Okay," she said, "but I'm going to head off in the next half hour."

"I'll go pack!" Rosalie rushed back into her room to grab some clothes.

And so they hit the road together. Kitty and Greg's house was an hour up the coast and it was a beautiful afternoon, so they drove with the windows open. Both seemed content watching the view and not talking.

Then Rosalie turned to her.

"Are you going to help pay for my window?" she asked.

"Your window? No. You broke it."

"No, I left it open, and because you or Elise left my door open, and the back door open it blew against the wall and smashed. So, it's both your faults."

"Rosalie. I'm not paying for your window" Harriet said sternly.

"Fine! Let me out then!" Rosalie said. Harriet ignored her.

"Let me out, let me out, let me out!" she started to shout and tried to open her door. Harriet swerved the car to the shoulder and came to a screeching halt. Rosalie leapt out and slammed the door and started walking back the way they had come.

Harriet accelerated away. If that was the way she wanted to be. Harriet was not paying for the window and that was that.

A couple of minutes later, Harriet started to feel bad. She had left the back door open when she and Elise had been having a cup of tea and that was why the window had smashed. She turned the car around and went back to find Rosalie.

She turned and pulled over next to Rosalie. Rosalie opened the door, collapsed in the passenger seat and took her shoes off. Harriet tried to breathe through her mouth.

"It's too hot out there" she opened the window.

"Are you starting the car or not?" Rosalie said.

They didn't speak for the rest of the drive. The evening wasn't much more of a success. Harriet decided that it may have been a mistake to bring Rosalie who spent the evening flirting with Greg and then wolfing down all the left-over takeaways.

Harriet was pleased to get home the next day and drop her off.

"I'm going to go stay at a friend's" Rosalie said, "there's no food here."

Harriet didn't disagree with her even though she knew that for once, there actually was.

And then the lawyer called and said that the owners would accept her offer if she increased it by two thousand. Which she just couldn't do.

When Elise arrived home, Harriet heard her coming down the hall and sniffled loudly. She heard Elise pause and then knock softly on the door.

"Come in" Harriet sniffed some more.

"What's wrong?"

"They turned me down again," Harriet said.

"Oh no! I didn't know you'd made another offer."

"Yesterday."

Harriet was annoyed Elise didn't seem to be sympathising with her but rather looking put out. She didn't have time for this.

"I'm sorry," Elise said, "I can make you a cup of tea and I brought a pack of biscuits."

"That would be nice" Harriet felt a tiny bit better already.

Fran's new career

Recommended listening: Talk Show Host
Released as a B side on the single Street Spirit
(Fade Out) by Radiohead.
Single released January 1996.
From the album The Bends released by Parlophone.
Then used in the 1996 film Romeo+Juliet by Baz Luhrmann.

"When they hired me, they told me and Harriet that we'd both be trainee managers. I found out the other day that was a lie."

Fran and Elise were at Eva Dixon's café. It was a Sunday morning, and they were splashing out on brunch. Eva's attracted the semi-alternative crowd. It was up on the first floor and the sun was streaming in. Fran had got there first and grabbed a corner table.

She had watched Elise come up the stairs and hesitantly peer around like maybe she hadn't been here before. But who hadn't been to Eva's? She came here all the time with Jill. It had the best coffee. But now she thought about it, it wasn't really the kind of place Elise would hang out.

But once Elise had seen her, come over and sat down they had got to discussing when they'd been hired to work in the bookshop.

They'd all been interviewed by the same two men; one was a part owner and the other they all decided later must have been the company accountant. Neither Fran, Elise nor Harriet remembered actually being told who was interviewing them - they'd all just been taken into a small office and told to sit in a chair while the two men had sat behind a desk shuffling papers and asking them inane questions.

"I don't think they felt any need to lie to me," Elise said. "When they interviewed me they just stared at how short my skirt was. I suppose it was quite short but that's not the point."

"I think it was legs for me too but probably boobs for Harriet" Fran shook her head. "It's so sexist."

"What always amazed me is that if you were trainee managers how come you were only on 50c an hour more than me, an uneducated lowly sales girl?" Elise asked. Fran knew that Elise had been to university, but she'd only passed a couple of papers before dropping out. Unlike Fran and Harriet who both had BAs, Harriet's was with Honours.

"Exactly!" Fran waved her spoon at her.

"So how did you find out they'd lied?" Elise asked.

"What can I get you girls?" the waiter was cute, and Fran had been making eyes at him across the room.

"Eggs Florentine for me" It was what Fran always had.

"Have you got bagels?" Elise hadn't even looked at the menu which was actually under the glass top of the table, along with amusing clippings from the evening paper.

"With cream cheese and salmon," the waiter pointed.

"I'll have that" Elise smiled up at him.

"Anyway" Fran interrupted "I found out that anyone with a degree was promised to be made Trainee Manager. So, we felt like our degrees were worth something."

"Something more than 50c more an hour?"

"Exactly."

And in fact, the Branch Manager had only told Fran about the fact she wasn't on track for management because the book chain had been purchased by another larger retailer. Never mind, Fran quickly told herself, she wouldn't think about it at the moment.

They talked for a while longer before the waiter brought their brunch over.

"Did you know I had to make eggs benedict when I was the breakfast chef at the Dixon Street Deli?" Elise said, starting to spread cream cheese on her bagel.

Fran frowned. She loved the Dixon Street Deli. It was the only deli in the city and was just down the road from where they were now. In the centre was a giant square glass counter packed with plates and bowls of meats, pickles, cheeses, and antipasto. Around the walls were shelves piled high with jars of sundried tomatoes, sauces and vegetables.

There were a few tables inside where you could have lunch or at the weekend brunch. Amusingly the deli also insisted on having several tables outside on the footpath for months and months even though for most of that time it was too cold and windy to ever eat out there. Of course, this summer was the exception and craning her neck and looking down the street, she could see people were sitting out there today.

"You were not a chef" Fran couldn't imagine it. She poked her fork into the egg and watched satisfied as the yolk slowly ran down the side of the bagel and pooled on the plate with the spinach.

"Well I only lasted a weekend before they decided to put my pay rate down so I stopped going." As she ate, Elise explained that she had told them she'd worked in a bakery but that she'd wanted to expand her skills. It had been a hard interview as the owner of the deli had taken her upstairs to the mezzanine which was not full height, and while he was short enough she had to bend down uncomfortably to walk. Even once he'd sat down behind his desk and Elise had taken the seat opposite him, she'd had to bend her head slightly because she was still touching the ceiling.

"When did this even happen?" Fran chewed.

"Before I started telemarketing. Last spring."

"But you only lasted the weekend?"

"Yeah, they asked me to bake a cake, but I hadn't used an industrial microwave before and so burnt the butter. That's when the owner told me he was reducing my pay rate as I obviously didn't know what I was doing. But we just had a normal microwave at the bakery. I didn't even know there was an industrial version."

"That's probably why they twigged you weren't a real chef" Fran firmly believed that there were some professions you didn't mess with without having some qualifications. It hadn't mattered too much that Elise didn't have a degree to work in a bookshop because at least she had read lots of books. But being a chef was different.

"The wanker never actually paid me for that weekend either" Elise piled the last scraping of jam onto the last bite of her bagel and popped it into her mouth.

"You should have gone in and asked."

"I shouldn't have had to."

"No, but sometimes you have to take the initiative." Like Fran was about to do. She not only knew she wasn't in line for a promotion but if some of the stores in the two chains were merged and if there were longer-serving employees in the other chain then she might actually get demoted. "If you don't, then you're likely to get screwed."

"You're not talking about me not being paid anymore" Elise had a mouthful of bagel.

"No, I'm not. The whole bookstore chain's been brought out. I might lose my job."

"What? When?"

"It's happening next month."

"What are you going to do?" Elise asked.

"I've had a look at publishing courses. I want to stay with books but I'd like to be involved in producing them, not selling them. I've found a two-year course that I can do and probably still work part-time and then hopefully get a job at HarperCollins or something."

"That sounds great." Elise looked impressed.

Fran rummaged in her bag and pulled out a brochure of the course that they'd sent her. Elise thumbed through it. Fran could see Elise was considering if it was something she'd like to do, but then flipped to the back and looked at the course fees. Fran knew there was no way Elise could afford it.

"What about you? What are you going to do with your life? You can't keep telemarketing" Fran said. She'd finished her brunch now and ordered a flat white from the waiter. She leaned back so the sun fell across her back. She put her sunglasses on. She felt like she should be an older sister to Elise here. Elise didn't seem to have much direction in her life and no-one telling her that she should get some. Harriet, who was older and should have been guiding her, clearly wasn't.

"Telemarketing isn't bad money. Ethan wants us both to apply for an American Express card. I don't earn enough but Alan said he'd do me a letter lying about my salary so I qualify."

"Getting a credit card that you can't afford, with a guy you hardly know is not a plan for your life," Fran said.

"I know. But it will be my first credit card. I'll actually be able to buy things."

"Didn't you have an overdraft on your cheque account that you didn't pay off?" Fran said.

"So?" Elise said warily.

"To get a credit card they'll do a credit check. And you'll have a black mark against you if you didn't pay that overdraft back."

"I couldn't pay it back!" Fran knew that Elise had got into a little bit of financial difficulty when she'd gone back to the UK last year. It had cost more than she'd really been able to afford so when she got back she had bounced a few cheques to pay for some food and clothes. Then she hadn't used that bank account again. The bank had written to her several times but then stopped so Fran knew Elise had decided it must have been okay. It was never okay though.

Fran decided now wasn't the time to burst Elise's bubble. "Anyway, I'm not sure you'll see that much of Ethan anymore." Fran took a sip of her coffee.

"What do you mean?"

"I told Harriet what happened," Fran said as matter of factly as she could muster.

Elise's face went white. "About what?"

"You know. About you and him." Fran shrugged.

"But why?" Elise cried out.

"I didn't mean to. But we were discussing him and Harriet was worried. And I had to tell her."

"No you didn't! What could possibly have made you need to tell her?" Elise's voice was raised and she looked embarrassed.

"She was going on about Jason. And how she would have forgiven me if it had been the other way around" Fran hadn't been going to explain but Elise seemed more outraged than she'd thought she would be. "So I said if that was the case, she'd forgive you for what happened with Ethan. I just forgot that she didn't know."

"You forgot?"

"It's not a big deal. Harriet was fine with it." It wasn't like Elise and Ethan were anything more than friends.

The waiter came over with Fran's flat white and putting it down looked between the two girls. Fran smiled back at him from behind her sunglasses.

Once he was gone, Fran slowly stirred her flat white.

"Okay I'm sorry," she said finally, looking up at Elise.

"Whatever" Elise shrugged and pretended to read one of the articles on the table.

Fran looked around and saw two of her friends arrive at the top of the stairs. She waved and they hurried over. Fran stood up and they all hugged and kissed.

"You guys have met Elise?" Fran said.

"Hi," Elise smiled politely.

"Come and join us," Fran said moving over so there was room on the padded bench.

"I'm going to go." Elise got up.

"Okay, I'll talk to you soon." Fran was already over Elise and her little sulk. Elise was going to have to grow up sometime and start handling life.

Fran waited to see if Elise would look back before heading down the stairs, but she didn't.

Elise hides out

Recommended listening: Slide Away & Underwear

Slide Away from the album Definitely Maybe, by Oasis.

Underwear from the album Different Class, by Pulp.

Why do you need to listen to both? Don't ask questions. Just do it.

"I need to hide out!" Elise said when Ethan opened the front door. He peered past her to the street, looking both ways, dramatically.

"Let me in you idiot! There's no one physically after me!"

He shrugged and opened the door wider so she could slip through. She hurried down the hallway to his room and when he came in after her, she was already sitting near the end of his bed, cross-legged.

"What is wrong with your bed?" she asked. It had some serious sag problems in the middle. It felt like the springs had gone entirely and if she wasn't perched on the end, she would sink down to the floor.

"The springs are fucked" Ethan shrugged. He got on alright sleeping in it. He sat down on the chair by his desk. "Who are you hiding from?"

"Rosalie. I'm supposed to go and meet her and Harriet at the flat with the lawyer. We've got to finalise the money stuff. The lawyer wrote and told us that it wasn't acceptable that the window was broken, and we'd have to pay for it. And we haven't paid our phone bill for months either. But I haven't got any money. So, I'm not going to go."

"Does Harriet know?"

"That I'm hiding? She will when I don't turn up."

"She'll get shitty."

"I know but I don't know what else I can do." Elise shrugged.

"I can go if you want. Just popping by to see if you're in. Then I can let you know what happens."

"Would you do that?" Elise actually thought that would be quite useful.

"Sure" Ethan shrugged. "When's the meeting?"

"In an hour. Thank you. That's really nice of you" Elise would have to think of some way to pay him back.

"I'll go and get us an ice cream" she decided and climbing off the bed, walked down to the corner shop and brought a couple of trumpets. When she got back, they went and sat out in the garden for a while, talking.

"Okay, well I guess I should head over there" Ethan looked at his watch.

"I might wait in your room." Elise had never been comfortable hanging out with other people's flatmates, especially not Ethan's. Not that there was anyone home at the moment, but you never knew when they'd arrive back. She decided to make a start on one of the huge piles of magazines he had stacked against the wall, while he headed across town to see if she was missed.

He was gone for over an hour and Elise started to worry. What was he doing over there? Had he told them where she was? No of course not. He was hardly likely to offer to go and see what happened and then blow her cover. Still, at least he had a good pile of GQ magazines that she was working her way through.

*

Ethan came into the room and closed the door behind him. Elise sat up. She had been lying on the bed reading about how to get a girl drunk by making pasta sauce with vodka in.

Ethan sat down in the chair by his desk.

"How did it go?" she asked.

"Well, they were pissed you didn't show."

"Who? Rosalie?"

"Her and the lawyer. He said you owed money for the window, even though it was Rosalie who busted it. Harriet actually raised that when they did up your bathroom, you'd hardly been able to use your toilet for a week and shouldn't have had to pay rent, but the lawyer just kind of talked over her. And Rosalie was pissed because you owe her money for the phone bill and it's in her name."

"I don't know what to do."

"Don't worry about the lawyer. If you didn't have a bathroom Harriet's right. You can't be charged rent. So that should cover the window. But if I was you, you might want to pay Rosalie off. Otherwise, she might hunt you down and make you smell her shoes."

"God, there could be nothing worse."

"Well, he and Rosalie have both gone now if you want to go home. I think Harriet suspects you'll be showing up soon. And by the way, she's okay about what Fran told her. About you and me."

Elise widened her eyes. She knew she was going to have to face Harriet about that soon enough, but she couldn't believe Ethan had brought it up. Although, if Harriet had told Ethan she was fine with it, maybe she actually was.

"Thanks," Elise said again although it didn't feel like enough.

She walked back across the city slowly. She was hungry but she'd wait until she got home. She and Harriet had said they would have a last dinner in the flat together, even though both Rosalie and Harriet had moved their stuff out now. In the end Harriet had taken a flat out near the airport on short notice, as she still hadn't brought a house. She'd gone to visit the flat, taken it, got a trailer and had Sean and Will come and move her stuff all within 3 days. Elise couldn't believe how fast it had all happened.

Elise hadn't been able to book the man and a van company until tomorrow morning. So, her last night in the flat she'd have to sleep there alone.

*

Harriet was waiting for her.

"You were naughty not coming" she scolded.

They still had the green chairs in the lounge which belonged to Elise. Apart from that the only furniture left in the house was Elise's bed, a few boxes of books, and her dresser. Most of the kitchen things had been Rosalie's or Harriet's.

"I'll have the money in a couple of weeks. I just can't pay Rosalie at the moment" Elise opened the hallway cupboard and found it empty. She wandered over to Rosalie's empty room. "Oh my god, it still smells in here," she said. "The next tenants will wonder what the hell it is."

She came into the lounge. She knew Ethan had said it was alright, but she wasn't sure if she believed it. She was nervous. She picked at the hem of her skirt.

She said hesitantly, looking at the floor. "Fran said she told you what happened. With me and Ethan."

"Yes, she did. You could have told me, you know." Harriet scolded.

"I didn't want to lose you as a friend." Elise finally looked up.

"Listen, Ethan and I are never going to be together again. We've both moved on. It's not a problem" Harriet assured her.

"Gwen thought it would be."

Harriet tutted.

"Did you just tut?" Elise laughed. It wasn't funny but she was just so relieved that Harriet was okay with this.

"I guess I did. You shouldn't always listen to Gwen." Harriet said. "And it didn't mean anything with you and Ethan?"

"No." Elise swallowed.

"Good. Now I thought we could get charcoal chicken. For old times' sake."

"That would be perfect!" Elise smiled.

"There's a phone message for you too."

"I'll check it later" Elise wanted to eat. They had left the mattress out on the deck. It had seen better days and Harriet had decided to buy a new bed when she got a new house. The flat she'd taken already had one.

So with the summer day fading in the sky above, they sat out there one last time, with the view of the washing line and the concrete, and ate their Charcoal Chicken roast meal.

"This feels like the end of an era," Elise said.

"It does. It's been fun" Harriet ate a forkful of peas. "I'll let you know when I'm having a housewarming."

Elise could see was completely confident that she would be in her own home soon.

"Good. Just make sure you're somewhere near the city then I can still come and visit you."

*

After Harriet left, Elise sat in the window seat and watched the lights of the city flicker on. She put on Definitely Maybe and rested her chin on her knees. She realised she was listening to Slide Away and thinking that everything was sort of sliding away. For once in her life, she wasn't sure that everything was going to be okay. Everybody was leaving. She had no-where to live past staying at Ethan's for a few days. And she kept falling for guys who didn't fancy her.

Maybe all her friends telling her that she had to get her life in order were right. Maybe she should.

When the album finished, she got up and packed the last few items into boxes so she was all ready for the morning and went to sleep.

*

It wasn't until the removal guy phoned the next day to say he was on his way that she heard the beeps on the phone. She'd forgotten that Harriet had told her she had a message.

She dialled into the account for the last time. It was a message from Shavaughn over at the party flat. It seemed that the first person they'd chosen for the flat had found somewhere else. Then Shavaughn and her boyfriend Craig had been visiting his brother and mentioned Elise.

"Anyway," Shavaughn said over the message "Craig's brother has met you. He said you're friends with Gwen, and he's married to Gwen's sister. So long story short, we'd like you to move in on Sunday if you're still wanting somewhere."

Elise could hardly wait to tell Ethan the news. When the man with a van arrived, she helped him load up. He'd had to use the front seat for some of her boxes, so she told him where Ethan's was and said she'd walk over. She said goodbye to the house, locked up, and left the key in the letter box. It didn't feel quite real.

It wasn't even like she'd lived here for years. It was less than 12 months, but she felt like so much had happened.

She shut the gate, hurried across town on the quickest way she knew, and found the van man was already half unpacked. Ethan's room was quickly becoming very full. She helped unload. When she came inside from paying, Ethan was looking at all her stuff.

"It didn't look like this much in your room," he said.

"My room was bigger than yours" she joked. Basically, all that was left of his room was a small corridor between the bed and the door. She could tell Ethan was perhaps having second thoughts.

"They called me from that party flat I looked at up the road and said I could move in on Sunday. So you'll only have to put up with this for 3 days" she said.

"That's good."

Elise wasn't sure if he meant it was good she'd got the flat, or good he would only have to put up with her and her stuff for a short time. Still, she had no choice.

"Thank you again for doing this."

"I have to go to work this afternoon" Ethan had only taken the morning off to make sure her move went okay.

"Yes me too" she had only asked Alan for the morning off to.

"I'll be back about 5. If you're earlier than that, someone might be home to let you in, or you can just wait for me" Ethan only had one key so couldn't give her one.

"Okay, I'll see you tonight then." Elise had a bit of extra time so decided she could walk to Alan's rather than catch the bus. In fact, once she moved into the party flat, she would be able to walk to work every day and not have to scrounge a lift from Alan. Which was good as things had got a bit weird with him. The other day she'd stood up and gone round the divider to ask him something and found that he was quickly shutting down some porn site.

Then the other day sales had been slow, so he'd asked her if she wanted to finish early and he could give her a ride into town because he was going in for a meeting. She'd agreed.

In the car, he'd showed her the new CD he'd just brought. It was Pulp. Elise had grinned.

"Yes, I've heard this."

"How? I got it on special order."

"My sister sent me some of the songs on tape. I'll go and buy it now it's out".

Alan had put the CD on random. The song 'Underwear' came on. It was a strange song about a guy wanting to see a girl in her underwear. Elise shifted uncomfortably in her seat. It was kind of an awkward song to be listening to with a guy you knew looked at porn a few feet away from you and then she'd been sure Alan had glanced across at her. She'd quickly looked out the window and was pleased to get out of the car.

*

Later that afternoon, she struggled back to Ethan's carrying the large, boxed present she had got him. It was just after 5 so she hoped he was home. When she knocked, he came and answered. He was in his jeans and white cow print t-shirt so must have been home a little while to change out of his suit.

"I've got you a little present," she said lugging it down the hall. She went into his room and dumped it on his bed. Ethan followed her in.

"You didn't have to get me anything."

"I wanted to say thank you in advance. Otherwise, I would be on the streets right now."

Ethan sat down next to it and ripped it open. It was a VCR.

"How did you get this?" he looked up at her.

253

She was grinning like an idiot. She knew VCRs cost heaps normally.

"Alan was going to throw it out, so I brought it off him. Don't worry, it wasn't much and he's just going to take a little bit out of my pay for the next few weeks."

"This is great, thanks" Ethan grinned. He took it over to the desk and started to hook it up to his TV.

"I've even got some movies I taped somewhere in one of these boxes" Elise pulled a box out of the pile and opened it up. Once Ethan had the VCR hooked up, he inserted the tape in the slot, and they played around with cables until suddenly the film came up on the screen. It was the Princess Bride.

"Have you seen it?" Elise asked. It was one of her favourites.

"I have, but I'll watch it again," Ethan said. "I was going to make you dinner first though."

So they turned it off and went into the kitchen.

Elise jumped up onto the kitchen counter and sat and watched as Ethan chopped garlic and tomatoes and made spaghetti. They took it outside to eat as no one else was home yet.

That night after watching the movie, Ethan picked up a pile Elise hadn't noticed at the end of the bed. It was a towel and a soap.

"This is for you to use. I thought you might have packed yours."

"I did. You're very sweet." Elise thought perhaps you shouldn't say that to a guy. But he was. She took them into the bathroom to get ready for bed.

*

Two nights in Ethan's bed and Elise hadn't slept well. The spring problem in the middle of the bed had meant she'd had to balance on the edge of the mattress if she wanted to get any sleep at all. If she rolled over in the night towards the middle, she fell down into the hole and woke up. Not that she could really complain, but she was looking forward to her own mattress again.

Sunday saw her and Ethan making journey after journey between his flat and her new flat, carrying boxes of books, the dresser, the green chairs, and finally her mattress. They were exhausted by the end of the day.

"Do you want to go and get some dinner?" she asked when they were done. She was sweaty and tired and really just wanted to collapse.

"No, I'm good. Will you be okay to unpack?" Ethan looked around the tiny room piled high with boxes. It was a mission to climb over them to get to the bed.

"I'm an unpacking whiz" Elise lied. But once Ethan had gone, she decided unpacking could wait until tomorrow and she had an early night. She climbed over the boxes to her bed and curled up and fell asleep.

Gwen & Greer fly away

Recommended listening: To the End
From the album Parklife, by Blur.
Single released in May 1994 and got to No.16 on the UK charts.
The single features a full orchestra and choric refrain in French by
Laetitia Sadier from Stereolab.

Greer had talked Gwen into baking a cake and icing it in the shape of the Union Jack. Now trying to carve the blackened edges off the cake, Gwen found she was covered in flour, had burnt one of her fingers, and felt sick from eating too much of the icing they had mixed up earlier.

She looked at her watch. The party was going to start in only a couple of hours and they were hideously unready.

"I think I may have done too much red" Greer came over with three bowls. One was white icing, one was blue and one was red. The red bowl was full to the top, but there was hardly any white or blue.

"It'll have to do" Gwen put the now slightly misshapen cake on a plate and they tried to make the Union Jack.

"Which bit is red?" Gwen asked. "Is the cross that goes across? Or diagonal?"

"I don't know" Greer stopped.

"Do you think they'll bar us at Heathrow if we don't know it?" Gwen pretended to be concerned.

"Yes, they're sure to. As well as a quiz on who the Prime Minister is."

"Who is it? Is it still Tony Blair?" Gwen realised she actually didn't know that much about England at all. Elise had barely told her a thing. Apart from about britpop.

They went in search of an encyclopaedia to look up flags and finally found one up in one of Greer's flatmate's bookshelves. They were having the party at Greer's flat as it was bigger and had a garden out the back. It was a BBQ and everyone was supposed to bring their own booze. Gwen was doing food. So far they had got a whole load of sausages, some kebabs, and some lettuce. It was looking a little dire.

They went back to finish the icing.

"Anyway at least I'll get to hang out with you again. All you've been doing is working" Greer said trying to ice the white cross.

"I've been working like a slave" Gwen had taken a waitress job in a café in the evening and weekends as well as working for 6 hours a day in the photo studio, and she'd saved every penny she made. It hadn't been fun, but it had paid off and now she had a nice little lump sum saved and had paid off her flights.

They were just finishing icing the cake, which looked more like an abstract Picasso than the flag when Gwen's sister arrived. She'd said she'd handle decorations.

"Everything ready?" she asked breezing in.

"The food is," Greer said, wiping blue icing across her forehead.

"I'll decorate then" Nikki had brought red, white and blue balloons and streamers. She hung the streamers up and put the balloons on the table.

"Right, you two need to help me blow," she said.

"We're going to put the food there," Gwen said.

"What have you got?" Nikki went and checked the fridge out and shook her head.

"This is pathetic. Why didn't you have this at mum and dad's? They would have put on a feast."

"I wanted to do it myself," Gwen said.

"Well, I'm just going to pop to the supermarket," Nikki said "while I'm gone, you blow up those balloons. I want them finished when I get back."

"Being married has made her even more bossy" Greer said.

"Shut up and blow" Gwen ordered.

*

They were groups of people sprawled around the garden on the grass, full of sausages and punch and chippies and cake and peanuts. Gwen was pleased. She'd got a few bon voyage presents from those that had already done their OEs. A neck cushion for the plane, a bum bag, a rough guide to London.

She came outside with a fresh glass of punch and saw Elise sitting over under a tree talking with a couple of her ex-workmates. She wandered over and sat down.

"We were just saying we're going to have to head off," one of them said. "We've got a dinner thing to go to."

"Oh okay, well it was nice to see you guys again" Gwen put her drink down, stood up, and hugged them. Once they'd headed down the path around the side of the house, she sat back down with Elise.

"Did you get enough to eat?" she asked.

"Too much" Elise rubbed her stomach. She was sitting, legs stretched out, leaning back against the tree and had her usual singlet and cream skirt on, although she was now far more tanned than when the summer had begun. "So what are you doing tomorrow?"

"Well our flight leaves at 11 am and we have to be at the airport three hours before departure. I just have to do a final check of my suitcase. I'm worried I'm going to forget something essential."

"Where are you storing the rest of your stuff?" Elise asked.

"In Nikki's garage."

"How long do you think you'll be gone?"

"I told you. I don't know. It depends on what jobs me and Greer get. And whether we meet anyone."

"You might find you get homesick."

"Maybe" Gwen shrugged. It was going to be too exciting to get homesick, but she had to make Elise feel better somehow. "Anyway, how's your new flat? How's the job?"

"The new flat's okay. My room is tiny but I'm not there that much anyway which is what Shavaughn wanted. It's basically their flat and me and the other girl are in the way. But we're paying rent so it's pretty rude really."

"Are you going to look for another place?"

"No I can't be bothered at the moment" Elise picked up her glass of vodka and lemonade. The ice in it had melted a while ago, but she still ran it across her forehead.

"Actually, maybe you could get Nikki to talk to Craig or Shavaughn for me."

"How does Nikki know them?"

"Craig's her brother-in-law. Actually, does that make Shavaughn her sister-in-law?"

"Did I hear my name mentioned?" Nikki was doing the rounds and came and sat down next to them.

"Elise is living with Shavaughn and Craig" Gwen explained.

"Yes, they came and visited us a few weeks ago and mentioned you so we said that we knew you and they should give you the flat."

"Thanks. I was going to be homeless otherwise."

"Elise was just complaining that they basically want her to be out all the time." Gwen was drinking cider. She didn't want to have a hangover for tomorrow.

"Yeah, they really don't want to have to have flatmates but can't afford not to" Nikki agreed. "It's pretty horrible. When you move in together you really want it to just be you two. I love having our own place. No weird stuff in the fridge. No having to wait to use the bathroom in the morning. You two should try it sometime. But I suppose you're both going to have to meet the right man first."

"Oh my god you are being such a smug married" Gwen punched her sister on the arm. Bridget Jones's Diary had been one of the books Elise had lent her last year which Gwen had then passed onto Nikki to read, and they'd been quoting from it ever since.

"And you two are being too Bridget Jones. You both need to have a proper relationship. You're going to get too old soon."

"Old? You're the old one!"

"If you're going to call me old, I'm leaving" Nikki got up. "Don't drink too much. You're flying tomorrow."

"Yes mum" Gwen pulled a face and Nikki swatted her. Once she'd headed off Gwen finished her cider, then lay down on the grass and propped herself up with one elbow.

"How's Ethan?" she asked.

"He's good." Elise took a sip of her drink.

"Just good?"

"Just good."

"That's good then" Gwen paused. Let Elise get all mysterious then and not tell her anything now she was leaving. "I was worried Brian might try and show up today."

"But he didn't?"

"He hasn't so far."

"Who hasn't so far?" Greer came over and sat down on the grass cross-legged. She was nibbling on a kebab.

"Just one of the other guys from work," Gwen said vaguely. Elise looked at her sharply and Gwen shook her head slightly. She didn't want to discuss it here and hoped Elise would get that. Elise nodded. She did. Not that Greer had even noticed anything.

"So I hear you're flying out tomorrow," Elise said to Greer.

"Yep. First stopover in LA for a few hours, then onto London" Greer said. "Then we're meeting up with this guy I know who's over there at the moment. He's living in a house with a few other New Zealanders so we're going to stay there a few days until we find a flat for just us. He works in a pub and said we can work there too until we get better jobs."

"So you're going for the perfect OE then?" Elise said.

"In what way?" Greer asked.

"Making sure the entire time you're there you never meet an English person" Elise grinned.

"We've already met an English person," Gwen said. She stretched and stood up. "I better go and talk to my family" she headed off across the lawn. Greer stood up too.

"I better go with her," she said.

"Sure" Elise shrugged.

*

The next morning at the airport they'd kept the farewells to a minimum by just getting Nikki to drive them out. She'd helped unload their suitcases, hugged them, and had driven off.

261

"I know I said it was a good idea to do all our goodbyes yesterday but now I feel like we should have crying family and friends begging us not to go," Greer said.

"Yeah, me too" Gwen hadn't really considered what they would do during the 45 minutes wait after checking in. It was a bit of an anti-climax when you wanted to be on your way. Then they would have to wait another 4 hours in Auckland for the actual flight to LA, then another 6 hours before their final flight onto London. All up it would take about 32 hours before they arrived on UK soil.

So they sat in the departure lounge feeling a bit despondent.

They both heard running footsteps and looked over expecting someone else to have a tearful family member coming to say goodbye. But it was Elise.

Gwen stood up.

"We didn't really get to say goodbye properly yesterday," Elise said and suddenly gave Gwen a hug. After a moment's hesitation, Gwen hugged her back and then found that she had tears in her eyes.

"Everything feels like the end of an era" Elise mumbled into her shoulder. Gwen pulled away.

"I'll write to you. It's not going to be forever and Ethan will look after you anyway."

"I know," Elise said. "He and Harriet dropped me out here and they're waiting outside."

"See you'll be okay," Gwen said.

"Make sure you look after her for me," Elise said to Greer who nodded.

"We actually have to board now" Gwen saw that the gate had opened and people were heading down the air bridge.

"Okay well have a great time. Write and send me photo's so I know what you get up to" Elise hugged her again.

"Okay 'bye," Gwen took her carry-on and followed Greer into the tunnel, looking back once at the entrance and waving to Elise.

and then
it was over

Recommended listening: Wonderwall by Oasis.

Single released October 1995.

From the album What's the Story (Morning Glory).

While the song was dedicated to Noel's girlfriend Meg, Noel said the media made up that it was about her. He says it was about an imaginary friend that will come and save you.

Elise woke up to hear the wind howling around the house. She hadn't heard it for so long that it took her a moment to work out what was different. She pulled the duvet up over her head, snuggling down. It sounded like it was cold out there. Perhaps a full-on change of weather was coming.

She heard Ethan mumble something beside her and she lifted the duvet like a tent above them so she could see him. He turned towards her and opened his eyes.

"Morning" she whispered. His face had a blue tinge from the light coming through the duvet material.

"Morning."

She watched him also realise that it was windy out.

"It sounds horrible out there," she said.

"We should both call in sick and go back to sleep" he grinned.

"I can't. I won't have enough for the rent otherwise. It's only wind. I'm sure we'll remember how to deal with it. It really has been so long though" she could remember the day when she'd felt like summer had arrived. She and Ethan had gone up to Mt Vic to pick parsley. It felt like a lifetime ago, not a few months.

"What's the time?" Ethan asked.

Elise pulled the covers down and felt on the chair by her bed for her watch. It was time to get up. She climbed out of bed, grabbed her clothes and towel, and went through to the bathroom to shower and dress. She had originally thought that when Ethan had insisted that he stay over, if she got dressed in front of him it might lure him into having sex with her. But at the last minute, she decided that that was just throwing herself at him. Over the last few weeks, it was clear that he really did just think of her as a friend.

He had started talking about this chick called Nicola who had started at his work. They had bonded when she had said her favourite book was American Psycho. She knew they had lunch together and had gone out for dinner so she guessed that was where Ethan's affections were. It was okay. She was happy with him as a friend.

She even liked having him stay over. It had been weird the first time. He'd been around watching TV with her. She'd got a tiny little 15-inch one that they watched sitting on her bed. It had got late, and Ethan had yawned and said could he just sleep here tonight.

Elise knew she'd slept in his bed with him and she had found it a little uncomfortable, and not just because of his incredibly saggy mattress. But that had been out of necessity. This was different and she didn't want him to. She wasn't why.

"No, you can't!" she'd said.

"But you had Blair stay over. And you said you'd slept in the same bed as Gwen."

"Yes, but that's different. They're girls."

"That's not fair!" he had pouted but also looked like he could be genuinely hurt, and Elise had laughed.

"I'll take you out for breakfast" he tried bribing.

"Okay, if you really can't be bothered walking home." Something about it made her give in.

That first morning, they'd both woken up with blue knuckles. For a moment Elise had thought she had some horrible disease, but it was just the dye from the new duvet she'd brought the day before. Another reason Ethan had told her later that he wanted to stay. It was warm under that duvet. His duvet was threadbare and thin.

Now she came back in dressed and ready for work.

"I'm going to catch the bus to Alan's," she said. "If you're going to shower here, you might have to wait for Shavaugn and Craig."

"No I'll go home first" Ethan had sat up in the bed while she had been gone and was flicking through a book.

"What are you doing tonight?"

"Possibly something with Nicola. Why?"

"No reason" Elise shrugged. That was fine. She hadn't been planning anything. Friends was on. It was the season finale, so she wanted to see that.

*

They ended up having a flat night watching it. Shavaughn was addicted to Friends and had taped most of the previous seasons. So Elise had made some pasta for dinner, and they'd all eaten together. It was actually only the second time they'd had a flat event. Even their other flatmate, the girl who no-one ever saw, was home.

Once they'd watched the finale, Shavaughn put on the first series. Craig went and made popcorn and they had watched several episodes.

The wind had died down earlier in the evening, and as the sun set, Elise excused herself from watching any more episodes of Friends, and took the book she was reading up the little lawn area behind the house up a flight of steps.

She hadn't even realised the lawn was there when she'd moved in until she'd had to hang some washing out and couldn't find the washing line. She'd climbed up the overgrown steps and found a concreted area for the washing, then after another flight of steps a lawn.

Now she escaped up there most nights. There wasn't much of a view as the lawn was enclosed by trees, but you could lean up against the retaining wall quite comfortably.

She was reading Banana Yoshimoto. It was on the author list that Fran had issued them all with. Elise was being naughty and not reading them in order. Instead, she was reading them as she found a copy in her favourite second-hand bookshop. Yoshimoto was the only female author they had come up with for 'Y'. Elise hadn't told Fran that she'd already read one of them.

She was enjoying it. Like the other one, it was set in Japan and the language was incredibly sparse. It was refreshing reading something that didn't have huge monologues in it but just described what happened.

She had been engrossed for some time when she heard someone coming up the steps. It was actually getting too dark to read and she realised she'd been holding the book centimetres away from her face. She put it down as Ethan came into view.

"I thought you might be up here," he said.

"I am."

He came over. He had on his ripped jeans and white t-shirt with the cow print arms. Out of all his white t-shirts, it was Elise's favourite.

"How was Nicola?" she asked.

"Oh, she didn't end up coming. It was just some of the others I work with. We went out for drinks and dinner at One Red Dog."

"We had a flat dinner," Elise said. "It was really weird."

"Who cooked?"

"Me. Now you've taught me to make pasta everyone was well impressed. Then we watched the Friends finale."

"What happened?"

They sat there together as the sky turned dark above them and Elise told him about Rachel and Ross breaking up as Ross had slept with the copy girl and Rachel didn't accept that they were on a break. She fell into silence and they watched the stars above get brighter.

"Did you know you can tell which are planets because they don't twinkle?" Elise said.

"You're a fount of knowledge" Ethan laughed.

The noise of a nearby party drifted down the hill behind them.

"I wonder if that's at Fran's place?" Elise hadn't seen Fran for weeks.

"What? Up on frump street?" Ethan asked.

"Don't be mean!" Elise punched him gently on the arm, but she was laughing. She loved his frump song. He had got her singing it too. And then as they lay there in the dark, Wonderwall came on. Someone cranked the stereo.

As Liam sang that today was gonna be the day, the entire party broke out into song. Singing along with it. She looked at Ethan next to her and he smiled at her and looked back up at the sky. They listened to the singing. It got louder when Liam got to the roads you have to walk are winding.

As they got to the end of the chorus, she turned her head to him again.

"Do you agree with them? That one person can save you?"

"No," Ethan said simply.

"Why?" she wanted to know.

"I think there are lots of people that you could be with quite happily."

"Not a soul mate?" Elise was disappointed. She thought there was someone you were destined to be with.

"It depends if you believe in free will. Are you creating the life you want for yourself or is all pre-ordained and you're just going along for the ride" Ethan said.

"Okay," she said thinking about it. This wasn't quite where she'd imagined the conversation going. "What I think is that you control your decisions but there are people you will meet along the way, and depending on the decision you make you'll just meet them at a different time and a different way. Did you see Sliding Doors?"

"No I did not."

"Well, I thought it was nice that in both parallel worlds, she still ended up with the same guy. Because it was meant to be."

"That's just trite."

"I don't think so" Elise felt like crying.

"Listen I could be completely wrong. Maybe one day I'll meet someone and fall so completely and utterly in love that we'll be together forever" Ethan said.

"You're making fun of me" Elise pouted.

"No I'm not. It could happen."

"It could happen!" she was indignant.

"That's what I said" he grinned. But she was not grinning. Wonderwall had finished and Elise shivered.

"I'm going inside," she said getting up. "See you later."

She didn't wait for him to answer.

*

She had just made four sales in a row, insurance deals galore, when she heard Alan on the phone. He popped his head over the partition.

"It's for you. It's Ethan."

"Do you mind if I take it?" she asked.

"Not if you keep making sales like that" Alan grinned. Elise came round to his desk and picked up the phone while Alan went off to the kitchen. "Hey," she said.

"Hey, I was wondering if you wanted to get some dinner tonight," Ethan asked. Elise figured he would probably realise he had upset her last night and make some effort to apologise. She had half expected a funny fax to come through, although he was taking it easy on those after the whole fax-waster incident.

"Sure, that would be nice."

"I thought we could go to the Lido?"

"Okay."

"I'm paying" he clarified.

"Damn, can we go somewhere where they serve lobster then?"

"Lobsters are terrible this time of year." He paused. "Listen I have to go. Meet you there at 7?"

"Okay," she said. She hung up and Alan came back in.

"Do you fancy a pizza for lunch?" he asked.

"Eagle Boys?"

"You got it" Alan picked up the phone. Once a week he normally ordered pizza for them and Elise always looked forward to it. The other days she made herself a sandwich but pizza was much better. And Alan always paid for it. She considered it a perk of the job.

*

"Is that a new shirt?" she asked as she sat down at the small outdoor table Ethan was sitting out. The Lido wrapped around the corner of the street opposite the city council and had several tables outside. This summer those tables had been very popular, and Ethan must have arrived early to make sure they got one. He was still wearing his suit but had on a dark blue shirt instead of his usual white one. He looked good. Really good.

Elise had worn her red tartan trousers and a singlet. She felt like perhaps she should have worn a dress. But then this wasn't a date. And she didn't own a dress.

"I tested my new credit card out today!" He grinned.

"Yikes…." Elise knew his shirt would probably have been quite expensive then.

She hadn't used the credit card yet. She was a bit scared of it. She'd always had to have enough money in the bank to buy something. Even when she'd had her cheque book, she'd never gone into overdraft until that trip to England. And when she wanted something that hadn't got enough in her bank account for, she'd put it on layby and paid each week until she could finally take the thing home.

She guessed she was worried about buying things and then getting a huge bill at the end of the month with interest on it. What if she didn't have enough to pay it off?

Yet when Ethan had suggested they sign up for American Express cards, she'd said yes. Despite all that. And Alan had been good on his word and written her a letter lying and saying she earned more than she did so she'd qualify. Ethan's was a supplementary card off her approved account as he didn't earn enough either. Harriet had warned that it wasn't a good idea, but Elise had ignored her. What was the worst that could happen?

The waiter brought them menus over.

"I normally just have the nachos," Elise said.

"Try something new," Ethan said "The green's getting it!" he tapped his wallet and grinned.

Elise ordered the pan-fried fish on potatoes with jus.

"What the hell is jus?" she asked. "It looks like just without the t."

"You are so uncultured" Ethan laughed. "It's a wine reduction."

"They should call it a wine reduction then."

"But that wouldn't confuse people and make it sound fancy!"

And dinner was a bit more fancy than usual, The food was really good. Elise had really only ever eaten the cheapest thing on the menu but paying a little bit more was worth it. It was one of the nicest meals she'd eaten.

Ethan also ordered wine. Elise hardly ever drank wine. Partly because it was too expensive but also because she didn't really like it much. She'd gone to a couple of wine and food festivals and had drunk so much of it that she got completely trashed, but she hadn't really enjoyed it. Vodka and lemonade was much more her style. But Ethan ordered a light red and Elise actually thought it was quite nice.

As dusk fell, they ordered hot chocolates.

They finished as it got dark. Ethan went in to pay and Elise felt odd waiting for him.

"Can I walk you home?" he asked.

"Sure," she stood up and they headed back through town. It started to rain. Gently at first then a little harder. It didn't matter right away as they were walking under cover. But then they reached Courtney Place. There was a huge stretch next to a vacant parking lot that was completely exposed to the elements.

"We're going to have to run," Elise said looking up at the sky. Even now it was night, she could still see the banks of black clouds that had set in. The rain drummed on the concrete and so Ethan took her hand and they dashed through the rain, laughing.

They reached the shelter of an overhanging shop front and stopped. They had both got a little wet but it felt nice. They wiped their faces and continued up Courtney Place and it wasn't until they were reaching the end, where the traffic lights were, and the road turned up towards Mt Victoria, and they would have to stop and wait to cross, that Elise realised Ethan was still holding her hand.

They were outside the theatre on the corner. The rain was coming down harder again and Ethan pulled her into the lee between two pillars where they were sheltered.

They were close to each other, and Elise realised they were still holding hands. She looked up at him.

"If this was a movie…." she said, trailing off.

"I'd do this" he said and leaned down and kissed her.

*

Harriet's VW was hurtling down the road towards Courtney Place, Harriet hunched forward over the steering wheel. Fran found herself holding onto her seat. The rain was drumming on the roof of the car and Harriet had the windscreen wipers on full.

"We're not going to be that late. You can slow down" Fran was worried that in the wet weather, the little VW might lose control. What she meant was that Harriet would lose control but she didn't really want to entertain that thought.

She had been up to Harriet's new house for dinner. She couldn't quite believe that Harriet was now a homeowner. It seemed too serious. But Harriet was very proud of her little townhouse and they had eaten and reminisced about old times.

Fran was pretty proud of herself. Her publishing course had started well and she'd already got an A on her first paper and she'd also met someone and was falling in love. Harriet had been pleased for her and when Fran had mentioned she needed to meet up with him across town, Harriet had offered to take her.

The lights ahead of them turned red and Harriet slowed to a halt, skidding very slightly. The rain seemed to lessen for a moment and Fran could see a couple making out under the shelter of the theatre overhang. They seemed to be going at it pretty hot and heavy.

The light turned green and Harriet turned right, taking the road up towards Mt Vic. Fran whipped around to try and keep the couple in her sights.

"That's not…." she started, as she suddenly realised.

"Who?" Harriet was concentrating and hadn't even seen.

"No one" Fran shook her head.

Harriet had the radio on very low volume and as they headed up the hill towards the monastery, the guitar strumming at the start of Wonderwall came on. Fran leaned forward and turned it up. This song now felt like summer to her, she'd heard it so many times.

As Liam started singing about today being the day, she wiped the window and looked out. The rain continued to lash down.

Autumn was definitely here.

Britpop summer was over.

Britpop summer

The full playlist

(to start) Champagne Supernova, Oasis

Girls and Boys, Blur

Common People, Pulp

She's Electric, Oasis

Charmless Man, Blur

Cast No Shadow, Oasis

Sorted for E's and Wizz, Pulp

High and Dry, Radiohead

Creep, Radiohead

Beautiful Ones, Suede

Cigarettes and Alcohol, Oasis

She Bangs the Drums, Stone Roses

Something Changed, Pulp

F.E.E.L.I.N.G.C.A.L.L.E.D.L.O.V.E, Pulp

Connection, Elastica

Married with Children, Oasis

Disco 2000, Pulp

Fake Plastic Trees, Radiohead

Bittersweet Symphony, The Verve

Alright, Supergrass

Country House, Blur

Talk Show Host, Radiohead

Slide Away, Oasis

Underwear, Pulp

To the End, Blur

(to finish) Wonderwall, Oasis

some thanks

There are a few people I'd like to say thank you to.

Firstly, to the bands.

Thank you for writing and playing the music that not just defined an era, but was THE soundtrack for a lot of Gen Xers. The nineties were an amazing time and you made it that way.

Thank you especially to the following: Oasis: Noel Gallagher, Liam Gallagher, Paul Bonehead Arthurs, Paul McGuigan and Tony McCarroll. Blur: Damon Albarn, Graham Coxon, Alex James and Dave Rowntree. Pulp: Jarvis Cocker, Russell Senior, Candida Doyle, Nick Banks, Steve Mackay and Mark Webber. Radiohead: Thom Yorke, Johnny Greenwood, Colin Greenwood, Ed O'Brien and Philip Selway. You were the ones I listened to most. You were the ones I loved the most.

Thank you also to Brett Anderson, Mat Osman and Justine Frischmann from Suede for starting it all.

For the writing, thank you to everyone involved in NaNoWriMo (National Novel Writing Month). I wrote the first draft of Britpop Summer during NaNoWriMo in November 2012, on an iPod. It needed to come out of me, and the whole structure of NaNoWriMo helped me get there in just 4 weeks. Thank you to everyone who was part of it that year.

To my first writers' group – Ron, Sarah, and Kineret. You helped me with the next draft of Britpop Summer. We were so bad at critiquing each other to start with but got so much better, and your feedback was part of this journey.

To the Bordeaux Writers Group – Matthew, American Pierre, French Pierre, Candice, Celine, Alaina, Claire, Erica, Jo, Lloyd, Vincent and Ela. I was so stuck and you inspired me to get this thing finished for once and for all. Thank you for some hilarious discussions, useful feedback and the motivation to get to the end.

And thank you as always to Fraser, who gives my life flavour, supports me in whatever I do and edits with love and a fierce eye.

also....

I couldn't leave without a special shout-out.

To Mr Liam Gallagher.

Britpop Summer was a long time ago and I know many Gen Xers are struggling with what we're doing and how we now make our place in the world. We remember the 90s because it was a special time in our lives. But we thought it was gone. And then Liam, you just picked up your guitar and started writing songs and brought it back for a second time.

Maybe we don't only get to do it once.

about angela

Angela Atkins is a proud Gen Xer.

Born in England, she grew up in New Zealand and has lived in California, the UK, Hawaii and South America. She and her husband currently split their time between France and Spain.

She is the author of four books of non-fiction including the best-seller *Management Bites*, and her writing has appeared in various magazines and other publications.

Britpop Summer is her first novel.

For more visit **britpopsummer.com**